USA TODAY BESTSELLING AUTHOR
Dale Mayer

SIMON SAYS...
JUMP

D1548051

A KATE MORGAN NOVEL

SIMON SAYS... JUMP (KATE MORGAN, BOOK 2)
Dale Mayer
Valley Publishing

Copyright © 2021

ISBN-13: 978-1-773364-77-3
Print Edition

Books in This Series

The Kate Morgan Series
https://smarturl.it/DMSimonSaysUniversal

About This Book

Introducing a new thriller series that keeps you guessing and on your toes through every twist and unexpected turn....
USA Today Best-Selling Author Dale Mayer does it again in this mind-blowing thriller series.
The unlikely team of Detective Kate Morgan and Simon St. Laurant, an unwilling psychic, marries all the unpredictable and passionate elements of Mayer's work that readers have come to love and crave.

Detective Kate Morgan has settled into her position and, although straining under her new caseload, is working hard. Simon is still a big question mark in her world—and his "gift" even more so. Dealing with a frustrating series of drive-by shootings has brought a three-year-old drive-by case to the forefront ...

Simon had hoped that his visions would have stopped, especially now that the police had solved the pedophile murders. No such luck. But these new visions are confusing, chaotic, and nonsensical. Unwilling to share yet more disjointed and meaningless information with Kate, he keeps it to himself. Until he sees a pattern and connects to a woman, ... one who is suicidal.

While Kate understands his physical and mental torment, she's underwhelmed by the lack of detail in his latest visions—until she looks into another issue and finds out that the number of suicides are higher than normal, as in way higher ...

Sign up to be notified of all Dale's releases here!
https://smarturl.it/DaleNews

A Behind-the-Scenes Glimpse into Dale Mayer's Simon Says Series

With this new Simon Says series, it seems some background information from me, the author, might be in order. For one, Vancouver is a city where I have many happy memories of my decade-plus years growing up there. As an army brat, I spent most of my childhood years in Vancouver, as I ventured into adulthood. For all the good memories I do have, several are not so good. That's partly what brought this series to light.

The city of Vancouver, like all big cities, has the wonderful surface layer that hides a dark underbelly. The contrast between dark and light has always interested me. I write on both sides of this coin constantly. The good against the bad, the light of day against the dark of night. The positive versus the negative. The funny compared to the dark. Laughter paired with suspense. It keeps me happy and the words flowing.

I was at a conference with several friends years ago, and I mentioned I wanted to do a new thriller series. The ideas easily flowed forth—which they do naturally with me anyway. But this time, my two main characters, Kate and Simon, fully popped into my mind, both the physical appearance of both as well as their personalities. I didn't touch the concept for another full year, until I sat down and wrote the first book, Simon Says ... *Hide*. Then self-doubt hit, and I pushed it aside, ignoring it for another year. But Kate hammered away at me inside my head, wanting more page time, so I sat down to write the next four books of this Simon Says series.

Writing fiction, particularly crime fiction, presents its own challenges, especially when you marry that with the fiction license—joining reality with imagination. Meaning, I did my best to line up truth and facts and yet kept my license to create needed bits of information to ensure that the story worked. Remember. These are stories. They are not real cases, not real people, nor real events. In fact, given urban density, at the time you read this story and the others in this Simon Says series, the Vancouver street names, traffic patterns, and even beaches and community neighborhoods could well have changed.

I do thank the Vancouver Police Department for their patience in answering my multitude of questions throughout the writing of this series. They were very helpful in sorting out the divisions between the various community and law enforcement groups that work together to protect and to serve and to keep safe Vancouver and all the neighboring cities.

Remember. All these people, places, events are fictional, creations of my mind. I wrote these stories for entertainment purposes only.

Enjoy!
Dale Mayer, Author of the Simon Says Series

CHAPTER 1

Vancouver, BC; Third Monday in July

D ETECTIVE KATE MORGAN, a homicide detective for just over four months of her thirty-two years of life, walked slowly across the Lions Gate Bridge—officially known as First Narrows Bridge. Parked off to the side were several cruisers, their lights flashing in the gloomy light. It was not quite morning, and vestiges of the night still clouded the air around her. But the pair of ladies' white three-inch-heeled pumps, placed carefully at the side of the railing of the bridge, shone with an eerie glow.

It was a well-known fact that suicide victims who jumped off bridges often took off their shoes, placing them to the side, as if shoes couldn't get wet. But nobody thought about their coats or anything else. Sometimes they left purses, keys, or wallets, anything to identify that they'd gone over the bridge, in an effort to help find closure for families and friends, if the body never surfaced.

As Kate walked toward the group of police officers, standing and talking in a huddle, one turned to look at her and nodded. "Good morning, Detective."

"Morning, Slater," she murmured, recognizing the officer from her earlier department, her gaze still on the woman's pumps. "Did we find the body?"

He nodded. "The divers are bringing her out now."

Kate stepped closer to the railing and looked over. "If she'd been any closer to the park, she would have hit the rocks first."

"Right," he said. "Most of them jump from the middle of the bridge."

Kate looked out and saw that they were not much farther than the lions mounted on either side of the bridge, heading toward West Vancouver. "Depending on the force of her fall, she might easily have hit the rocks, just under the surface," she murmured.

"We'll find out soon enough," he said.

"Any identification left with the shoes?"

"Not that we know of."

Kate nodded. "Sure seems to be an awful lot of jumpers already." She had done a quick search a few days ago, and the stats had stuck with her.

"This year has been pretty tough on everybody."

"I know, but we've had what? A fifty percent increase in jumpers from last year?"

Two men nodded. "A lot of businesses went under, and people are suffering financially, not to mention the mental health aspect."

She sighed. "And there's never enough we can do for them either."

"Were you called in on this?"

"No, I heard it on the news. I was already close by."

"Ah, that explains it. I'm surprised to see you here so fast."

She waited until everything was dealt with as much as they could on scene, while they waited on the coroner. At that point, she walked back to where she had parked up the hill. Not very many places to get out of the way of the normal heavy traffic, but she'd parked on a service road. She would have to go across the bridge in order to get back where she needed to go. But that was all right; it wasn't a very long turnaround.

She quickly drove across the bridge and turned around to head back into Vancouver. Instead of going to the office, she headed to False Creek area, to a small harbor café that should be open by now. She parked, got out, and walked, the brisk air hitting her senses, the saltwater breeze lifting her hair. She watched as the sun rose, its light shining on the city she loved so much.

Picking up a coffee, she found a bench and sat. She had a morose feeling inside, once again confronted with the realization of just how many people willingly took their own lives because they felt that was better than any other option, unable to see a way out of whatever hell they were in. It made her sad, but it also made her angry.

She'd never gotten to that point herself, but she'd gotten close, and she certainly could understand it. As she sat here, she recognized a man's voice behind her, ordering coffee at the counter. She waited, knowing that he would come in her direction.

Finally he stepped up beside her. "May I sit?"

She nodded with a half smile. "Why not?"

"I haven't seen you in a few days."

"It's been busy," she said, with a wave of her hand.

"Why are you here so early now?" Simon St. Laurant asked.

"Why are you?" she replied, her eyes going wide.

He smiled. "Deflecting a question with a question, huh?"

"Are you a lawyer now?"

"No, God help me," he said. "That would not be what I would choose to do. Not in this lifetime."

"Neither would I," she said. "In some ways it was simpler in the olden days. Guilty was guilty, and they were swiftly handled," she said, shaking her head. "Now the lawyers get in on it, delaying justice, and criminals carry on with their lives, without ever being punished, filing one appeal after another."

"It doesn't sound like you have much faith in the judiciary system."

"Oh, I have a lot of faith in it," she said. "It's the process that I struggle with sometimes."

He nodded slowly. "It's got to be frustrating when you keep taking bad guys off the streets, only to see them there again, free to commit more crimes. Then it's up to you to go back out and hunt them down once more."

She looked over at this man, someone she was struggling to keep at arm's length. But the more she tried to do that, the less it worked. After all, she'd found her way to his corner of the world, hadn't she? As if her body had a mind of its own. She sipped her coffee and studied him over the rim of her cup. "Why are you up so early?"

"Couldn't sleep," he said. He spread his arms along the back of the bench, studying her. "Why are you?"

She shrugged. "I was awake already and heard news on the scanner about a jumper."

He winced. "That's always tough, isn't it?" Then his gaze sharpened. "But you're a homicide detective," he said. "So surely suicides don't come under your domain."

"All unattended deaths are investigated."

"So you just follow police scanners for fun? Don't have enough cases now, so you have to go find new ones?"

She laughed.

"You're just not ready to tell me."

She shrugged. "It's probably nothing. I guess I'm wondering if there's anything to be done for the mental health problems we have in town," she murmured, giving him a partial answer.

He looked over at her, then reached a hand across to cover one of hers. "You know that you can't help everyone, right?"

"Wasn't planning on it. Yet I care about a lot of things," she said, "and kids are number one."

"Missing kids, you mean."

She glared at him. She still couldn't believe she had opened up enough to tell him about Timmy. Then, given Simon's history, it had seemed like a good idea at the time.

"That's better," he said, with a nod. "I was wondering what was going on that made you look so maudlin."

"I wasn't," she protested.

"Were too."

"Was not," she snapped back. He left it at that. After a moment, her shoulders eased. He was right. "I guess just seeing another jumper ..." she said. "I mean, it's like there's one every day right now."

He looked startled at that. "Is it really that high?"

"Not quite. If I were to count all the bridges on the Lower Mainland, it's especially bad," she said. "It seems much higher than normal."

"Well, last year was bad overall, and this year has been a pretty ugly one so far too."

"I know," she said, "and I get that people are losing their loved ones, their businesses, their homes, plus their families are breaking up. We didn't even need the pandemic for all that to happen, yet just so much else is going on all the time. The pressures of today's world are immense, and handling it all seems to be a special skill set that a lot of people don't have. And, all too often, I think drugs and other enabling issues help bring it all down too."

He shrugged. "And again, there's only so much you can do."

"I know," she said. "A whim sent me down there. I hadn't been there at that wee hour of the morning in a long time."

"Why would you ever be in that area at that hour?" he asked in surprise.

"When I was a teenager," she said, "sometimes I would go sit on the bridge." He sat back and stared. It wasn't hard to understand what he was thinking ... She shrugged. "I never really considered suicide," she said, "but I did know several people who had completed the job, and it always shook me to realize that death was the best answer they saw. I'd sit there and ponder what the attraction was. That water is cold, dark, and often rough. What a way to go."

"I'm sorry," he said. "I didn't know."

"You didn't know because I haven't told you. I haven't told you much," she said, with a shrug. "It's not like we know each other."

He snorted at that. "Knowing each other requires taking time to be with each other."

"You mean, not just screwing like minks when we're together?"

"Well, okay, that's pretty damn nice too," he said. "But getting to know each other, that's a process that takes time."

"Well," she said, "it's also a process that requires I open up a little bit—and you too."

At that, his lips turned down, and she nodded. "Right," she said, "not exactly your style either."

He frowned. "Maybe," he said, then turned the subject away from him. "Was there anything different about this suicide scenario?"

"No, not really," Kate said. "She was pretty close to the shore and got caught up in some driftwood. So, instead of floating past or sinking, she was held right there for the divers."

"At least her family will get some closure and can lay her to rest," he said.

"True, yet it still makes me angry."

"Except anger isn't the emotion I'm seeing on you right now," he said. "It's more what I would call *defeated*. As in, already too emotionally involved."

She shook her head. "I'm definitely not," she said, with half a smile. "But maybe weary. I just turned in all the reports and follow-ups on the pedophile case, which was a long and difficult case."

"You solved it pretty damn fast, considering."

"It should have been solved a long time ago," she said, staring off into the distance. "So many more victims because it wasn't."

"And again, not your fault. You weren't even a detective then. What's it been? Four months now?"

She nodded slowly. "Four and a half."

"Well, you've already shaken things up in the department and earned a commendation for having done so well."

"Yeah, and I appreciate that," she said, "but I wish instead that the kids had been helped."

"Don't we all," he said heavily.

She smiled at him. "See? You're no better."

"Hey, you're the one who's making me depressed this morning."

She laughed. "Well, I'm heading off to work anyway."

"Did you get any sleep last night?"

"I did," she said, "but it was a …" She shrugged. "It was a rough night."

He frowned, as she got up and walked away. "You could say goodbye, you know."

She reached up a hand and, without turning around, called out, "Bye."

She walked to her vehicle and then drove on to the station. She needed to shake off this funky mood, but just something bothered her about the last case and the final paperwork she'd had to hand in. The court cases would go on forever, since they had unearthed so many perverts who were involved in the pedophile ring. That was the good thing. It was a good thing, yet, at the same time, it was difficult because none of the bodies had been that of Kate's long-missing brother. And even though Simon St. Laurant, a reluctant psychic, whose abilities had just blossomed in this thirty-seven-year-old developer and philanthropist, had mentioned the name *Timothy* from his visions, it had been a different child.

There had never been any other mention of her brother Timmy, who had gone missing so many years ago from the schoolyard. He'd been supposedly under her care—though she herself was only seven at the time. Still, her mother had blamed Kate for the rest of her life, and it was just one of those things that Kate didn't shake off easily. Having this last case involve a child with the same name had opened old wounds. She could ask Simon if he had any information on her brother, but could she accept whatever he might say? She struggled to understand and to believe the little he'd offered on the case as it was.

As she walked into the station and headed to her desk, Andy was already there, and he looked up in surprise.

"Wow, you're early."

"So are you," she said, noting his usual overly coiffed hair and well-dressed self did not seem so pristine today. Was that mustard—or egg—on his tie? "Shouldn't you be dragging your ass in here late, after a wild date?" As far as she knew, he hadn't changed his ways, still in the hump-and-dump stage of adjusting to divorce—where his wife chose his best friend instead.

He shrugged. "Bad night."

"Ditto," she said.

He looked over at her. "Are you okay?"

She nodded. "Yeah. It's just finishing up all that paper-work on the pedophiles, and ... you know." She shrugged.

"I'm sorry that you never found your missing kid brother in all of this."

"Me too," she said. "One day."

"That's got to be tough. All you can do is keep looking."

"Of course," she said, "but it does give me a certain empathy for the families in similar cases. I know what it's like to not have answers. I know what it's like to be looking for that closure that never comes."

"Still not a healthy way to go through life, always looking for a ghost."

Well, that was a conversation stopper if there ever was one. He turned back to his work; she got up, grabbed a coffee cup, surprised to see a mostly full pot sitting there, just waiting to be consumed. Deciding that maybe she should be nice, she grabbed another cup and brought Andy one at the same time.

He looked at her, surprised, a smile breaking across his face. "Thanks."

"No problem," she said. She sat down at her desk. "How many open cases do we even have right now?"

"Six, I think," he said.

She nodded. "Hopefully most of those will go by the wayside pretty quickly."

"Maybe, maybe not," he said.

She looked over at him, seeing the fatigue ravaging his face. "How are you doing?"

He looked up, saw that she meant it, then shrugged and said, "Well, I'm working on getting time with my kids now," he said. "I'm starting to find a pathway forward. It's tough though."

"Sorry," she said. "I can't imagine."

"Yeah, I had no idea, but suddenly it becomes your reality, and it doesn't matter if you're prepared or not because it's up to you to start dealing with it. And I am the parent *supposedly*."

She nodded slowly and said, "As long as you are dealing with it, you're moving forward—toward something better."

He nodded with a smile. "The kids miss me," he said, "and I miss them, so it was really nice to see them this last weekend."

"Did you have them for the whole weekend?"

He laughed. "Yeah, we spent a lot of time at Stanley Park area. Second Beach has always been one of their favorite places to go."

"Good," she said in delight. "That's a great place for kids."

He nodded. "It was nice. Like I said, it's progress."

She nodded slowly and returned to her files. Her email was overflowing as usual, but she dove in and soon got through it. Toward the bottom was one with a picture. She opened it up and froze. It was a picture of her standing at the bridge before dawn today, just staring at the shoes. Under her breath, she whispered, "What the hell?"

"What have you got?" Andy asked from behind her.

She twisted her monitor slightly and said, "An email with a creepy picture."

He got up, walked over, and said, "What the hell is that?"

She sighed. "I couldn't sleep this morning. I heard on the scanner about a jumper on Lions Gate Bridge, so I headed down to the spot."

He looked at her in surprise, but she shrugged and said, "I've spent more than a few days sitting there myself."

"Ouch," he said. "We need to talk."

She laughed. "Really?" she said. "Are you really saying that to me *now*, with you dealing with your divorce by hooking up with nameless women nightly?"

He winced at that. "Okay, so I've been a mess lately. I get it, but I haven't been suicidal."

"There are a lot of ways of killing yourself," she said, with an arched eyebrow.

"Yeah," he said, "okay, but back to you. So you went down there and then what?"

"I talked to the cops. While I was there, the divers were bringing up the body."

"And she left her shoes there?" He tapped the picture on his monitor. "I've always wondered about that. Why do they leave their shoes? I mean, if she's got on a good pair of shoes, doesn't she have on a beautiful dress to match? Why don't they take that off? Do they take off their jewelry? No," he said. "It's like the shoes have some weird significance."

"I know. But speaking of weird significance," she said, pointing at the picture, "why is somebody taking a picture of me standing there? And then sending it to me?"

He sat back, studied it, then her. "Just because I gotta ask, were you doing anything wrong being there?"

She shook her head. "No. I wasn't so much curious as solemn and maybe more than a little disturbed by the harsh increase we've had in suicides this last year."

"Right, I noticed the numbers have gone up." He shook his head at that. "I mean, it is a little macabre that you go down to the spot, but it is what we do."

"Exactly," she said. "And, at the same time, it was like a visit to a place that I had been to before but will never go back to again. At least I hope not."

"But you never tried to jump, right?"

She shook her head. "No," she said. "I never did. I wasn't really suicidal but knew several who had jumped."

"So why do you think this guy took a picture of you?"

"Not only did he take a picture of me," she said, "but he then emailed it to me. And it's my work email."

"The address isn't all that hard to figure out," Andy pointed out. "If a person had any dealings with the department before, all the email addresses are in a pretty standard format."

She nodded. "And I get that, but why? Why does anybody care enough to send it to me and to let me know that I was seen?"

"That's why I was asking if you had any reason *not* to be there."

She shrugged. "Not that I know off. Did I break some

rule? Is a homicide detective not allowed to go to another scene like that?"

"No, no rules like that," he said, "not that anybody would care if there were."

"Well, that's what I thought. But obviously somebody seems to think differently."

"No message?"

She shook her head.

"What email address did it come from?"

"Jumpers.com," she snapped. "Info@jumpers.com."

He looked at her and said, "Please tell me that's not a real group."

She said, "I just checked, and it's not. It comes up as a blank website, but, hey, it's full of ads for building a website, if I want."

"Well, thank God for that," he said. "So, a joke maybe? I don't know."

"Maybe somebody related to another case?" she suggested. "Maybe one of the pedophiles?" she added. "Like somebody who is absolutely certain we must have fixed the case and their poor little Johnny is being framed?"

"You know what people are like," he said, shaking his head. "There will always be family members who can't believe that somebody in their family did something wrong."

"I know," she said heavily. She frowned. "Well, I'll just park it off to the side and see if anything else happens."

"You need to tell Colby and the others."

She looked at Andy in surprise. She hadn't considered the need to tell her sergeant, but maybe keeping Colby in the loop could be helpful. But more likely not. "Why?"

"Just in case," he said. "That's just smart."

She shrugged and agreed; then she never thought anymore about it, until after the team meeting. While Kate still wrote down notes of everything they had to work on today, Andy spoke up. "Everyone, Kate has something to say."

She looked at Andy in surprise. "I do?"

He nodded and said, "That email."

"What email?" Colby asked Andy, then turned to Kate.

She wrinkled up her face and said, "Oh."

"You would like to ignore it," Andy said, with emphasis, as he rolled his eyes, "but I don't think it's something we ought to forget."

Colby turned toward her. "Kate, what's up?"

"I got an email this morning," she said, "with a picture of me that goes back to about an hour and a half before that email."

Everybody immediately stood around her, and she brought up the email on her phone.

They said, "What the hell is that? You were standing at the bridge?"

She nodded. "I had a really shitty night's sleep. I woke up early and was sick of tossing and turning. Then I heard on the scanner that a jumper went off the bridge, so, for whatever reason, I went down there to take a look."

At that, she felt several of them stiffening around her.

"So, as a matter of full disclosure, way back when at one point in my life, I spent a lot of time myself on that bridge. No, I never jumped, and, no, I don't think I ever seriously considered jumping, but I knew several who had jumped. I never saw anybody commit suicide there, but, because I'd spent quite a bit of time there myself, the whole scene drew me.

"As I walked over, I noticed a beautiful pair of white shiny women's pumps sitting there, carefully placed off to the side. Already several cruisers were there. I talked to an officer briefly for a few minutes and was told the body had already been found, and they were bringing her up. At that point, I headed back to my car and drove down to False Creek and had a coffee, watching the city wake up."

There were a couple not-so-hidden smirks at that.

She ignored them. "From there I came into the office, chatted with Andy, checked my email, and this popped up."

"So somebody saw you there and thought enough to take a picture of it and email it to you?" Colby asked.

"Yes," she said. "What I don't know is why they would think that I would care or what the message could possibly be behind it."

Colby stepped forward, looked at it, and said, "That makes you wonder."

"I know. Presumably there's a meaning behind it," she said. "But honestly I don't know what that could be. Am I supposed to think that this suicide was a crime? Is this a family member, saying, 'Hey, she didn't commit suicide.' Or is this an observer, just saying, 'Hey, you got nothing else to do with your time, maybe you should check this out.' Or ... who the hell knows." She raised both hands in frustration. "Like we have time for anything extra."

"Right," Andy said behind her. "So bizarre."

"But then people are bizarre," she said.

Colby frowned at her. "Keep us informed, if you hear anything else, and watch your back."

"I always watch my back," she said calmly. "I don't think I'm being targeted."

"Well, I'm not sure what else you would call it," Rodney said pointedly. "When somebody sends you a picture like that, it means that they've gone to the time and the energy to take your photo and then to let you know that they saw you."

She stared at him. "It sounds a little creepier when you put it that way."

"It is creepy," Rodney said. "What was this guy doing out there at that hour anyway? I'm just saying, let's be smart about it, okay?"

She didn't have any argument with being smart about it, but it just seemed like everybody was making a bit bigger deal out of it than there was reason to support.

Colby said, "Log in the email and open a file, just in case."

She groaned and said, "That's just extra paperwork."

"Do it," he said. "No arguments."

She flipped her hands, palms up. "Fine." And rose, headed back to her desk, got down to work. After making sure her requested file was complete, she carried on with her day. "Where are the witness statements, from that drive-by shooting down on Hastings Street?"

"They were supposed to come in last night," Lilliana said. "Did they not?"

Kate shook her head. "I wasn't tagged on them, and they haven't been dropped into the file. Let me check," she said. It took a few minutes for her to shake down the officer out canvassing the neighborhood. "He apologized, said that they'd been out all night with a different case, and hadn't had a chance to send them to us."

"So, is he sending them now?"

Kate nodded. "Apparently. They should be in the file within a few minutes."

"Good enough," Lilliana said.

"I wonder what other case they had?" Kate asked. "I

didn't get tagged. Did anybody else?"

Everyone shook their heads. Lilliana said, "Maybe check the computer."

"Well, they get called out on plenty that has nothing to do with us, don't forget."

It took about twenty more minutes before they had all the statements that had been collected on the recent drive-by shooting.

"What's the point of a drive-by anyway?" Kate mused out loud.

"To murder and to get away with it," Rodney said, glancing over at her. "Hands off, easy escape."

"I get that, I do, but it's not very personal. You do get a split-second chance to see who it is you're shooting down, but there can't be much job satisfaction in that."

"You mean, it's not up-front and personal? Yet it is in a way," Rodney said. "When you think about it, you get to pick the victim. You get to see the shots fired. There is that sense of power, the sense of control, but, at the same time, you have speed on your side, so you get the hell away safely. And, as you can tell with this one, we haven't got very much to go on."

"That's the other thing I don't understand. I mean, normally we have cameras everywhere, and, while we're still lobbying for more cameras for this area, it's one of the heavier populated downtown streets. So we know for a fact that witnesses are around somewhere. Witnesses with cell phones. What are the chances of the shooter getting away with this?"

"Good enough to take the risk apparently," Rodney said. "If you think about it, their getaway vehicle would be ditched in no time, and they would change to something else. So we'll have a pretty rough time proving that they were the ones involved."

She frowned at that. "Not if we can pinpoint who was driving on one of the city cameras, particularly in that area. Then, if we can put that vehicle at the scene of the crime, even better."

He nodded. "And I get that," he said, "but things never seem to line up quite so nicely. Remember that."

She winced. "I know. I know," she said. "We've still got one drive-by from a few years ago that we never closed, don't we?"

"Exactly," he said. "You never know. This could be the same players though."

She looked at him in surprise. "Why is that?"

"Both ... involved old Chevy trucks," he said.

She stared at him. "Well, in that case, they could easily be connected."

"Not necessarily," Rodney said. "I'm mean, sure it's a similarity, but it's not enough. The trucks were different colors. I don't have any confirmation of what years they were, and we don't have any ID on the driver from the first one—or for this one, for that matter. If I understand it right, the victim was standing outside, smoking a cigarette."

"Where was he?"

"He was on the same block as a popular nightclub. So it could have been random, I suppose."

"Or it could have been targeted."

"Both possibilities are still on the table right now."

"But the shots were also well-placed, correct?"

He nodded. "Yes, the victim died at the scene."

She nodded. "And what about the one before, ... the older open case?"

"Same thing," he said, looking at her in surprise.

She shrugged. "It's just one more consistency between the two cases, that's all."

He frowned. "That's pretty thin as far as consistency goes, even more than the Chevy."

"Hey, *thin* is my middle name," she said, with a laugh. "Let me go through these statements. I'll see if anything's there."

"Yeah, thin ice maybe. Good luck with that. Most of the statements came from the partiers who were going in or out of the nightclub."

She nodded. "The thing is, somebody saw something. It's just a matter of finding out who saw what, and, if they saw what they said they saw." He blinked at her several times, frowning, but she just waved a hand. "Don't worry about me," she said, with a chuckle. "You carry on, and so will I."

━━━∾∾━━━

AFTER THE EARLY morning start, Simon carried on through the downtown area. He had several addresses he needed to look at, to consider for purchase. One was for rehabbing; another was a potential rehab or drop. He wasn't sure which it would be. The Realtor had tried to tell him that she already had offers coming in, and, if he was interested, he needed to make an offer soon. If that were the case, she shouldn't have called then because he didn't do anything under pressure and never just because somebody else told him to.

Breathing deeply of the fresh morning air, he stopped at the first place on Hastings and looked at the surroundings. This area was really up for a lot of renewal, and it was happening, just very slowly. A lot of these buildings needed complete remodels or rebuilds, but the businesses were either older, gone, or at the lower end of what he wanted to be associated with. A sex shop was in the middle of the block and what looked like a pawn shop right beside it, with multiple For Lease signs on other windows.

He frowned at that and studied the huge building that reminded him of the brownstones in England, where they were pinched between two other stone buildings. This one looked to have been built around 1960, and he checked his paperwork to see it was 1965. He nodded to himself. "Everything will have to be redone, from plumbing to electrical and probably even structural."

He let himself into the building, as the Realtor had told him it was empty. As soon as he saw just how decrepit the structure actually was, he moved swiftly through the place. It was probably 50-50 on costs as to whether this one needed to be dropped or rebuilt as it was. With the property prices in Vancouver skyrocketing in the last five years, the price they were asking for this piece of crap was unbelievable.

He put a question mark beside the listing, but he sure as heck wasn't in love with it, and he knew, if he decided to take it on, it would strictly be a financial decision and none other. He felt no joy in this building, and trying to restore her would be very expensive. She'd been unloved for a long time, and, although it was unfair to her, he wasn't sure he needed to take on every building crying out for attention. He would have spent a lot more time and way more money if that had been his agenda.

As he headed toward the next address on his list, he noted it was now midmorning. He'd spent longer at the last building for sale than he'd intended, so something there must have drawn his attention. As he passed a coffee vendor, he stopped, snagged a coffee, and carried on. A bench was just up ahead. As he got closer, he almost stumbled, making him stop and collapse onto the bench with more force than intended, as a number slammed into his brain. The number thirteen.

"What the hell does that mean?" he asked out loud. He set his coffee beside him on the bench and rubbed his face.

The coffee vendor raced toward him. "Are you okay, sir?"

He looked over at the young girl with a smile, then nodded and said, "Sorry, I'm fine. I just tripped."

She looked like she didn't believe him. "Are you sure you didn't have a heart attack?"

He winced at that. Did he look so old? "No, I'm fine," he repeated, then pointed. "You've got another customer now."

She turned, but looked back at him doubtfully, and then headed over to her next customer.

Simon sat here for a long moment, more pissed at what appeared to be happening again than he could have imagined. He had thought the whole psychic thing was done and over with. After all, he had a logical connection to the last case. He had congratulated himself on avoiding his grandmother's prediction of a one-way street down the psychic pathway because, ever since they'd found the pedophile ring, he'd been sleeping perfectly once again. No nightmares, no more visions of boys, nothing—well, except for that one black-and-white vision. Otherwise awesome. He'd thought it open and shut forever.

As he sat here, trying to regain his equilibrium, all he could do was watch as a series of thirteens slammed into his brain in a repetitive motion—just like when you finished an online game of solitaire, and the cards did a weird little shuffle pattern at the end of it. But, in his case, every card said thirteen.

Not knowing what to do with the information, he did what he always did. He pulled out his phone and texted the number to Kate. And then he laughed because no way she would have any clue what that was all about. Hell, he didn't either, and that was the problem. She always expected him to have some idea, and, of course, he didn't. He was hoping this would mean something to her. It often had, but no guarantee that it would this time.

And, of course, bringing her back to mind also brought back their conversation from this morning and had him wondering about her mood. The knowledge that she had wandered that bridge earlier in her life, contemplating the suicides of her friends, had him off-kilter. It just was a bit hard to imagine. She said she'd never gotten that far herself, but to have been there at all said a lot about where her mindset had been.

It couldn't have been easy being blamed for the loss of her younger brother, particularly when she'd been only a child herself. But since her mother couldn't accept any of the responsibility herself, it had been much easier to push it off on her other child. And the fact that Kate got some closure for the families in some of these pedophile cases, yet nothing that had anything to do with her own brother, just made it that much harder. The wounds would still be raw for her. Simon hated that she did so much work for so many other people, but just no justice was out there for her. He hoped that one day there would be, but that could be a long time coming.

When his phone buzzed, and he saw a question mark from her, he just laughed and sent a smiley face and a message. **No clue but that's what came up.** And he carried on. Hopefully she'd come up with her own answer. He had a lot of work to do yet and was tired and getting cold. He raced through the next couple potential buildings for purchase and ended up seeing more than he had planned when the Realtor had reached out and suggested a couple more that he should take a look at. Since he was already here, and his mind was on the work, he went through all of them and then started back home again. He had gotten a bit farther from home then he'd intended to, so he grabbed a cab and got dropped off outside his place. It was almost dinnertime.

By the time Simon entered the lobby, Harry, his usual daytime doorman, smiled broadly at him, until he got a good look at Simon.

"Oh dear," the doorman said. "Long day?"

"Yeah, long day," he said, shaking his head. "Some of them are just that way."

"I hope you picked up a meal for yourself."

"Nope. I didn't get that far," he muttered. "Though I should have."

"How about I order something in for you?" he said immediately. "You know you can't keep working like this, if you don't feed yourself."

Simon laughed at that because it was one of the arguments he always used against Kate to get her to eat properly. She was always on the go and missing solid meals. The last thing he wanted to do was follow in her footsteps in that regard. Besides, anything from Mama's place was to die for. He nodded. "The special of the day at Mama's would be great. If you could bring it up," he said, "I'll pay you then, if that works."

"Not a problem," Harry said. "We've got a fund here for just such emergencies."

"Well, I'm glad to hear that," he said. "Otherwise I can pay you right now."

"Let me bring it up, and then we'll know what it actually cost."

With that, Simon headed upstairs, the rain starting just before he made it home. He threw off his suit and hopped into a hot shower. By the time he came out, dried off, and had redressed in gray slacks and a black turtleneck, he felt 100 percent better. When the doorbell rang, he walked over to his penthouse elevator door, checked the peephole, and opened it to the doorman. "Wow, that was fast, even for you, Harry."

"That's Mama for you. The minute she heard it was for you, she was all over it."

Simon laughed. "What would we do without her?" He checked the tab, then pulled bills from his pocket. "Here's for the meal and a tip for you and a tip for her."

"Thank you, sir," he said respectfully. "I'll make sure this gets to her."

"You do that. You know I'll ask."

The doorman laughed, knowing full well Simon would do no such thing because they had a mutual trust and respect that didn't require it.

With that, Harry headed out swiftly.

When the elevator door closed, Simon locked it behind him and took the very large container to the kitchen, where he placed it on the counter and opened it up. Mama always sent far more food than was necessary. He didn't know if she thought he kept a harem at his place that she had to feed at the same time or if she figured he could at least eat good food two days in a row. Regardless he had to appreciate it because her food was always good home cooking. She was Italian and had married a Mexican man, and the two of them had somehow created a special cuisine between them that worked. Simon didn't even know what to call it, but it was good. It was hot. It was fresh, and, as always, it went down with joy.

Even hearing that phrase made him want to laugh and to cry at the same time. He'd heard it time and time again. Some Japanese woman was all about joy and finding joy in the day, in your life, even in your possessions, and making a fortune with that.

He looked around and smiled. "Well, I find joy in my location. Does that count?" There was some merit to what he said because he definitely only liked to take on buildings where he found joy in their rehab because it was one of the things that he loved to do. He loved to see something old and broken-down be fixed and brought back up to their former glory again. Or sometimes they just needed to be completely dropped and rebuilt in the same space, but that didn't give him the same sense of accomplishment as a restoration.

And, as such, he wasn't too thrilled with three of the buildings he'd looked at today. One of the latter ones held the most promise, but still he wasn't into getting pushed by the Realtor. As he sat down to his meal, the Realtor called him. He looked at the number and just let it ring. No way he would answer her call and ruin what was no doubt the best meal he'd had in several days.

He wasn't a bad cook, but he didn't particularly enjoy

cooking if it was just for him—any more than he bothered about eating sometimes if it was just him, which put him in the same category as Kate. Only she didn't eat because usually she overworked herself to the bone and had no time to eat or no time for a good meal, or she didn't care because she was already past hunger and looking at the next job on her desk. He'd given her enough shit about it that he pretty well had to make sure he stepped up and looked after himself; otherwise he was being a hypocrite, and she'd be the first to call him on it too. He laughed at that.

When the phone rang a second time, he pushed away the empty plate away, looked at the number, and answered it. "Hey, did you figure out what that number meant?"

"No," Kate said crossly. "How about a little more explanation?"

"I got nothing," he said. "It literally was a case of that number damn-near dropping me in my tracks," he said. "I didn't like it either because I figured all this woo-woo stuff had gone bye-bye, and I was free and clear." Hearing the frustration in her voice, he asked, "Where are you?"

"I'm still at the office," she said. "We had a couple drive-by shooting cases that broke open today but not enough to close them quite yet."

"Well, that's good," he said. "You seem to be busy, as usual."

"As long as assholes are out there killing each other," she said, "I won't run out of work anytime soon."

"Sorry about that," he said. "It would be nice to think that they'd take a holiday once in a while to give you a bit of a break when you're tired."

"Nah, if they thought I was tired," she said, "they'd be in there looking to do some serious damage to everybody they hated."

"Unfortunately that is quite true."

"Anyway," she said, "I was just checking to see if you had any clue what that number meant."

"Nope," he said cheerfully. "I'm tossing that on your plate."

"*Great*," she said, "the least you can do is make it a useful toss."

"Always," he said. "There's got to be something you can do with it."

"Not yet," she said, "not yet." And, with that, she hung up, as was her custom.

He smiled and looked down at the spaghetti, thinking he should have asked if she'd eaten. He was thinking about calling her back when his phone rang yet again. He groaned and noted it was the Realtor yet again. He answered it and said, "I haven't made a decision."

"Well, you need to do it fast," she said, "because I've got other offers coming in."

"Good," he said, "you better take them then."

There was silence at the other end. "Seriously?"

"Sure," he said. "Depends on which buildings you're talking about of course. But, if somebody else wants it, I won't sit here and get into a bidding war over those decrepit shacks."

"Hey, they're really good real estate," she said. "These prices, you know they'll only go up."

"That's the amazing thing," he said, shaking his head. "I can't believe we've been talking these kinds of millions."

"We are," she said, "and I'm loving every minute of it."

"Sure, you get a commission on every sale," he said, "but I won't get pushed into anything."

"That's fine," she said comfortably. "If you want something, let me know."

"Will do."

And then she stopped and said, "You know, the offers are only on two of them."

"Yeah? Which two?" he asked, sitting back. When she listed the addresses, he smiled. "What about the other one you mentioned?" he asked and gave her the address for clarification.

"No offers on that one," she said. "It's been on and then pulled off the market a couple times."

"Pulled off why?"

"Because they couldn't sell. They decided they would go and rehab it themselves, then decided it was too costly. Now they'll try and sell it again," she snapped. "Honestly I really wish they'd just make up their mind and stick with it."

"Well, it depends on whether they really want to sell or not," he said, "but I can put in an offer." He went on to give her an amount well below the asking price.

She gasped and said, "Are you trying to insult them?"

"Nope," he said, "it's worth that to me and not a penny more. Talk to them, see if they want anything written up," he said, "but that's my offer."

With that, he ended the call. He chuckled because, as much as she didn't like his offer, if she could make the deal happen, she'd like it very much because it still brought her a ton of money. But he wasn't interested in the place unless he could get it at a price that allowed him to make a profit on it. With building costs going up, and supplies being a huge issue right now, absolutely no way would he pay more than he needed to for a building like that. And, if they'd had it on and off the market multiple times, then the sellers were willing to accept a lower price than they had in mind earlier—something this Realtor didn't want to hear. Either way, he was prepared to let it go if he couldn't get it for what he wanted. But, if he could, then he'd take it. Other than that, no way.

He cleaned up after his meal, then poured himself a glass of wine and made his way over to the couch, where he sat down to stare out at the beautiful view. He was tired after all the walking today, weary after having that number slam into his consciousness, and more upset than anything over that vision because he had thought his psychic events were a closed chapter of his life. He just wanted to relax. But it wasn't to be.

When his phone rang again, he stared at it, pissed, because this time it was his ex-girlfriend. He refused to answer it, and, when he didn't, a text came through.

Thank you again.

He rolled his eyes at that.

No way he was opening that door. He knew what she meant, in that he'd been instrumental in finding her nephew. She'd been derelict in her duty, and the boy had somehow slipped into the hands of a pedophile. At the same time, if Simon opened that door to Caitlin and even acknowledged her words, she would feel that she could contact him anytime. And she most definitely could not.

It was all water under the bridge, and it had taken a long time for her to get out of his life as it was. When he didn't respond, another text came through.

At least you could acknowledge that you received my message.

He stared at it and wondered. "And why the hell should I?" he murmured out loud. Then another text came through.

I really am sorry. I treated you like shit, and I shouldn't have.

He laughed at that. "You think?"

He got up, put on some music, and sat back down again, shutting off his phone. He liked an awful lot of technology, and one of the best ways to enjoy it was when it was time to shut it down. He closed his eyes and rested.

CHAPTER 2

Kate's Tuesday Morning

TUESDAY WAS A repeat of the day before. Time went by in a blur of cases and research. When Kate got some time, she'd gone back to the original drive-by case that Rodney had mentioned. She walked over to his desk with the file in her hand and said, "So a couple more similarities are here."

He looked up at her in surprise. "What are we talking about?"

"The Chevy trucks and the drive-by cases."

He frowned, his mind shifting gears, and said, "We've been busy since we talked about that last."

And their desks were piled high. Plus, the detectives had added pressure to maintain the good press the department had just received for breaking up that pedophile ring. It was still in the media, still all over the news, and they were still being hounded by people for interviews.

"Similarities? Like what?" he asked.

"The same color," she said, "aqua blue. That's a fairly unusual color."

He nodded. "Huh, I thought it was black."

"According to what's here," she said, "it says aqua blue."

"Interesting. Okay, so what else?"

"It didn't have a bed liner, but it had hooks on the sides.

Metal ones, like *T*s coming up off the bed."

He nodded. "Tie-down hooks?"

"Yeah, something like that," she said.

"So, it could be the same truck," he admitted. "Although there's how many models in the Lower Mainland like that?"

"If we could narrow down the year," she said, "I could spit out a run, and we could check on them. But other than it being clunky and old looking, I'm not getting any clue on how old it was. I could pull several images and see if I can get any of our witnesses to narrow it down again."

"Yeah, that would be good," he said. "Get any of the witnesses to take another look."

She nodded. "I'm working on one of the paint programs to try to get the color right. And add a few dents, if I can." She laughed. "Everybody seems to remember it was dented, but nobody could really say where the dents were."

"And, of course, nobody ever has a picture," he said.

"Always," she said, with a shrug.

She headed back to her desk and brought up several of the old Chevys around in the 1960s. She printed it off when the model changed in '63 and then another for the few tweaks made in '67. Other than that, she had four different prints in color. She had to send them to a different part of the office, since they didn't have a color printer in their area. With that done and the printed copies in hand, she headed back to the files for the witnesses' phone numbers and contacted a couple previous witnesses. She got through to two, who agreed to let her email them some photos of trucks.

She fired off the emails and, while on the phone with one woman, said, "Okay, so do you recognize any of these as the truck?"

"Honestly I don't remember," she muttered. "It all happened so fast. The color seems right, but I don't know about the truck."

"Okay, is there anything about the truck that you think isn't right?"

"The front," she said. "The grille on the front. I think it was more vertical looking. The ridges were sticking up somehow."

"Okay, good enough. Thank you."

The second one said something similar but wasn't sure about the color. Even by the time she left messages for the third and fourth witnesses, Kate knew it was probably a long shot and wouldn't come anywhere close to giving her more details. Then she moved on to the second drive-by case and contacted anybody associated with that one. Another four witnesses had seen the shooting, and, by the time she phoned them and had them take a look at the truck photos, she was pretty bummed because she wasn't making any progress.

Rodney looked over at her, shrugged, and said, "You know that it's really hard for people to remember details of vehicles, unless they're car buffs."

She nodded. "And what are the chances that any of these people were one?" she muttered. She still had a couple more, and, just when she was running out of options, she got an email back from one of the ones she had emailed the photos to.

It was the second one. But the dent was in the front, and there was damage to the grille. I remember that specifically because, at the time, I was dealing with a problem with my own grille, and I thought he must have smacked his up too.

She picked up the phone and called him and asked, "Did you put that in your statement?"

"I don't know," he said, "but seeing that picture reminded me."

"Good enough," she said. "Any chance it jogged any other information you can think of?"

His tone was thoughtful when he said, "I'm looking at the picture now. The color is close but not quite right. It was a long time ago. But that's an odd color."

"Do you think it was a custom paint job?"

"No," he said, "I doubt it. I'm not sure it's quite the paint that was used in that year though."

"Right, I can get the manufacturer to give me a better idea on the colors back then."

"Yeah," he said, "it was also, you know, I hate to say *faded*, but it was faded."

"So, maybe just old paint?"

"Well, it was definitely old paint," he said. "I don't know. It's hard to tell. It's close to this, but it's not exactly." Then he asked, "Why are you worried about this now?"

"It's not that I'm worried about it now," she said, "but we've had another drive-by shooting, and there are a few similarities."

"That son of a bitch," he said. "He gets away with it once and then tries a second time?"

"Which is why we're checking everything again," she said.

"This one was really funny. He drove up slow to a bunch of people on the sidewalk," he said. "I was on the opposite side of the road, and, as he drove up, it was like he was just looking for somebody. Searching the crowd maybe."

"Meaning, it was targeted?"

"Well, targeted somewhat, like, you know, if there had been a group of six kids, I got the feeling he might still have picked out a kid from that group. It's like he was looking for something or for someone to fit, and that one was close enough. He just fired off a bunch of shots, and he tore out of there. I don't remember the whole license plate, but there was something with a *G* in it."

At that, her eyebrows shot up. "I've got your statement here. There was no mention of seeing the license plate."

"No, because I couldn't see the whole thing," he said, "and I didn't think that a lone *G* would help."

"Well, it's something," she said, and she started typing her notes. "And it would give us an idea. I mean, I can run that down for any of the trucks of that vintage and see if something comes up."

Her witness added, "I didn't think it was much help. Sorry about that. But it really pissed me off, you know, the way the guy just didn't give a shit, and then he just killed that young guy. We always wondered if that young guy had been the intended target in the first place or not."

"We'd like to think so because otherwise we could have some asshat just running around, shooting people. Now three years later," she said, "it's possible he's doing it again."

He swore at that and said, after a moment, "Part of the problem is also that I think they were using different parts from different trucks."

"What do you mean?"

"I remember thinking at the time that the driver's door wasn't from the right model of truck," he said, "but again, I don't remember more details about it. Once the shooting started, everything else fled my mind."

"Good enough," she said. "You've been a great help, thank you."

"Well, I sure hope you find the shooter. The last thing we want is to have somebody else get mowed down just because they were walking on the sidewalk."

"Is that what you think the reason was?" she asked curiously.

"I have no idea," he said. "It probably was something much more involved than that, but it didn't make any sense. He just looked like he was searching for a target. In this case I think that guy was not so much the one he was looking for but one that would fit the mold, you know?" And, with that, the guy rang off.

She sat back, turned to Rodney, and said, "That was an interesting conversation." And she relayed the information he'd provided.

Rodney nodded. "Some guys are really good at picking out car parts," he said. "And, if that's the way it appeared to him, that's good to know."

"But," Kate replied, "it also means that, if there is a connection between the two cases, this guy has waited three years to do this again. Why?"

"Well, maybe the first time he got so panicked that he took off, waiting for the cops to come to his door. When we didn't make a connection, he got cocky again," he muttered. "Sometimes it takes them a while to work up the nerve to try again. Maybe something made him angry, and he's looking for a target. Who knows?"

"Which would make him a random serial killer," she muttered, shaking her head. "That would be depressing."

"More than depressing," he said, "he'd be hard to stop because we need more than just a vehicle. That vehicle could go into a garage and be completely unseen for the next three years."

"And, if that's the case," she said, "the insurance on it won't be his either. This one witness mentioned a license plate with the letter *G* on it."

Rodney shrugged. "You can run it," he said, "but you'll get way too many options."

"But maybe not with these other details," she said. Determined, she started to run a match through the license plate database, checking to see what might pop up. She could ask Reese to do this too, but—as the one analyst shared among all three VPD Homicide Units—she was swamped, and Kate liked to find out information herself. She was quite surprised when, a few moments later, it spat out a list of matching vehicles. "Now this is interesting," she said, "there's only forty-two. I was expecting three times that or more. But one of them is flagged as stolen."

Immediately Rodney got up and walked over. "Which one was stolen?" She pointed it out to him. "Follow that up," he said with a frown, "because that could easily be the one we're looking for."

She frowned at that. "But, in this case, do you think he stole the truck or just the license plate and put it on his truck?"

He shook his head. "No idea, but either way it would be good to know, right?"

She followed up, and, by the time she reached the person who owned the truck that had been stolen, she ended up getting his son.

"I'm sorry," he said. "My dad passed away last year. It was his truck. He had kept it in the garage, uninsured for a long time."

"Uninsured?" she asked.

"Yes, up until not too long before it was stolen. Out of the blue he decided to get it insured and to clean it up a bit, maybe to sell it. He knew his health wasn't good, and he was trying to take care of things, so my mom didn't get left with all that to deal with. Of course he left it too late, and, by the time he dealt with the truck, he was already in poor health."

"Sorry to hear that," she said.

"Well, at least he enjoyed his last few years."

"And there was never any news on your stolen vehicle?"

"Nope," he said. "We weren't exactly sure what happened to it. We got up one day, and it was gone."

"So, it was kept in the garage?"

He answered clearly. "Yes, it was kept in the garage, and my dad hadn't taken it out in years. So I'm not even sure who would have known it was there."

"And, of course, if the garage door was closed—"

"Well, it was supposed to be, but I'm not sure," he said.

"So it's possible somebody saw it there?"

"Yes, and it's quite possible that someone walked in, started it up, and drove it out of there. Both my parents are hard of hearing. They didn't like the hearing aids, so they'd take them out as early in the evening as they could."

"Right," she said, "so stealing this vehicle wouldn't have been that difficult."

"No," he said. "Not at all."

"What about the license plate?" she asked.

"My dad's name is George, and he ended up with one that had a G at the beginning."

"Perfect," she said. "Do you happen to know the rest of the plate numbers?" She looked down at the list in front of her.

He said, "I don't, but I have it right here. Just a second." Moments later he reeled it off for her.

"Perfect, that lines up with what I've got here."

"Does that mean you found the truck?"

She hesitated. "No, but it could very well mean it was used to commit a crime."

The younger man on the other end of the phone gasped. "Well, if that's the case," he said, "I'm really glad my dad is not around to hear it. It would break his heart to think of his old baby being used that way."

"Well, we're not sure just yet," she said, "but we're doing our best to track it down."

"Good luck," he said. "Give me a call if I can help in some way."

"Was it dented?"

"The front grille had a dent," he said. "It wasn't too bad, and Dad was looking at replacing the parts. But, as it turned out, they were quite expensive, according to my father, so he had decided to sell it as is."

"Okay, what about the doors? The same model as the vehicle itself?"

He gave a bark of laughter. "Oh my, how did you know? My dad replaced one of the doors on it. I don't even know where he got it, but it could have been at one of the pick-and-pull places, I'll bet."

"Good enough," she said. "Thanks for your help."

And, with that, she rang off, then looked at Rodney and said, "Bull's-eye."

He grinned. "Well, that's interesting. So we have a stolen vehicle, likely used in the first drive-by from three years ago. Now we need to corroborate that information and then confirm if it was used in the second one, the recent one."

"I hear you," she said. "I'll get there." She looked over at him. "What are you working on?"

"The victims," he said. "While you were working on that, I figured I'd drill down on the victims to see if any

39

connection was there."

"That's a good idea. It seems so strange to think that, if you had this need to kill somebody, you would go pick a complete stranger off the street."

"But, if you think about it," Lilliana said, from her desk behind them, "it's the easiest way to not get caught. If there's no connection, there's nothing for us to find."

Kate frowned at that but nodded. When her computer chimed to say an email had come in, she popped it open and sat back with a low whistle.

"What's up?" Andy asked, as he walked into the bullpen area, starting his day late, probably from all the time he spent on his hair. Or maybe it was a kid-related thing. "That was an interesting whistle."

She looked up at him but was a little disconnected over what she'd seen. "Remember that email I got yesterday?" she asked, and the others looked at her.

"The one with the picture of you at the bridge?" Andy guessed.

"Yeah," she said, with a nod. "I'm not sure what the hell is going on, but I just got another email."

"What does this one say?" Lilliana asked, getting up and walking over to take a look. She too whistled when she saw it. "Well, that's a strange thing to put in the subject line."

It said *Maybe not* and attached a picture of a bridge and another pair of shoes.

"You're not in this one," Rodney murmured, joining them around Kate's desk.

"No," she said, "I'm not. I don't know anything about it, like what bridge this is or when this was taken," she said. But then she looked at it again and said, "Wait. A time stamp's on the photo. It's from this morning."

"Wow, let's check to see if we had another suicide this morning," Lilliana said, looking at the date stamp. "Why the hell is he sending this to you?"

"I don't know," Kate said, "and what is 'maybe not' supposed to mean?"

"I don't know either," Lilliana said, "but I don't like it. Send that around to all of us, so we can each take a good look. Let's get on the horn and check if anybody's gotten notice of a suicide. Anybody recognize that bridge?"

"I wondered if it was the Port Mann," Rodney said. "But not enough of it is in the photo to tell. And the other email didn't have a message, did it?"

Kate said, "No, it didn't. At least not that I saw, but we better check." She brought up the first email and cast it to a big projector on the front wall. "Can anyone see one?"

Rodney got up, walked over, and pointed. "Do you guys see this?"

At the bottom of the first picture, blending into part of the bridge railing, it read *Finally*.

Immediately Kate cast the second photograph to the big wall screen and asked her team, "Is there anything on this one?"

They all looked, and then Rodney shook his head. "No, but, if he thinks you didn't see his note on the first one, he put it in the subject line of the second one to be sure you did this time. So it's 'finally' and 'maybe not,' right?"

"*Maybe not* what though?" Owen asked, listening in to the whole conversation, and now speaking up.

"I don't know," Kate said, as they stared at her. She rubbed her temples. "This doesn't make any sense." She double-checked the sender. "This is from the same email address."

"And, if you send a reply, it'll go somewhere right into cyberspace," Andy muttered.

"But that doesn't mean our cybersecurity team shouldn't check it out anyway," Lilliana warned. "And now that you've got a second one, you better let Colby know."

Again Kate nodded. "I really don't need this right now," she muttered. "I was happily working along on the drive-by case."

Just then, Colby walked in, usually the last one on each shift. "Hey, what about that drive-by? Did you catch a break on it?"

"I don't know if it's a break as much as another distraction," Kate said.

"Oh, now there's an interesting point." Lilliana spun on her heels and looked at Kate.

Kate stared at her teammate and shook her head. "No, I don't think these emails are connected at all to the drive-bys," she said, her mind immediately puzzling away on it. "How could they be?"

"Hey, hang on a minute," Colby said. "Does somebody want to fill me in here? What's happening?"

Rodney spoke up first. "She got another email."

He turned to look at Kate and asked, "Another picture of you?"

"No," she said, shaking her head. "That's what's weird about it. It's not of me at all, but it looks like it's another bridge scene and potentially the aftermath of another suicide."

At that, Colby's eyebrows shot right up. When she pointed and cast the second emailed picture on the wall screen again, he turned. He moved closer to it and said, frowning, "That's the Second Narrows Bridge."

She shrugged. "And it's a photo of a pair of men's work boots, so that would imply a man had gone off the bridge."

"That's the theory," Colby said. "I don't know how many people planning to commit suicide would put somebody else's shoes there."

"But why send that photograph to me?" Kate asked.

"And then you have to consider the message," Rodney said.

"What message?" Colby asked.

"We didn't see it at first," Kate said, "but Rodney just saw now, on that initial photograph. Written at the bottom by the railing it says 'finally.' And on today's photo, there's no message on the photograph, at least none that we can see, but 'maybe not' is in the subject line of the email."

"*Finally* you're involved, and then number two photo, without you in it, so *maybe not* involved?" Lilliana said, thoughtfully tossing out ideas. There was a moment of silence, as everybody stared at each other.

Then Kate groaned. "Please tell me that it means that they thought I would be involved in the investigation of the suicides because I was seen at the first and then, when I didn't show up at the second one, they assumed that I'm not involved." Her gaze went from one to the other. "The only reason I would be involved is—"

And they all jumped in. "They weren't suicides."

<hr />

Simon's Tuesday Morning

SIMON WOKE UP Tuesday morning, his head full, his mouth dry, his tongue swollen, seemingly wrapped in fuzzy cloth. *Uh-oh.* He had been watching for weird symptoms to see if they were precursors to visions. *Hopefully not.* He got up, brushed his teeth thoroughly, and had a hot shower. When he stepped back out again, he still felt a bit woolly-headed, but, once he was dressed and headed to his kitchen for coffee, he hoped for the best, though he had a long day ahead of him. He had barely seated himself at the kitchen table when his phone buzzed. Seeing it was his ex, he put it on Silent and shoved it off to the side.

He hadn't even checked his emails or messages yet, something he needed to do. But this time in the morning, with a cup of coffee, needed to be honored and appreciated before the day closed in on him and went to shit right afterward. He clicked on the news and checked that everything in his world was fine. Only as he heard word of another suicide did his heart stop, and slowly he looked at the scene, so similar to what Kate had seen yesterday and had shared with him. It was a different bridge and a different pair of shoes but the same theory, and he knew she would have an ugly day because of it. He immediately grabbed his phone, turned the sound back on, and sent her a note. **Sorry, just heard there was another suicide. Don't let it get to you.**

And he let it go at that.

As soon as he started his workday, his papers all packed up in his portfolio, he headed on foot to the one building he was still considering buying. He hadn't heard back from the Realtor. It could be a done deal or a dead deal; he wasn't at all sure, but he had several meetings he had to accomplish with his own builders, as they rehabbed other projects currently underway.

There was never a time when he had nothing to do. He also needed to do some banking, and that was always fun. Moving money is what he called it, but people had to be paid, and people of all kinds needed to be kept in the loop. Paychecks were important, and he couldn't stand to see anybody not getting what they were due. Plus, a lot of people just needed help. Speaking of which, he thought about a couple he knew on the streets, as well as a women's shelter, that could always use a little more money. He added a few notes to his To Do list on his cell, then looked at all of it and winced. "It'll be a damn long day again," he muttered.

Still, if need be, he had leftover spaghetti and meatballs, even some salad and garlic bread too. He shook his head at that. He was worth millions and was happy because he had leftovers for later. He sagged. "One of these days you'll have to start looking after yourself." It was so reminiscent of what he told Kate over and over again that he laughed. "Fine, but, if she ever finds out, you're in trouble."

CHAPTER 3

Kate's Wednesday Morning

P ROGRESS HAD COME to a dead stop on the drive-by case. Kate couldn't locate the vehicle. Reese hadn't found anything either, which frustrated both of them. None of the current witnesses had anything to say, other than it was an older faded-blue truck. Kate groaned at that and headed toward the morgue. It's not that she had a gruesome bent by any means, but she liked to see the damage for herself. She liked to see and to understand the angles and to figure out in her head just how somebody did this ... and why.

Rarely did she get the answers that she needed, but it did give her the motivation to keep going and to find the asshole who thought life had so little value that they could just shoot somebody down in the street in broad daylight, for no other reason potentially then just because they were there. Reese was still working on the victims involved, from years ago and from the current shooting, looking to see if she could find any connection between the cases, but, so far, nothing had popped. And Kate was afraid that, as time went by, nothing would happen with it—until the next time this guy decided to come through with another drive-by shooting.

She had no way to know for sure that these drive-by cases were connected, but she liked the concept. She really liked the idea, but what she needed were facts. Cold hard evidence was the only thing that would help in a case like this right now. If only she could get what she needed. As she neared the hospital, she saw the flashing lights and heard the sirens, as vehicles headed off in another direction. "Crime just never takes a break, does it?"

But then she also knew, from working in a variety of law enforcement departments, that somebody was always out there, causing chaos for somebody else. Not everything ended up with a murder, but almost all cases ended up as a crime. That kept everybody busy, even if they didn't want to be. By the time she made it to the morgue and headed to the autopsy room, she stopped just outside, looking for Dr. Smidge.

He looked up, caught sight of her, and narrowed his gaze.

She shrugged. "Just wondering how the autopsy on the drive-by was coming."

"What do you want to know?" he asked, motioning to a table off to the side. "I just finished."

"Anything unexpected?"

"Nope. A healthy twenty-three-year-old male, who didn't look to have any lingering illnesses of any kind. Died at the scene from three bullets to the chest. I would say instantly, but, of course, nothing is instant."

She nodded. "I got it."

"Have you found out who your shooter was?"

She shook her head. "No, I'm wondering if it's connected to a drive-by from three years ago."

His gaze narrowed at her. "Why would that be?"

"Possibly the same vehicle for one thing."

He shook his head. "Doesn't make a whole lot of sense."

"No, but not a lot in this world does," she fired right back at him.

He groaned. "Isn't that the truth. Well, let me know when you get there."

"It's the bullets I'm looking for."

"Ballistics has them," he said.

"Right, I'll wait on that then."

"It was three bullets here. How many did your victim die of before?"

She turned, looked at him, and said, "Three."

He frowned. "Damn. How old?"

"In his twenties too. The shooter drove slowly up and down the street, either looking for somebody or for an opportunity that would work, then chose his victim and shot him."

"So random killing, random timing?"

She nodded. "That's what it looks like—at the moment at least."

"Well, if it's connected," he snapped, "we need to find him before he does this again. Senseless killing always pisses me off."

"Any killing," she said quietly. "But, yeah, the ones like this are so much worse." She turned to walk back out again, already dialing Ballistics. "Do you have anything on that drive-by?"

"Not yet," Daniel said. "Do you want us to do something in particular when we get there?"

She said, "I want you to check it against a cold case from three years ago." She gave him the case number.

"Interesting," he said. "Well, it'll come up in the database."

"But that might take extra time," she said. "Check it

against the ballistics when you can, please."

"Will do," Daniel said.

She smiled and kept on going. She had a sense of freedom and accomplishment being where she was in her job as a detective. She also had a ton of hard work and responsibility that really didn't go down as easily as she had hoped it would. But she was here, and she was doing the job; there wasn't anything else she could ask for.

Out of the blue Kate wondered what the hell the number thirteen was about that Simon had texted her earlier this week. She was always wary with any information that came her way, but some of these random things of his had proven valuable, but she just wasn't prepared to automatically count all of it as being true. Then again, he had never asked that of her either, and that was nice too.

As she headed to her vehicle parked outside Vancouver General Hospital, her phone rang.

"We've got another drive-by," Rodney said.

"Shit. Really?"

"Yes," he said, "and another old blue truck, according to the witnesses."

"Crap, can we get it on video at least? I'm heading out now. Tell me where."

"Texting you the address. I'll meet you there."

Getting to the scene took her a bit, as traffic was heavy. When she finally arrived, she parked at an angle across the road, thankful that the scene was at least blocked from traffic, as she headed over to Rodney. "What have you got?"

"Four witnesses off to the side," he said, pointing at them. "They were all out walking. The victim is a friend of theirs."

She looked at the young man lying on the street, a sheet

partially tossed over him. "Same age group as the other two?"

He nodded. "Doesn't mean they're related though."

"Nope. It's just one more similarity."

"Meaning he picks victims who are young and healthy."

"Oh, that's not a bad thought," she said, turning to look at him, considering.

He frowned. "What do you mean?"

"Maybe he's aging or diseased, or he's the same age and is disabled and is taking out his anger at the world on healthy people around him."

"Well, that would suck. So just because you're having a shit life, you turn around and make others pay for it?"

"Well, we've seen a lot worse," she said quietly.

"Doesn't mean I have to like it."

"No," she said, "none of us do."

Rodney shook his head. "Well, we don't really know what's going on yet, so let's keep an open mind."

She walked over to the first of the four witnesses and pulled the woman aside. "What did you see?"

"Just this old truck," the young woman said, tears streaming down her face. "We were all just talking and laughing."

"Were you laughing at the truck?"

She looked at Kate sideways. "Maybe. It was one of those really old beaten-up trucks, you know? Nothing special."

"Do you think he heard you?"

The girl looked at her, shocked. "Oh God," she said. "I don't know. Is that why he shot Billy?"

"I don't know," Kate said quietly. "We're looking for a motive."

The witness shook her head. "Well, we wouldn't have

said anything if we thought he would react like that."

Kate wondered how many times people had to get a bad result before they would understand the effects of their shit talking. Sometimes you don't get a second chance to change. Like Billy. "Have you seen the guy before? Did you recognize the truck?"

The young woman shook her head. "No," she said. "I've never seen it before." She started to cry.

"Okay, what do you know about the victim?"

She wiped her eyes. "He's a friend of my brother," she said. "We were just going to the mall. I wanted to go, but I'm not allowed to go alone, so they were walking me there. I never want to go to the mall again now."

"Take it easy," Kate said quietly, "this isn't your fault."

"But you said maybe it's because we were laughing at the truck."

"No," she said firmly, "that's not what I said. And, even if that were true, you're not the one responsible. The guy who did this shooting is responsible. Remember that. But next time somebody drives something that you think is funny, or you want to make fun of someone, maybe just keep quiet."

The younger woman nodded. "I will," she promised. She looked over at Billy. "He was a really nice guy," she said. "He's the reason we're walking because he wouldn't let me go alone. He said it wasn't safe anymore and that the world was different now."

"And he's right," Kate said sadly. "Unfortunately his death proves that."

The girl started to wail again, while Kate moved on to the next witness and then the next, the brother of the victim, who sat off to the side, stunned. She looked over at him and asked, "Are your parents on the way?"

"Yeah, they are," he said, "but I don't want to leave Billy like that."

"The coroner is coming too," she said. "There's nothing more you can do for Billy now, except help us catch this guy."

"I don't even know who it was," he said, staring up at her face. His eyes were wide and dry, from holding back the tears, but his anger kept his spine stiff. "I've never seen the guy before."

"Did you get a good look at his face?"

He shook his head. "No, he was wearing a baseball cap, pulled down low."

"Of course he was," she muttered. "What about the truck?"

"It was an old Chevy. Beat-up. The front grille was bashed in. I noticed that. Billy and I were talking about the repairs it needed. One of the doors, the driver's side door, looked like it was a different year or style than what was originally on it."

"Do you think the driver heard you at all?"

The brother looked at her in surprise. "I—I don't know. I don't know why or how he could have. We were on the street, and he was driving by. An old truck like that... chances are he wouldn't have heard anything outside of the cab."

She just nodded and didn't say anything. "And, as far as you know, you've never met this guy before? And I don't suppose you would have any idea if Billy had met him."

"He didn't sound like he did," he murmured. "He didn't say anything about it at all."

By the time she was done, and everybody had been interviewed, she headed to where Rodney stood. "It looks very similar to the drive-by we had a couple days ago. Same truck description too."

He nodded. "We're pulling the footage from all the cameras we can find," he said. "That should help us to tie it in."

"And hopefully tie these current cases into the open one from three years ago."

He looked at her and shrugged. "That'll be a lot harder."

"Maybe," she said. "I guess one of the biggest problems is that three-year break in pattern, isn't it?"

"Yeah," he said. "Why would there be three years between shootings and then only two days now?"

She shrugged. "I have no idea, but it seems like something significant happened to change his timing."

"Maybe," Rodney said, but he was distracted, as he looked at the sheet-covered form in front of him.

"Or are there other cases that we haven't connected?"

He looked at her and shrugged. "I don't know if there are any others—cold or not. And it could also be that our database isn't as complete as we'd like. Maybe they came from Surrey or Richmond or somewhere else."

She nodded slowly. "I was thinking of that too. We need to pull some more data, before this gets too far along. I'll contact Reese." She pulled out her phone.

"Too bad we hadn't pulled it before," he said. "This guy is just a kid. He'll never grow up and live a normal life. He'll never get married and have kids," Rodney said, shaking his head, his lips thinning in anger. "It's senseless!"

"Look at who he is shooting," she said. "Why is he picking healthy young men? Like we discussed earlier, maybe the shooter is not young, not healthy himself? Is he making his victims pay a price for his own ill health or something?" she asked. "What's his motive?"

"And the killing is fast and simple. He gets to see it happen, but maybe that's all he can do."

"Exactly," she said. "Maybe he's not physically capable of getting out of the vehicle and taking these guys down."

"Maybe he doesn't have the skill, the strength, or maybe he doesn't even have the guts," Rodney added. "You know, like a scaredy-cat killing. From a distance, largely undercover, with an easy getaway, so there's very little chance in his mind that he'll get caught. So he's pulling these stunts and taking down people just because he can."

Noting his reaction, she put in the call to Reese, requesting to get as much as the VPD analyst could find on similar cases in Vancouver and all surrounding areas.

PREPARED, SIMON HEADED out for the day, going from one area to the other, slowly taking things off his list. When he walked down the back alley of one of his favorite places, he quietly knocked on a subdued and partially hidden wooden door. When he heard a woman's voice on the other side, he said, "It's Simon."

A little window opened at the top, and a woman's face peered through. He held up a roll of bills. "Something to help you out for the next month."

Immediately she opened the door and accepted the money with a big smile. "You know, if it wasn't for guys like you, I don't—"

"I get it," he said, with a nod. "Get back in there before anybody sees you."

And, with that, she closed the door, and he kept on going. He had a soft spot for women's shelters and an even softer spot for kids who found themselves in tough situations. He helped out all kinds of charities, but he was committed to seeking out those who needed help but didn't fit into the existing charity systems. Those were even harder to find. Simon knew several street kids and several sex workers he would help, especially if they pushed the money along to the kids. Paying it forward was an unspoken agreement. He would ignore their illegal activities among consenting adults, and they would keep him out of the loop of all the lawbreaking, providing that they held up their end of the bargain, and the bulk of the money went toward the kids in need. There were always kids in need.

As Simon made his way back to the building that he was looking at buying, he heard a voice in the background.

Do it.

He frowned, stopped, and looked around, trying to see who had said it. Finding nobody close to him, he finally muttered, "Do what?"

And there came the voice again.

Do it. A hoarse whisper, pushing him to do something.

He shook his head. "Well, I won't do something just because you say so, asshole."

And the voice came again. *Do it. Just do it.*

He frowned once more, not exactly sure who was talking or where the voice came from. And knowing he would likely experience more crippling visions—if that's what this was—he went into a small park and sat down on a bench, slightly out of view from anybody, in case he fell unconscious for a moment. He was tired, but he wasn't that tired that he would fall asleep outside.

Although he was more tired than expected, and that

could be why this voice was creeping into his space. It was not anything that he was comfortable with. He closed his eyes and tried to empty his mind, sending the message to go away.

But instead the voice whispered, *Come on. Just do it.*

Simon shrugged. "You know what? You're really pissing me off," he muttered. "Go away."

And he reached up mentally and slammed the door. Almost instantly a sense of peace entered his mind. Beaming, he hopped to his feet. "Got that fixed." And he laughed. He kept on walking, feeling better, although in the back of his mind was that little concern because he had thought he was clear of all this psychic garbage. And it wasn't garbage. He got that. But he didn't want anything to do with it either. He kept on walking, and suddenly the door in his mind burst open again.

Do it! This time the voice was harder and stronger.

He frowned, froze, and looked around. "Do what?"

CHAPTER 4

Kate's Thursday

A FTER ANOTHER LONG day, Kate had an ugly realization. She'd followed all the leads and had done everything she could on the recent drive-by shooting cases, and, when she finally closed the file and dropped it at the side of her desk with an ugly sigh, Rodney looked at her and said, "It happens that way sometimes."

"It's just so frustrating," she muttered. "Somebody knows something."

"Somebody always knows something," he said, nodding his head. "But getting those people to talk, that's a different story."

"It's about asking the right questions too. I mean, you think about everything that you could ask, and then you realize that maybe you need to frame the question in quite the right way. Maybe they didn't realize what you were asking, and maybe they didn't think of something else because of it," she said. "It's incredibly frustrating."

He laughed. "It is, indeed," he said, "and you're not the first or the last person to find that out."

"I know," she said, with a groan. She looked at him. "I guess you didn't come up with anything new."

"Nope, I would have shared if I had," he said cheerfully. "Go home. Take your mind off it. Maybe something will come to you then."

She nodded, but her lips were in a grim line.

"I'm heading out now. Come on. I'll walk with you to our cars."

She thought about what he had said all the way home. The atmosphere these days in the bullpen was completely different than when she had first started here as a detective, and that was good. The team had pulled together, compiling an incredible amount of work already and had solved all kinds of cases. It's just that the crimes never let up, so there never seemed to be any end to it all, and that was frustrating too. She wanted to go home at the end of the day, satisfied with what she'd accomplished, but always had that uncertainty, wondering if she may have missed something else, something that she could have done more of, and that hurt.

The stress was real. As she rolled her neck and shoulders, while unlocking the door to her apartment, that thought immediately reminded her that she'd let her judo practices slide. She'd picked up an interest in it as a teen for that extra exercise and for the chance to kick ass somewhere. With that in mind, she quickly got dressed in her exercise gear and went back out again, walking to her favorite club.

When she walked in, her sensei looked at her, smiled, and said, "There you are. I haven't seen you in a while."

She nodded. "I know," she said. "I'm so sorry. But I need to be here tonight."

"If nothing else," he said quietly, instantly understanding the tension in her system, "it's really good for stress relief."

She smiled. "And that's good because I could use some of that right now."

He said, "Great. Let's give it a hard run then."

And a hard run it was. By the time she was done, she was groaning, prone on the floor, and he was smiling, offering his hand to help her up.

"Hey," he said, "you've got to get back in here a little more often if you want to knock me down."

"I know," she said, waving away his hand. "That was evident tonight."

He burst out laughing. "No," he said, "you still had some moves. It's just you're a little out of practice."

"Too much so," she said, still on the floor on her back, staring up at the ceiling. "I need to get here more than just weekly again."

He nodded. "Yes, you do. In order to keep it flowing the way you want it to flow," he said, "it's pretty necessary to be here consistently."

"Yeah, if only my workload would allow for it."

"I get it," he said. "Believe me. I do. You're doing a very important job, and it comes with an awful lot of challenges, and one of them is time."

"Time, energy, and mental health," she said. "I'm slacking on the mental health side as well."

"You've got to watch that," he said, "and find a way to figure it out. I understand your misgivings about seeing the department's mental health doctor, but find some other way. That is way too important to let slide."

She smiled. "It's an occupational hazard, but the job doesn't exactly come with any manual on how to deal with it."

As he thought about it, he frowned and said, "No, and it's a real problem, isn't it?"

She nodded. "It is, actually. You do your best, but sometimes you come away thinking that you're not getting anything done."

"Well, we know you are," he said. "It's just a matter of staying positive."

At that, she laughed. "If it only were that easy."

He chuckled. "Still, it's not all bad news."

"If you say so," she replied, with a big grin.

"Well, when you've got time," he said, "I've got time for you. So do the best you can."

And, on that note, he headed over to work with other students.

Too tired to shower here, she walked out the door. The air was fresh, and she stood still for a few long moments, just taking in deep breaths. When a shadow detached from the wall beside her, she was momentarily startled, only to realize it was Simon. "What are you doing here?" she asked bluntly.

He winced. "Always rolling out the welcome wagon, aren't you? But anyway I'm here," he said, "and it doesn't look like you're in any shape to walk home."

"That bad? I could catch a cab or maybe the bus," she said, with a shrug. "Honestly I just needed to come and to blow off some steam."

"Hard day?"

"Frustrating," she said. "We can't get any answers, and apparently you aren't getting anything on this one. Maybe it's only when there are children at risk," she said, with a side glance at him.

"I hope so," he said casually. "I'd just as soon never have that happen again."

She nodded. "And that's what makes you so unique."

"Not unique enough," he said. "It's still disconcerting to

have any of this happen."

"Sorry about that," she said, but her tone was so obviously unrepentant that he had to laugh.

"You could make it sound like you care a little bit at least," he said, chuckling.

She gave him a wave of her hand. "Trying not to lie."

"How was your session?" he asked, nodding his head at the club doors behind her.

"Really good, but, as I stand here, I'm realizing you could be right about my ability to make it home, at least walking."

"No, I'm not walking for sure," he said. "Come on. My car is around the corner."

"You don't have to keep looking after me," she said in exasperation, yet inordinately pleased that he cared enough to. It's like she craved what wasn't good for her. Or what she was trying to convince herself was a bad idea—but was it? Still?

"Well, if you—uh—managed to look after yourself," he said, "I wouldn't have to."

When she glared at him, he chuckled. "Come on. Don't be stubborn. There's a time and a place, and this isn't it."

"Says you," she muttered.

He gave her a flat stare, and she groaned. "Fine, I am tired."

"Right," he said, "at least we can agree on that."

She just tipped her head side to side and rotated her shoulders.

"You should really get a massage."

"Yeah, well, that's not likely to happen," she said, waving her hand. Then realizing she was being ungrateful, she said, "Look. I'll take the ride home, if you've got time, but that's it. I'm going to bed and crashing."

"And that's a hint for me, I suppose."

"I've told you that we aren't a good idea."

"Keep on telling yourself that."

She glared; he shrugged. And finally she just said, "I'm too tired right now to have this conversation."

"Got it," he said, "and you don't ever need to have an excuse. Believe me. I'm all about you taking care of you."

"I take care of me just fine." But lately it was hard to do. At his flat stare, she groaned. "Okay, so it's been a busy day, you know? Some weeks, some lifetimes are like that."

He nodded. "I get it. I really do because some of my nights are like that too. But it doesn't change the fact that, if you don't take care of yourself, nobody else will."

She nodded and got into his vehicle quietly. He was right, and she knew it. But the last thing she wanted was to be chastised like a child tonight. When he pulled up outside of her apartment, he looked at her and said, "I'd like to come in for a moment."

"But—" And she hesitated.

"I get it," he said. "I promise. I just want to come up and have a cup of coffee with you."

She looked at her watch and nodded. "Fine, but you're not staying."

He grinned at her.

"I mean it," she said. "Last time it happened, and it wasn't supposed to."

He shrugged. "I'm not pushing. I already said that."

"I know you *said* that," she replied, "but it seems like that's not how it ends up."

"That's not fair," he said. "I promise I'll be good."

She rolled her eyes at that but let him come up. She said,

"You put on the coffee. I'll go have a shower. Some things just don't feel right unless you can get clean."

"Go."

And, with that, she headed for the shower, enjoying the feel of the hot water sluicing down her back. She stepped out a bit later to find the coffee still dripping but only just started.

"What's the matter? Did you forget how to make it?" she asked in a teasing voice. Looking around, she found him stretched out on her couch, studying his phone. "Anything interesting?"

He said, "Unfortunately too interesting. You might get another phone call here soon."

"Why?" she asked, wrapping a towel around her head. Just then her phone rang.

"That's why."

Frowning, she looked at him and picked up the phone. "Hello."

"This is Dispatch. We have a DB. We're texting you the address and the details we have."

"Okay," she said, closing her eyes, wishing she didn't have to go out tonight, but then someone didn't want to die tonight, and they didn't get their wish either. "I'll head down there now." She called Rodney.

"Yeah, I just got it too." He said, "One other thing though, I was talking to somebody else earlier today."

"Oh, what's up?"

"There's been another jumper."

She stopped and winced. "Damn," she said, "that bridge is getting heavy use."

"It was a different bridge, so a different department's jurisdiction, which is why it didn't cross our desks," he said.

"Not that it makes any of it easier."

"No, it doesn't," she said. "I wish I knew what was bringing on this rash of jumpers."

"Does anything have to be bringing it on?" he asked in a dark tone. "Seems like there's always more than enough strife and ugliness in the world for people to find a reason to choose a different route."

"Maybe," she said, "but I'm really not liking these numbers."

He laughed. "Nobody likes the numbers."

"Okay, I'll meet you down there."

"Good enough," he said, "but I'll be going right past your place. I'll pick you up."

"Fine," she said, "give me ten."

"You got it."

She quickly dressed, and Simon still reclined on her couch. "You have to leave," she said, without preamble.

He hopped to his feet. "I know. I know. I was just waiting for you to be done."

She rolled her eyes at him. "I'd really rather that my teammate not see you."

At that, Simon's gaze narrowed.

"No, I'm not trying to hide the relationship," she said, "but, at the same time, I don't really want to answer any questions about it right now."

He nodded slowly. "That'll do for the moment."

She wasn't exactly sure what he was trying to push but figured that, when they had time to talk, he would open up a little bit more about it. Still, she figured that she wouldn't like it any more than she did now. "That reminds me. How did you know?"

"From one of my jobs. It's close to one of the houses I

was looking at rehabbing. I was texting the Realtor about it, and she said a swarm of cops was around what looked like might be a murder down the street."

She looked at him in surprise. "Of course you'd be involved," she muttered.

"I'm not involved at all," he said. "And, just for the record, I've never been involved in something like that."

She flashed him a smile. "I'm really glad to hear that." Because she was running behind, she stopped, looked at him, and said, "You need to lock up."

He nodded. "Go," he said. "I'll take care of it."

"Fine," she said. "It's not like I've got anything here to steal." She laughed in his direction, as she ran out of the apartment. Down on the street level, Rodney was just pulling in. She jumped into his vehicle, and they headed downtown. "Do we know anything about this one?"

He shrugged and said, "I heard it looks like a murder-suicide and have the address."

"Do we know anything about the other jumper you mentioned?"

"No, not a thing. Just that there was one." He looked over at her, with concern. "I hope you're not getting too worked up about them, are you?"

"Well, I hope somebody is," she said. "Somebody needs to give a damn."

"Lots of people need to give a damn," he said quietly, "but that's a big issue for one person to tackle."

"I know, but we have to start somewhere."

"What will you do? Give mental health workshops or something?"

"That's definitely not something I would handle very well."

"Maybe not," he said, "but I'm not so sure about that. You do pretty good with that psychoanalyst stuff."

"Hell no," she said. "I really suck at that."

"I don't know," he said. "I think you're a dark horse."

She laughed. "Nothing dark about me. I'm just what you see, ... an open book."

"No," he said forcibly, "that's the last thing you are."

She looked at him in surprise. "What do you mean?"

"There are depths to you that, even if we worked together for ten years, I highly doubt I'll ever get to know."

She was surprised to hear him say that. "That's an odd thing to say."

"Not at all," he said. "The fact of the matter is that most of us don't quite understand what makes you tick. We're just glad you joined the team, so you're on our side."

⁓

CURIOUS AS TO what Kate and her partner would see, Simon followed the news, while he headed back to his place. He'd rather have spent time with her. She was definitely more intelligent than his usual dates. And he loved her lively curious brain; even her natural crankiness appealed. Although talking hadn't been the prime activity before. He was a sexual creature and thoroughly enjoyed letting loose.

He understood that Kate didn't want their relationship to become an issue at her job; he just didn't see how it would. He didn't know any of the people she worked with, but, because of their prior association on the pedophile case, and what you might call his unconventional way of offering assistance, there was definitely some hesitation on her part to bring all that back up again. He could respect that. It was also frustrating. He'd love to have a little more of her in his life, but, as long as she kept him at arm's length, it wouldn't happen.

She was fiery, yet uncertain, was easily startled, and would bolt at this stage, if he pushed it. And he'd do a lot to avoid making her feel that way.

Rather than going straight home, he headed down in the area with the building he wanted to buy and drove past to see cops still everywhere, including her. The last thing he wanted was for her to think he was following her. He had been hoping to take her out for dinner, but that had all gone sideways when she went for a workout, and then he'd seen the fatigue and the weariness on her soul. The job was demanding and had to be stressful. The fact that she was doing so well was amazing, but he saw that it was taking a toll.

That was something he would have to deal with probably all of his life, if he planned on staying close to her. Which he did, at least for the foreseeable future, and wasn't that something? Kate was the opposite of what he'd historically had for lady friends. Kate also looked to be a lot of work. He wasn't sure if that was good or bad, but it's what it was, and, because that was where his interests had landed, he was willing to work with it.

As he finally drove toward home, he heard another report on a jumper. He frowned at that and called someone he knew in law enforcement in West Vancouver. When Ben asked him what his interest was in the jumper, he said that there just seemed to be so many of them right now that he wondered if the city needed something extra to help those people in need.

"Wouldn't that be nice?" his friend said, an age-old weariness in his tone. "I'm not even sure how to tackle something like that, but mental health is a huge issue right now."

"Right now? I think it's all the time, isn't it?"

"Probably," Ben said. "I mean, when you think about it, if it comes to that, you know—in some people's minds— there are just no other options."

"That's the part that just blows me away," Simon said quietly. "I mean, how is it that there are no other options?"

"Because these people either don't have money, don't have facilities or support, or they're missing something major that would help them to avoid this last step."

"Well, surely there are at least online chat groups for support," Simon said.

"Sure, but unfortunately there are also online chat groups of people supporting the decision to do it as well."

"Ouch." Simon winced. "That should be monitored."

"Yeah, except then we're infringing on personal rights and privacy." With that statement, Ben's wariness and frustration was evident. Simon was sorry he'd reached out to his friend.

"Well, if you think of anything I can do to help," Simon said, "let me know."

And, with that, he rang off, as he headed back to his penthouse. He walked upstairs, still thinking about it.

Was there something he could do to help? This was not an area he'd ventured into, but that didn't mean he couldn't, if only he found a way. And that was always the problem— trying to figure out just what he was supposed to do, what his role in all of this rightly was. Generally he liked to stay well and truly clear of being in the public eye, but, on some things, he couldn't. Some things were just too much out of control, hurting so many people, and maybe that's where he was at right now. He didn't know, but it was a struggle sometimes.

On instinct, once he got inside and settled, he turned on his computer and sat down, looking at some available suicide resources online. What was immediately apparent was you could join a lot of groups on social media and otherwise. A million therapists advertised their skill sets on the internet as well. Whether they were any good or not left a lot to be interpreted, and by people who were the most vulnerable. He wondered just how anybody was supposed to evaluate these services, especially if they didn't have the money to try them out. That had to be difficult because did you just go talk to all these people? Not likely. If you were already struggling, the last thing you wanted was strangers digging into your mind and your thought processes, yet who else was there?

He kept searching and reading, and finally found on one of the sites a commemorative list of the names of people who had committed suicide. Frowning, he looked at the names and kept scrolling down the page. It was a group trying to support each other after a loss to suicide. When he got to one name, he stopped and frowned. He quickly made a phone call and said, "Louisa, this is Simon."

She immediately started bawling. "Hi, Simon," she said in between hiccups.

"I just saw something on the internet," he said, hating to even bring it up, since obviously she was traumatized by whatever was going on.

"So you heard," she said.

"I guess I did," he said again hesitantly. "Is it true? Did he commit suicide?"

She started to cry even harder. "Oh my God," she said, "it's been the worst few days of my life."

He looked at the list, noted no dates.

"When did this happen?" he asked.

"Just a few days ago," she murmured. "I knew he was upset about something but to commit suicide, to jump? He was afraid of heights," she cried out. "Why would he do that?"

Simon tried to console her as best he could, but not a whole lot he could say, and he was in shock himself. When he finally got off the phone, he sat down and pulled up all the information he could find, but there wasn't very much available, and that was something else that just blew him away. When these suicides happened, did nobody keep track? Did nobody look into their lives to see why, or did it become just another statistic? Just somebody else who didn't want to live and who took care of the job themselves?

More than a little stunned and upset, knowing that his friend had been a very vibrant guy, Simon couldn't imagine why he wouldn't have reached out and said something to him? Then Simon checked his email and looked at the last few he had from David and found nothing suspicious, absolutely nothing to suggest trouble of any kind. Simon didn't know what to say; there wasn't anything really, but it made him even more aware of the problem. Yet it was this big blank in his world.

He saw the result but didn't really know what was causing the problem, and that bothered him even more. He did a bit more research and found a few more places that had support for spouses of people who had committed suicide. He emailed those to Louisa with a note. *If there is anything I can do to help, please let me know. I had no idea that David was even in trouble.*

And, of course, maybe she hadn't either, so she'd be left

with survivor's guilt, something else that wasn't fair to her as well. He didn't even know what to say or to do and was still flabbergasted by it all, even when he woke the next morning.

***

Simon's Friday Morning

DETERMINED TO FIND out more, he contacted a couple lawyers and asked them about the suicide issue.

The lawyers had very little information either, with one saying, "Suicides are suicides," he said, "almost in a world unto themselves."

"But these people need help before they start jumping off bridges."

"I know," he said. "Right now there seems to be a rash of them, and they're getting in the news, and unfortunately that sets off a new rash of suicides," he muttered. "But I'm not sure that it's this bad all the time."

"How bad does it have to get?"

Not liking the lawyer's attitude about it either, Simon rang off and sat down, wondering if he could do anything further. He wondered about the women's shelter. He made a couple phone calls and ended up talking to his contact there. "Lisa, is there any help for some of your women, if—um—if they're really depressed?" ·

"There is some help," she said. "We have a group of doctors who work with us, some counselors."

"Good," he said in relief. "I've just become aware of the rash of local suicides lately, and I'm finding it a bit shocking."

"It is shocking when you first become aware of it," she said, "but honestly it's something that a lot of us have been dealing with for a long time."

"That just makes me feel worse," he said. "I had no idea the issue was so bad. I just found out a friend of mine, somebody I've known for years, jumped off the bridge a few days ago."

"Oh, my goodness," she said immediately, with sympathy. "I am so sorry. I think suicide is one of the hardest things for the survivors to deal with. It's like, *Why didn't you say something? Why didn't you tell me that it was that bad? I could have helped.*"

"Exactly. I'd have sworn he wasn't the guy to do something like that."

"Well, unless you know exactly what was going on in his mind at the time, it's really hard to say that."

"I know. I know," he said, "and now I feel like it's too little, too late."

"Hence the whole problem with suicide," she said quietly. "Honestly, when you have a friend in trouble, it's just important to even talk them down off the bridge, if that's what they need."

"The trouble is," he said, "I had no idea this guy was even in trouble."

"And that's probably the same for his wife too."

"Absolutely. I just got off the phone with her last night, and she was completely unaware of what could have been so bad that he would do this, and she's beating herself up for it."

"That'll be really hard on her," she murmured. "Hopefully she has some support."

"Well, I'll be there. I've known them both for fifteen odd years," he said quietly, "so she won't be alone right now."

"Just be aware that her survivor guilt could take her

down a path where you don't want her to go."

"Ouch," he said. "All the more reason to stay in touch."

And, with that, he hung up.

CHAPTER 5

Kate's Friday Morning

RUSTRATED AT HAVING come to a dead end on the hunt for the drive-by shooter, already dealing with a murder-suicide on her case list and what looked like another child killing, Kate sat down with a heavy sigh and picked up her extralarge cup of coffee and took a sip.

Rodney sat down at his desk in front of her. "How are you holding up?"

"Sometimes this job sucks," she said, "but I'm holding."

"Yep, it does," he said. "The successes, although there are many, sometimes feel like they're few and far between."

She nodded. "Just when it seems like you're getting somewhere, everything stops. You think that people are cooperating, and the next day nobody has anything to say. You go through twenty, thirty, even forty interviews with people, and nobody saw anything."

"And you're always looking for the one person who saw something, even if they didn't know it was important," he said.

She stared at the stack of files in front of her. "We have a lot of cases right now," she said, "and those are just the current ones from this week."

He laughed. "And then there are the current ones from last week. And unfortunately there will be current ones for next week as well."

She nodded. "I guess that's why it's bugging me. They just keep stacking up."

"Don't let it get to you too much," he said.

She looked at him and said, "You've been here in the unit for what, ten years of this?"

He nodded. "Ten years in homicide."

"How do you handle it?"

"One day at a time," he said cheerfully. "You understand there are wins, and there are losses. You had a big win right out of the gate," he said, "and now we're in an ugly spot, where it just seems like the cases are piling up, and we're getting nowhere."

She pinched the bridge of her nose, giving herself a mental headshake. "I guess that's a good way to look at it," she said and then stifled a yawn.

"You've got to make sure you get rest in between everything else," he warned her.

"And how do you do that, when the faces of the dead wake you up in the night?"

"You say, 'Thank you for reminding me of your existence. Now please let me sleep, so I can better fight for your cause tomorrow.'"

She stared at him in surprise. "Wow. That is good advice."

He laughed. "I'm not just a pretty face around here," he said, waggling his eyebrows.

She laughed at that.

"Have you gotten any more weird emails?"

"No," she said, "thank God. I have enough things to deal with without some weirdo."

"I get you there."

She added, "But, then again, I haven't opened up my email today."

"I do it when I first wake up," he confessed.

"I used to. Then I decided I needed to have that bit of distance, so I don't look at work emails until I come in to my desk."

"That's probably smart," he said, "unless you're expecting information, and then you'll need to be into it all the time."

"Well, it's a fairly recent attempt," she said, "so I don't know if it'll work or not."

He shrugged. "It seems like, most of the time, information comes in at odd hours, so you'll have to be a little flexible with it at least."

"I know," she said. "I was just struggling and trying something in the way of boundaries."

He nodded. "And I get that. I really do," he said. "You've just got to find a system that works for you and keeps your head above water."

She smiled, nodded, and opened up her emails. And when one came in with something odd in the subject line, she said, "Uh-oh. Look at this subject line. 'Are you there?' it says." She snorted. "Like where else would I be?"

He turned and looked at her. "Did you open it?"

She said, "It's just opening now." She picked up her coffee, took another big sip, and almost spewed it back into the cup. "Shit," she said.

He slowly turned, looked at her, and asked, "Is it another one?"

She nodded. "It's another one." She studied the image in front of her, a growing disquiet inside. "Looks like the Lions Gate Bridge again," she said, "and, although it's a picture of shoes, I can't tell the sex of the wearer from these. It's a pair of runners." She frowned. "Looks like maybe a wallet or something is stuffed inside them." She scrubbed her face and said, "What the hell is going on?"

"Put it up on the wall screen, and let's see if there's anything else."

She quickly transferred the desktop image to the screen on the wall. Two others in their team walked in just then, talking, Lilliana and Owen. They stopped when they saw the photo. Lilliana's gaze zoomed in on her. "Another one?"

Kate nodded, as she stood and walked over to stand in front of it. "I just found it."

"Why is somebody sending you pictures of the aftermath of a suicide?" Owen asked, not expecting anybody to give him an answer.

"This one had a subject line," Rodney said, coming up beside her, his tone grim. *"Are you there?"*

"What the hell does that mean?" Owen asked.

"What it means," Kate said, "or at least what my churning stomach thinks it means, is that somebody is killing people and making it look like a suicide."

Colby walked up right behind her. "Please tell me that you didn't just say that."

Her shoulders hunched. "I got a third email today," she said, nodding at the front wall.

He walked up to take a closer look. "Jesus. Confirm that a jumper was there overnight," he said. "And then we need to have a talk about it."

"Talk about what though?" Kate asked. "If this is murder, I don't even know what to say."

"It's probably not. Odds are it's just some asshat messing with you," Rodney said. "They know that first one got to you a little bit because they saw you down there, and now they just want to jerk your chain a little bit."

"Meaning that it's just a sicko playing games?"

"Well, the other alternative," he said, "is that we have a serial killer."

"That's not anything anybody wants to look at either," Kate muttered.

"But burying our heads has never helped," Colby said, his voice quiet. "This needs a full investigation, if only so we can write it off."

Kate nodded. "Fine," she said. "I'll add it to my stack of paperwork."

He looked at her and said, "The case files not going anywhere?"

She shook her head. "It seems like nothing's going anywhere at the moment."

"Well, maybe this will help, and you'll find something about whatever it is that's going on," he said. "Who knows? Maybe it'll produce something fresh enough to work."

She nodded. "That would be nice." She tossed one last look at the picture on the wall and said, "I'll send these off to Forensics."

"Good idea," her sergeant said. "Did you send the others?"

She nodded. "But I'll tag them with this third one, and then I'll check in with the PD and see what we've gotten overnight for jumpers."

And, with that, she sat down, ignoring them all, as she took care of everything else going on in her world. But, inside, she was using it as a means to escape their looks and their curiosity as to why she had been targeted for this.

She truly had no answer, but that wouldn't make a

damn bit of difference to whoever was doing this. They had a reason; she just didn't know what it was yet, and that was quietly terrifying. She hadn't done anything wrong in her world that she knew of, but it wouldn't change anything.

Several calls later, she'd done what she had set out to do, but the information was oddly disquieting, even though she had the confirmation she needed.

Rodney turned around to face her. "Anything?"

She nodded slowly. "They're still searching for the body. It was on the Lions Gate Bridge, so West Vancouver PD responded to the call." He sat back and exhaled. She nodded. "I know. And there was something in his shoes, like we thought. The officer in charge hasn't seen the report yet and wasn't on the scene, so he didn't know more, but they will forward the details as soon as it's logged."

He nodded. "And what do you want to do now?"

"I want to go to all three of the jumper scenes," she said quietly.

He looked at her in surprise. "They're hardly crime scenes."

"We don't know that, do we?"

He looked at the front wall where the latest jumper's shoes picture was no longer visible, and he said, "You know something? It might be good to go anyway." He hopped up, grabbed his jacket, and said, "Come on. I'll drive."

"I can drive," she said.

"*Can* and *should* are two separate things."

She glared at him. "It's not a problem."

"Hey, when suicide pushes your buttons, then we do the best we can to make sure they aren't pushed any further."

"It just makes me feel like a wimp," she said. "I should have gotten over it."

"When a friend goes that way, I think we're all left with a question mark as to why and what we could have done," he said. "Nothing like guilt to rack you over, time and time again."

"And the stupid thing is, even after all the years, you still don't know, you still don't understand. So you still have questions."

"And that's human nature, right? And when you care, not a whole lot you can do about it. You just keep asking the same questions and never get any different answers. Maybe this time you can get a different answer."

She looked at him in surprise. "But these aren't people I know."

"No, but they're people that other people know."

She winced at that. "Ouch. That's part of the problem. The friends and families are out there, waiting for somebody to come home or waiting for an answer or waiting for something we can't give them."

"Well, maybe this time we can," he said, with a bright smile. "Remember. Stay positive, and let's keep hacking away at it."

"Oh, I'm positive," she said. "Positive we'll figure out what the hell is going on." And she was. This guy was starting to piss her off.

Rodney looked at her as they walked out. "Now you're getting angry."

She laughed. "Yeah, I am," she said. "He's yanking my chain, and I don't like it."

"Good," he said. "Get angry, get angrier, get really freaking angry, so that, when something does break, you're in the right mind-set to deal with it. When somebody targets you like that, it's easy to slip into the mind-set of a victim, and it makes everything in your world seem wrong."

"And that's exactly what I've been feeling like," she said.

"Good reminder."

"Hey, no problem," he said, with a shrug. "You can talk to Dr. Rodney any old time."

At that, she burst out laughing. "Hey," she said, snickering. "I get that wasn't meant to be super, super funny, but I'm sorry. It's hysterical." And, with that, she burst into another fit of giggles.

"However you want to take it is okay with me," he said, with a big grin. "And you're not hurting my ego in any way."

When Louisa called Simon, it took him a moment to reorient himself. He was standing in the middle of one of his big buildings, looking at the massive staircase going up inside, wondering why the hell he had decided that this was a good deal.

"Hello," he answered distractedly.

"Simon, it's Louisa," she said. "I wondered if you could take a look at something on David's laptop."

He pulled himself together and shifted to look down at his phone. "Sure. What do you want me to look at?"

"Well, I don't recognize a whole lot here," she said. "I didn't think that he would keep anything from me, but now I'm not so sure." A slight hiccup in her voice said that she was either on the verge of crying or had just stopped. "I really don't know what to make of it."

"Are you home right now?"

"Yes," she said. "I'm off work until I can deal with his funeral arrangements and everything."

"Right," he said, wincing. "How about I come over in

about an hour?"

"Thank you, that would be great," she said gratefully. "Honestly I don't know anybody else who could look at this."

"It's business stuff?"

"I don't know what it is," she said quietly. "I'd just feel better if somebody else would make sense of it and tell me that it's nothing."

"Okay, I'll take a look," he said. "I'll be there soon." He hung up, then took one last look at the staircase and shook his head because it would be a massive job to fix, which meant expensive as all hell too. Groaning, he shook his head, wondering what he'd been thinking. He knew that fixing the staircase was doable; it would just cost a lot more than he had initially planned for.

He took his leave of the building and headed over toward Louisa's house. He didn't know what she wanted him to look at, but they'd all been friends for a long time. If something was there that she didn't understand, he was more than happy to help out. He would be astonished if it was something he didn't understand.

David had been a hell of a guy, but he hadn't delved much into business. At least not that Simon knew of, but maybe he'd sunk some money into an investment and had lost it all or something. That could account for why he'd decided that life wasn't worth living after all. If that were the case, Simon sure as hell wished his buddy would have contacted him. Simon could have bailed him out or at least helped him find a path forward.

As he walked up the front steps and knocked on the door, he turned to look around. Nobody was nearby, but Simon had that weird sensation in the back of his head. And just then came a whisper.

Do it. Just do it.

"Simon? Simon?" Louisa said in a louder voice.

He gave a headshake, turned to look at her, and said, "Sorry, I was off in another world."

"You looked like it," she said, with a half smile. She reached up, gave him a hug, and said, "Come on in."

He stepped inside, noticing that it was the same as the last time he'd been there. "So what's this all about?" he asked, as he walked in.

"I've left David's laptop open on the dining room table," she said, pointing over at it. "If you want to take a look, I'll go put on some coffee."

He would never say no to coffee, so he nodded and said, "Sounds good." He walked over, sat down at the dining room table, and took a look. She was already logged in, but he didn't even know what security might be here, if any. His friend was not really a business guy but had dabbled around in some online stocks and did a few bonds. He kept a few high-interest savings accounts, but that was about it. He worked for a car dealership as a salesman, working off commissions and generally had a solid reputation.

Simon wasn't sure at first what he was looking for here. He checked all the open tasks on the taskbar, and they all appeared to be chats.

When she came back and sat down across from him, he saw she was nervous. "What is it you're expecting me to find?"

"I'm not expecting you to find anything," she said. "But it looks like he belonged to some groups that I wasn't aware of. And there are conversations with some people I wasn't aware of."

"Sent to his usual email?"

She shook her head. "No." She pointed to a small black book that Simon hadn't paid much attention to on the side of the laptop. "I found that in his night table when I was cleaning it out. It's a bunch of log-ins," she said. "I'm too scared to check them all out."

"Why?" he asked, settling back and looking at her.

"I'm afraid he was having an affair." At that, tears welled up and poured down her cheeks again.

"Well, I would be very surprised if he was. I know he loved you very much."

"If that's the case, why did he leave me?" she said flatly.

He nodded because that logic was irrefutable. He opened the book and noted some of the log-ins and then checked it against some of the websites. He nodded and started logging into the first one.

"Well, this one is a chat group," he said, "for men," as he read his way through. "It's discussing marital problems, how to handle different issues." He checked David's username, checked on some posts. "His last post was at Christmastime, trying to figure out what to get you for Christmas."

She gasped, and her tears ran freely this time. "Is that all?"

"For that one anyway," he said. "I don't know what else I'll find. Give me a few minutes."

She nodded and settled back, looking a little bit more relaxed. When the coffee was done, she got up and poured them both a cup. When she returned, he said, "The next one is on a men's group, asking about fertility testing," he said, looking at her. "I gather you were having trouble conceiving."

She nodded slowly. "I told him that it didn't matter to

me."

"But it mattered to him," Simon said, with a nod. "It affected his masculinity."

"And yet it didn't have to. And, if that's why he killed himself," she said, "I'd want to kill him all over again for being so stupid."

He gave her a small smile. "Well, let me keep looking. So far though, nothing indicates that he was having a relationship with anybody else or that he wanted to."

"And that is truly good news," she whispered.

When he logged into the next one, he frowned.

"What is that look for?"

Simon sighed heavily. "It's a suicide group."

She gasped in horror and started to cry, getting up and racing away. He wasn't sure what he was supposed to do about that, but it was certainly not in him to hold back the truth from her. Even though it was tough, the truth was necessary for people to face. In this case maybe it was a little bit too much. He checked to see if there were posts from his friend, and, sure enough, there was one saying that David was struggling, that things were looking pretty dark and gloomy, and that he wasn't sure even why he was on the forum.

Others responded, saying, "Hey, it's okay. You are in the same boat we are. Not exactly sure why we're here but always coming back because, if nothing else, here we are understood."

As Simon kept reading, he felt the darkness that had crept into the soul of his friend. Sadness that David couldn't have children and his inability to face a life without them. Several times he posted that *My wife said it didn't matter and that she's okay with it, but how do I explain that I'm not?*

Others responded that adoption was always an answer, and he said, *No, in our case it's probably not*, he wrote, *because I've got a prior conviction.*

At that, Simon's eyebrows raised because he hadn't been aware of that. As soon as he found that, he looked over at Louisa, when she joined him again. "He talked about adoption not being an option."

She sighed and said, "No, probably not."

"He mentioned a conviction."

She winced at that. "You know that stupid charge. He was caught drunk driving a few years back. It was after a bender, when he found out that he couldn't have children," she said. "But, of course, that went against us, when people are looking at ideal parents."

Simon could imagine. And he said, "I'm sorry. That just compounded his problems, didn't it?"

"Yes. You didn't know?"

He shook his head. "No, we haven't stayed in touch all that much on a regular basis. We hit the highs and lows in life—I thought anyway—but apparently I didn't hit very many of the lows. Not if these chats are anything to go by."

"And I didn't know how low he really was," she whispered.

He nodded and said, "I have a couple more here to check."

She nodded and said, "I'll just grab my laptop too. Something to keep my mind off what you're doing." She got up and walked around him, going upstairs. He went to one website, which turned out to be another suicide one. He had avoided going to it at first because something was familiar about it. He thought he'd seen a corresponding email address in David's emails. But Simon checked it out, and, once again, his friend was talking about how the world would be better off without him and how his wife would find somebody else to be happy with and to have children with.

Simon swore at that because, if Louisa wanted one thing, it wasn't life without David. She would never choose children over having a life with him. On the whole, it sounded like David was working his way through it in some of the conversations. Simon checked the dates, and nothing there suggested that anything had triggered this suicide action or that he was close to taking that final walk off a bridge.

When Louisa sat back down again, Simon asked, "Was there any trigger or anything upsetting him this last week?"

She looked up and shook her head. "I've asked myself that a million times, wondering what would have set this off," she said, "but I don't know of anything."

He nodded slowly. "And—" Then he stopped and said, "I don't even know how to ask this, but, outside of the parental thing, can you think of any reason why he would choose to do this?"

"I would never have imagined he would ever choose this," she cried out. "I know in the past he's made a couple dumb comments, and I'd shut it down really fast," she said, "because who wants to hear anybody talk about suicide? That's not funny," she said, "so I didn't think anything of it or put any credence into it because he would only bring it up when he got depressed."

"Interesting," he said.

"Why? What are you thinking?"

"I'm just not seeing anything that shows a trigger for why he did it. I can't imagine that, from one day to the next, he just woke up one morning without any reason to live."

Somebody had been talking to David in the one chat on a private message board. It took Simon a moment to figure out how these boards worked, but he found the one message with a response at the top.

Go ahead and do it.

His friend had responded. *Hell no, why should I?*

You should.

David's response was clear and succinct. *Fuck off.*

Simon smiled. "Well, he said fuck off to somebody pushing him to commit suicide," he said to Louisa. She gasped in joy. And then she looked at him, the smile falling away. "So then why did he do it?"

"I don't know," he said. "I'm still looking." He went through it, and then, taking note of the one, he checked the other message board. And found the same type of message from somebody else.

Go ahead and do it. You'll feel better. Everybody'll be better off without you.

Simon frowned at that and went to one of the others. And it was the same thing. In each case, always somebody who private-messaged him, then said how it would be much better if he did it. That he would feel so much better and that his family could move on without this curse. Somebody was actively encouraging David. Simon's fingers thrummed on the table as he thought about that. Then he went to the emails. "Did he have more than one email address?"

"Yeah, he had a couple anyway," she said. "I don't know all of them. Check the book."

Simon flipped through the book and, in the back, were the email accounts. He checked the first one, but it's the one that he used all the time, and there didn't seem to be anything in it. When he checked the other two, one was completely blank and empty, and the last one appeared to be the one he used for all these chats.

Simon checked and found several messages from several different senders, all saying some version of *Hey, dude, you should.* A few were supportive, saying things like, *Don't, the world is still a brighter place, and you'll be happier if you're in it.*

And then the last one was very different.

Do it or else.

Alarm growing deep inside him, Simon opened it up to see a picture of Louisa, sitting right across from him, only this time, the photo had been doctored, and a bullet hole was in the center of her forehead.

He slammed the laptop shut.

CHAPTER 6

KATE WALKED THE first suicide scene, remembering how she had felt that morning. She stood back in the same position, where her memory said she must have been when the picture of her had been taken.

At her side, Rodney asked, "Were you standing there?"

"I think so."

He immediately shifted to look up in the hills behind him. "He could have been anywhere. Probably took multiple attempts."

"And a lot of people were here," she said, "so it could have been from a vehicle across the street too."

"Agreed. Wouldn't find much at this point." Rodney added, "It'd be pretty murky at this point in time."

But she walked over to the bridge railing, took a closer look, and said, "If he picked her up and tossed her over, he'd have to be sure that nobody was here, and this bridge is superbusy. Has anybody checked the cameras?"

"We need to double-check whether they have or not." Rodney nodded. "I can do that."

She said, "Let's go on to the second site." It took longer to cross town than she expected.

They went to the second jumper scene, and, although she only had a vague idea of where the jumper dove off the bridge, based on the shoes she had seen in the photo, she could walk to within ten feet of the spot. She looked over the railing, saw the flowing water below, and winced. It bothered her to imagine such an end. "The water's not as high today, but, if caught in that heavy current down there, it would be pretty rough. They wouldn't survive for long."

"Hard to imagine jumping, isn't it?"

"Most bridge jumpers don't make it at all," she said. "And, in this case, it was a healthy thirtysomething male. And that I don't get," she said, turning to look at Rodney. "I mean, if we were talking murder, and somebody tossed the body over, there should be something else to show as a sign of death. Surely a struggle? Defensive wounds? The victim wouldn't be an easy target, right?"

"Being a jumper," he said quietly, "no tox screens are even done, and visible signs of trauma, outside of ... what?" he asked, raising both hands. "I mean, what damage would there normally be with a jumper? Wouldn't there be bruising from hitting the water? I mean, hitting water at a distance like this is like slamming into concrete."

She nodded. "I don't think it breaks major bones, ribs yes," she said hesitantly, "but I'm not sure about the rest. We'd have to talk to the ME. Not only that, you know that there are rocks, trees, other debris in the water. He could easily have tumbled around in there and picked up all kinds of bruising. But they would be post-mortem."

"Not necessarily. Death isn't always instantaneous."

She turned to look at the traffic, heavy in both directions. Then it always was, unless in the wee hours of the morning. "And again," she said, "if somebody else is murdering these people, he—or she—must pick up and toss the victim, while ensuring nobody saw. And that would be difficult. This is a very heavily trafficked area. So we need to check the overnight cameras."

Frowning and still unsettled, they headed to the third jumper's scene. This was the same bridge but farther down, on the opposite side. "Another female, I presume?" she said, turning to look at Rodney. "We need to confirm that."

"Regardless, we've got both sexes so far."

She nodded. "Which doesn't help at all."

"The truckers are through here at those hours all the time. And, of course, nobody reported any such scene."

"No. We should also check the weather," she murmured, as she searched the area, her gaze automatically going to the sky, even though it wouldn't give her past weather.

"Are you really taking this seriously?"

"I'm not sure how not to," she said. "Somebody is sending me those damn pictures for a reason, and, as much as I wish they'd stop, it doesn't change the fact that he's sending me a message of some kind."

"No," Rodney said, frowning, "you're right. Not to mention the fact that notes have been on every one of those pictures he attaches."

She said, "Exactly. Frustrating as hell but definitely not something to ignore."

By the time they were done, she walked back to the car, tired and stressed. Somebody had once told her that stress was basically just a cover-up for fear. At this point in time, the fear was that they could have a serial killer and not know it because the victims were already counted as suicides, under an almost expected headcount. And didn't that sound terrible? There was an expectation that a certain number of suicides would occur annually, regardless of which month of the year.

Based on past years' data, the statistics showed those suicides would fit into the norm of reasonable error of data. And even if somebody were tossing people off these bridges, even impacting the normal data, it still wouldn't be enough to rouse eyebrows enough to start an investigation.

As she made her way back to her desk, she retraced her steps down the hallways of her mind, replaying what she had just observed at the three scenes, wondering just what she had learned, if anything, when her phone rang in a frantic manner. *Frantic? Yes.* She stared down at it, wondering how she always knew when it was Simon and when it was urgent. His issues always impacted her cases. She answered the phone, her voice terse. "What's up?"

"So ... I don't know," he said, "but I've just found a few photos." His voice suggested he was rattled.

"Photos of what?" she asked, curious as to what had upset him.

"Look. A friend of mine, he ... her husband committed suicide a few days ago."

"Was his name David by chance?" she asked, her stomach sinking.

"Yes," he said, "that's exactly who it is. How did you know?"

"I was just at the site."

"Oh," he said in surprise. Then sounding bewildered, he continued, "Well, his wife asked me to take a look at his laptop to see if anything would explain things or if she needed to deal with or know about something unexpected."

"And?"

"He did belong to several groups, chat groups, ... on suicide."

"I'm so sorry then," she said sincerely. "I think battling this is something so much bigger than us, and it makes it so hard to tackle."

"Yes, but I found signs that he was pulling away from those suicidal thoughts. He was getting support from various people, but, within each one of the groups, somebody was being an absolute dick, pushing him to go ahead. To commit suicide."

"We've heard of that happening too," she said wearily. "Sometimes people are assholes."

"Well, in this case, I'm afraid somebody might have done more than push him," he said. "I need to send you this stuff."

"Okay," she said, "go ahead and send it. I'm almost at my desk right now."

"Good," he said, "it'll be in your inbox in a couple minutes." And, with that, he hung up.

She raced to her desk, impatient for the emails to load. How terrifying. She had heard all kinds of horror stories but had yet to come up against a case where somebody had coerced someone else into committing suicide. She could only hope that people were not the complete shits that she thought they were.

As she got into her office, her rapid steps raised eyebrows around her, and heads turned as she tore off her coat. She sat at her desk and immediately started clicking away.

"Wow, somebody is hot on to something. You want to fill us in?" Lilliana asked behind her.

"In a minute," Kate said, "depends on what the hell I see here." She brought up the email from Simon, studied the message, and then looked at the pictures. He'd sent all kinds of screenshots as well. She shook her head. "Son of a bitch," she muttered.

"Something break?" Rodney asked, coming up beside

her. He looked at her screen and whistled. "That's nasty looking."

"Yeah. Not only is it nasty looking," she said, "it could be a threat. Or was it just done in somebody's idea of sick fun? I don't know what to think of it."

"You want to explain?" Lilliana asked.

Kate turned, dug into the physical files at her side, and pulled up what she had just collated on the current suicides. She flipped through to the second one, held it up, and said, "Remember him? Suicide number two of three in this last week?"

The team gathered around her and nodded. "Simon is friends with the family."

At that came some rolled eyes and raised eyebrows. She ignored them all.

"This guy, David, his wife asked Simon to come take a look at some stuff on his laptop. Simon said that she was afraid there might be something of a sexual nature that she didn't want to stumble across on her own, like an affair or if he was gay or even had lost all their money. Some explanation. She didn't know, but she didn't want to go there on her own, and she'd found a bunch of log-ins and password information that she didn't recognize.

"As their trusted friend, she wanted Simon to do it instead, so at least she'd have some support. What he found was membership in several suicide-related online groups and chat sites, which makes sense, considering he committed suicide. Simon also found that somebody was pushing him to do it, not just one person but several different people pushing for him to go ahead and do it, like the world and his wife would be better off if he were dead. Things like that."

"We do get a certain amount of that," Rodney said quietly. "Some people are just dicks."

"I get that. But then Simon checked David's email accounts against the one email address that he had from the chat, and, of course, that then is something trackable, except that the message wasn't in David's normal email account. It wasn't one that he used for everyday occurrences. You might wonder how Simon accessed all this stuff, but David had left the log-in data all right there in a black book. Simon found three email accounts. One was unused and empty. One was the current one he used for almost everything, and the third was the one that David used only for these chats. In that inbox was a message with a subject line *Do it or else*. There was also a picture attached. Take a look." And she clicked on the image.

"So you're saying that this guy, whoever he is, was telling David to commit suicide, and, if he didn't, his wife would get a bullet?" Rodney asked, shocked.

"That appears to be what this message is saying," she said. "Now, was it just for shock value? Was it a real and substantial threat? I don't know."

"And, even if it wasn't," Lilliana said quietly, "the fact is, this guy did commit suicide. It could be that he did it in order to save his wife."

"But how would he know that his wife would be safe, even if he did the job?" Kate asked. "Because that's the worst thing, isn't it? You do something. You try to keep your family safe, and then you turn around and find out—of course this guy wouldn't find out anything because he's dead—but you find out that it was a lie all along, and they were planning on killing the wife anyway." Kate took a long, very long, deep breath and let it out slowly. "Either way," she said, "I really feel like we need to check into the other two recent suicides and make sure we don't have something similar."

"Good," Colby said, making her spin around. He gave her an approving smile. "It's an angle. I don't know that it's a good angle, but it's an angle."

"But it does mean," she said, "that these suicides—"

"—are no longer suicides," he said. "It sounds suspiciously like murder to me. We'll snag these cases as ours."

She nodded slowly. "And it would mean that nobody would have had to see these bodies going over the bridges because there wouldn't be anybody helping them over. No struggling. No defensive wounds. These people would be willingly throwing themselves off a bridge and committing suicide in order to save their families."

"After being coerced by a threat, and, therefore, that's murder," her sergeant said. "It might not be the easiest thing to prove, unless we get something forensically, but emails like that are a really good start."

"Yeah," she said, "but whoever it is remains hidden behind this email."

"Well, we have a team just for that," he said. "Did you send them the other emails and the other images from your computer?"

She stopped and stared. "I wonder," she said. "Shit, I just wonder. What an idiot I am."

"Wonder what?"

She sat back down in her chair, clicked away on the keys, bringing up the emails. "Crap. Remember the headlines, the messages? Each one was specific, like the last one was, 'Are you there?' As if to say, 'Hey, I killed somebody. Glad you're finally on board, or maybe you're not on board, and now it's, 'Hey, do you see this?' Right?"

Colby took several steps forward, looked at them over her shoulder, and said, "You're saying that he's egging you on to see if you're in the game, to try and catch him."

"I'm afraid so," she said quietly. "And it really makes my stomach churn."

"But she did get a lot of notoriety over that pedophile case," Rodney said quietly. "And most of us have had a sicko target us at one time or another for something."

She looked at him in surprise. "You have?"

He nodded. "Yeah. It's never fun, but they always seem to think that the name of the game is to stay out of jail, but that alone is just way too boring for some. So they challenge us, almost to make a game of it."

She shook her head. "You'd think that they would just want to disappear. They got what they wanted. The guy kills himself, tormented right to the last moment. Why the hell can't these dicks just disappear and be happy that their sick game worked?"

"Not only can they not just disappear but they seek out the notoriety that goes with it," Lilliana said. "They want to know that somebody realizes what they've done, and, if they can't tell anybody because they don't have anyone they can tell safely," she said, "then they need the police involved because that keeps us engaged with them too."

Kate sat back, looked at the most recent jumper's shoes photo, and said, "So that's why the killer's sending me the pictures. He thought that I might have seen something, and that's why I was at the scene of one of the jumpers. So, the first one, he sees me there and covertly says, 'Finally,' thinking that now the game will get going. But I'm not there for the second one, and he says, 'Maybe not,' and then, on the third one, he's basically mocking me, with 'Are you there?' suggesting I don't even get it."

They all just nodded.

"Ah, crap," Kate said, sitting here. "I really don't want to be responsible for anybody else dying."

"And you aren't," Colby said sharply. "He is, so get that thought out of your mind."

She nodded. "I can try just because you say so, sir, but it's really not that easy."

"I don't care if it's easy or not," he said. "You stop thinking along those lines. You are not responsible for the actions of this asshole."

"I get that in theory," she said. "I really do. But, past the theory part, it's really hard to stomach."

"So, you start with Forensics," he said. "You start with Computer Forensics. They get to take a look at this. They take a look at everything you've got to share. And we'll need that evidence from Simon."

She nodded, picked up her phone, and, when Simon answered, she said, "I need you down here with David's laptop and that black book."

He didn't answer immediately.

"No," she said. "It's bigger than just your friend. I need both."

He said, "On my way."

She looked over at the others. "Okay, he's coming down now."

"Good," Rodney said, rubbing his hands together.

She glared at him. "Oh, hell no."

He nodded. "Oh, hell yes," he said. "Simon got his nose into that other case, and now he's got his nose into this one. How do I know he's any good for you?"

"The last time I checked," she said, "I was an adult, and

eighteen was a hell of a long time ago."

"Nope, nope, nope," he said, with a big grin. "You don't get out of it that easy."

She sighed. "It would really be good if you'd let it be."

"Not happening," he said, "and you should probably stay out of this case yourself, now that you're involved to this level."

"Stay out of the case, my ass," she snapped. "I can't do that, and I'm not. This is too important." At that, everybody turned to look at Colby.

He narrowed his gaze and said, "No point in taking her out because, if we did, this guy is likely to just keep killing if she doesn't interact with him. I mean, in theory he'll stop, but all he'll stop is interacting with her. He might start with somebody else, and he might say, 'Screw it, I'll just keep killing because nobody can stop me.'"

"And maybe it's a plea for help," Kate said, stopping and turning to look at her sergeant. "It wouldn't be the first time somebody said, 'Somebody stop me. I can't stop myself,' would it?"

"No, it wouldn't," Colby said, with a heavy nod. "Good, it's settled then. And you should go talk to our new shrink."

She winced at that. She remembered the last one. The sister of two pedophiles. Not someone she wanted to talk to.

He said, "The new shrink, remember? The other one is busy dealing with her own legal issues."

She snorted. "That woman is a psychopath."

"Well, she was certainly the twin of a pedophile psychopath," he nodded. "And definitely aware of his crimes and their brother's too. Now you need to go talk to Dr. Abrams."

"Will he give us a profile?"

"Don't know if it's a profile we want at this point in

time. He'll probably say we don't have enough data but try. Get your head wrapped around the psychology behind somebody like this."

"Fine," she snapped. "Really not what I want to do though."

"Doesn't matter," he said cheerfully. "Maybe you can tell your woes to the shrink while you're there. That's the way the cookie crumbles."

She sighed. "I'm not sure that cookies are a really good topic right now."

As her stomach grumbled, he laughed. "Didn't you get down to the bakery?"

"Not yet," she said, "we didn't pick up anything while we were out, and, yeah, I'm hungry."

He nodded. "Well, Forensics first," he said, "and you can look after your stomach afterward."

She didn't have much to say to that. She just nodded and took off walking. As soon as she got to the Computer Forensic Division, she explained to Stoop what was going on, forwarded everything from her cell as she spoke. There were a couple questions back and forth as Stoop looked at her and said, "Seriously? You think somebody is trying to get others to commit suicide, based on threats against their family?"

She nodded and said, "Yes, we do."

"What's the motivation driving the nutjob behind that?" he exclaimed.

She sighed. "I don't know. I'm supposed to go talk to the new shrink about it."

He laughed at that. "Wasn't it you who got the last one canned? That should be a great meeting."

She winced. "Do you think he knows that?"

"Oh, you can bet on that," he said.

She looked over at him. Stoop was a teenage girl's wet dream. He looked like a movie star from the '60s, with the lock of hair falling on his forehead and a smile that could melt hearts. But behind all that was the clear-cut, claw-like gaze that looked at everything analytically, rarely seeing flesh and blood.

"Well," she muttered, "that will set a nice tone for our first meeting." She knew the sarcasm was wasted on him, but she turned and walked out without a word anyway.

SIMON SHOULD HAVE expected it, but somehow, he hadn't really thought it through. He groaned as he headed out with the laptop and the black book. He gave Louisa a gentle kiss on the cheek. "I need to take this down to the police."

She nodded slowly. "You haven't explained everything."

"There's no point yet," he said, "because I don't know if it has anything to do with his death or not."

"I would give anything to find out that it wasn't intentional."

He gave her hug and said, "Leave it to me. I'll talk to you as soon as I know something, but I do have to take all this down to the police station."

She nodded and held the door open for him as he walked out. "I really wish you'd tell me something though."

He shook his head. "Not yet," he said. "No point in upsetting you, however it comes out, until we have some facts." And, with that, he left her. He hopped into his vehicle, headed straight toward the police station, and pulled into the parking lot around back. As he hopped out with both items in his hands, he headed toward the reception area. There he asked to speak to Kate. At the use of her first name, the officer's eyebrows shot right up.

In a smooth move he said, "Detective Kate Morgan requested these." He held up the laptop and the book.

At that, the woman nodded and sent a message through. He waited and waited, and, when Kate didn't show up, he pulled out his phone and texted her himself. He got a message back not too long later.

Coming.

"Good," he said to himself. "Obviously that works better than anything else." At least he hoped so. Though he still had to wait another ten minutes.

When she came through the connecting door, she apologized. "Sorry, I was in a meeting."

He understood that, as he had plenty of those himself.

She took one look at the laptop and the black book, then reached for the black book first and checked the pages and nodded. "Good," she said. "I'll log this in and get it to Forensics." She accepted the laptop and turned away.

"Do I get a *Hi, Simon. Nice to have coffee. Thanks very much for bringing this.* Anything at all?"

She stopped and glared at him.

He waved at her and said, "No, no, you're welcome. It's all good." And, with that, he turned and walked toward the door. But he was chuckling, and he heard her sigh from down the hall, before he heard her call out.

"Thank you!"

He caught the officer at the front desk, looking at him speculatively, and, with laughter in his gaze, he kept on walking. He wondered just what kind of relationship Kate had with the rest of the department. But then she was still fairly new, so maybe they hadn't seen her with anybody with whom she had a personal relationship with. And, considering what she'd said to him, that made the most sense. She also hadn't particularly wanted anybody to know that she might be involved with someone.

He winced at that because it was probably just a little too late for that. This exchange would stir the pot of questions and gossip, and he hadn't done anything to mitigate that. He sent her a quick text. **Sorry, but it looks like the front desk is a little too interested in us. Whatever.** Kate added a frowning face emoji, apparently just tossing it off.

He grinned at that. He wasn't even sure what the hell they had, but he was willing to take the trip to see where it went. As he headed to his own car once again, he stopped, searching for that little deli somewhere around here. He reoriented himself and walked across the street to pick himself up some food. As he stood in line, his phone rang.

"Where are you?"

He said, "At the deli."

"Shit," she said, "I'm on my way."

Surprised at that but not exactly sure what was going on, he thought about it as he got up to the counter, and, when it was time to place an order, he placed it for two specials. The employee didn't say anything and served up everything he needed. He paid the bill and took it over to one of the small empty tables at the back. When Kate dashed in, he called her over. She sat down in the opposite chair, with a look of complete exhaustion on her face.

"You okay?" he asked in concern.

"Yeah." But she didn't look it. "I booked it down here to get one of the specials. They run out so damn fast." She stared at the two plates on the table and then looked up at him.

He smiled and said, "I hadn't eaten, and I thought maybe you could use some food too." Then he nudged one of the plates closer to her.

Her face lit up, like a sunrise in the morning.

He stared, enchanted. "Wow," he said, "if that's all I have to do—"

She pulled the plate closer. "That's one of the reasons I came running," she said. "The specials were always gone early in the afternoon."

"They didn't say anything about it." But, even as he looked up, an employee posted a sign, saying that the day's special was sold out. "Wow," he said, "good timing." They both sat here and enjoyed their lunch. He wasn't even sure what kind of soup it was, but it was delicious, and a huge thick slab of bread rested beside it. He was happy to watch her eat the rest of hers. "You're inhaling that."

"I try not to," she confessed. "It's always so good, and it seems like I have so very few minutes in a day for a break."

"That's because you do," he said, with a smile. "Unless you change that."

Soon the food was gone, and she sat back with a happy smile. "Thank you," she said sincerely.

He nodded in wonder. "First," he said, "I wasn't expecting that your rush down here was to get lunch. Second, I wasn't expecting that your full-on rush would completely stop when food was put in front of you."

She chuckled. "It's been one of those days."

"Did the laptop help?"

"I won't know for a while yet," she said. "It should be a huge help, particularly that email. It's taken us in a direction that we hadn't considered. Honestly I really don't want to go there, but—"

"Who would?" he said. "Louisa is a friend of mine. So was David. I had no idea what was going on in his life. I feel terrible about it."

"That's another reason," she said. "I didn't even think to ask her any questions. I don't know if the officer who informed her of her husband's death did or not. Even if he did, he likely wouldn't have asked the questions I want to ask."

"Go ahead and ask me," he said. "What do you want to know?"

"Just about the relationship, what their marriage was like, things like that."

He nodded. "I guess you have to ask that stuff, don't you?"

She nodded. "It helps to set the scene, and it lets us know what's going on."

"Right."

She brought out a notebook and asked, "How long have you known him?"

"David?"

She nodded.

"Easily fifteen years," he said. "Beyond that, I don't really know."

"Good enough," she said. "And his wife?"

"They've been married about twelve years I think," he said thoughtfully, "so probably two years before that. Let's call it fourteen years, give or take."

"Any altercations, any problems between them?"

He looked at her in surprise and said, "Not that I know of. I've never seen any sign of it. You don't think she's responsible for any of this, do you?"

She looked at him and said, "I have to ask questions."

"I get it," he said, "but they're disturbing."

She nodded. "But, at the same time, she's the one who gave you the little black book."

He stared. "Which is why I would have said she was completely in the clear."

"I get that," she said, "but please, I just need to ask the questions."

He settled back and answered a few more. "Yes, as far as I know, they've been happy. No, they have no children. I hadn't realized that was an issue, but apparently it was."

She looked at him in surprise.

"It's in the chats," he said. "One of the reasons he was there looking for help was the fact that he couldn't have children. He really wanted children and felt like less of a man, unable to give her what he felt she wanted. But I don't think she gave a crap."

"Meaning that she didn't want kids?"

"No, just that she didn't want him to be so upset by it. If they came, great, but, if not, she was okay with it."

She nodded. "Not everybody is meant to be a mother."

"He definitely wanted to be a father."

"And that makes it all the more difficult," she agreed.

By the time they were done with the questions, Simon felt like he had pried into his friend's life more than was even acceptable, even given the circumstances. When Kate was finally done, he said testily, "That was really uncomfortable."

"Yes, I know," she said, "and unfortunately I'll have to ask all of those questions over again to Louisa."

He stared. "I thought the whole point of doing this was so she wouldn't have to be put through it."

"This starts the process, but I have to confirm from her

that this is all the truth. We have to investigate David's death. The last three jumpers are with my team now."

"So I suppose, if she lies, you get her caught out in it," he said in disgust.

"I don't do this on purpose, nor do I do it lightly," she said. "There are other aspects to this case that you don't really know about and that I can't really share at this point in time."

He pinched his lips closed and glared at her. "Well, you need to give me a hell of a lot more than that," he snapped, "because a hell of a lot more is at stake here."

"And I get that," she said gently, "and I guess, at this point in time, I'll have to ask you to trust me that something else is going on and that I need to at least write her off."

"And doing this writes her off?" he asked in surprise.

She nodded. "Yes. These are the types of answers I need."

He shook his head. "I'll never understand the world that you live in."

"And I probably won't understand yours either," she said, "and I get it. I really do. But this *is* my world."

He sat back, stared at her, and said, "And, if I want anything to do with you, I have to live with your world, is that it?"

"No, not at all," she said. "We don't have to have anything to do with each other. That's what I keep telling you."

"Oh no, you don't," he snapped. "You don't get rid of me that easily."

She stared at him in surprise, and she said, "Maybe you should give it some thought."

He shook his head. "No, I'm not even talking about that right now," he said. "Yeah, I'm pissed, and I'm not thrilled that you'll take this information and put my friend through hell over it, but you'll do it no matter what I say," he said. "So, am I at least allowed to give her a heads-up?"

She frowned and said, "I'll tell you what. Why don't we both go over and talk to her together?" He stared at her in surprise. She shrugged. "It would probably make her feel better if you were there for support."

"Yes, it definitely would, although she's likely to be quite pissed at me for having brought this down on her head."

"You didn't bring it down on her head."

"Okay, so her husband then," he said. "How will that make her feel any better, considering her husband is dead?"

"Well, hopefully we'll end up with some answers about her husband's death because of this."

He shook his head. "Those answers wouldn't come anytime soon, and it'll just cause her a lot more torment."

"The end result unfortunately in this case," she said, "justifies the means." But she wouldn't say any more.

He glared at her, which was useless. If there was one thing she would be solid about, it was defending the truth and the integrity of the case, until she could tell him something.

"Fine," Simon said, looking down at his watch. "Let's do it now." Then he got up and led the way out of the restaurant, not giving her a chance to argue.

CHAPTER 7

KATE KNEW SIMON was upset with her, but she really had no other option. She just needed to make sure they didn't waste their time looking at the wife. Wives were statistically a lot less likely to be a murderer as compared to husbands murdering their wives. But she couldn't take that chance right now because encouraging a suicide, something manipulative like this, could be done by all kinds of people.

By the time they got to the property, Kate looked around the area and saw that it was not a high-end place by any means, but it was a good solid family housing area and would have served David and Louisa well, if they had grown their family.

When Simon knocked on the door, and Louisa opened it in surprise, another woman stood there, with her arm on Louisa's shoulder. Louisa looked back at her friend and said, "This is Simon."

Simon nodded. "I think I've met you before," he said, with a frown. He appeared to think for a moment and then said, "Helen, is it?"

"Helena," she said, with a hand out, shaking his. "I've been friends with Louisa for a long time," she admitted. "Since grade school," she said, looking over at Louisa, who smiled and nodded.

"Yes, that's correct." She faced Simon and Kate. "What's

the matter? Why are you back again?" Her gaze narrowed, and she said, "I don't think I know who you are."

"Detective Kate Morgan," she said, holding out her badge. "I'm investigating your husband's death."

The woman looked at her in shock. "Police?" she said, then looked at Simon.

"I told you that I was taking David's things to the police," he said.

"Yes, yes, of course," she said, with a shake of her head. She glanced around at the neighborhood and said, "Please, come in."

As they stepped inside, Simon explained further. "Kate just needs to ask you some questions."

"Oh," Louisa said, staring at Kate in horror. "You know that I already spoke to an officer, right?"

"Yes. I promise it won't take long."

"Everybody says that, don't they?" Helena said.

"I don't know," Kate said, "but, in my world, questions are one of the basic elements of getting to the truth."

"Well, I don't have anything to hide," Louisa said, still staring at Kate, obviously perturbed.

"Good," she said, "maybe Helena could give us a few minutes, and we could just go over them."

"No, no," Louisa said, immediately reaching out a hand for her friend.

Kate studied her friend and saw Helena's hand instinctively take Louisa's. "That's fine," she said. "Most of the questions are pretty general." She pulled out her notebook.

"Oh, come on in," Louisa said. "I'm sorry. We don't need to stand in the hallway here. Let's go into the kitchen. I'll put on some coffee."

Realizing the woman needed something to do to keep

busy, Kate followed Simon, who followed Helena.

As they stepped into the kitchen, Helena glared at Simon. "Why did you have to bring the police in on this?" she snapped quietly.

"Because of something I found on David's laptop," he whispered back. She looked at him in surprise. He just shrugged and didn't say anything more. "Keep in mind, his death was already something the police had to look into."

Kate appreciated that. If everybody stopped assuming that they knew what was going on, Kate might get to the heart of the matter and be on her way. But, at the same time, she didn't have a whole lot that she could share at the moment either.

The coffee now dripping in the pot behind her, Louisa turned around nervously. "So what can I help you with?"

Kate started with the easy questions and went through the simple ones, about how long they had been married and how long they had lived at the address. When she got into the more troublesome ones—about if they had any problems in their marriage—she saw the jolt of surprise in Louisa's face at the question.

She stared in horror at Kate. "You don't think I had anything to do with his suicide, do you?" Her bottom lip trembled, and immediately Helena raced over.

"No, of course she doesn't. Nobody would think that," Helena said. She turned a hard glance toward Kate. "Do you?" she challenged.

"We're checking into all areas, also some information that we received."

At that, Louisa turned to look at Simon in shock.

He shook his head. "Just answer the question. She's not looking at you for complicity in anything." He tried to say it reassuringly, but it was obvious that the woman was still struggling.

Kate decided to carry on with the last of the questions. By the time she was done, Louisa was almost comatose with shock. Kate turned to Simon. "That's all I need."

He nodded and said, "I'll see you to the door."

"Good."

At that, Helena broke away from Louisa, raced to the front door with them, and she said in a harsh whisper, "Make sure you don't come back," she snapped. "That's the last thing she needed."

"Maybe so," Simon said, his voice equally hard. "But sometimes this shit has to happen in order for us to get to the bottom of the problem."

"There is no problem here. Isn't it enough that he already betrayed her by committing suicide, and then you just throw acid into the wound by bringing up all this stuff? The last thing that she wants to discuss is their marriage or anything else. She already feels guilty enough," she snapped.

"I get it," he said, his tone still hard, "but *you* don't know the whole story."

"Well, explain it to me then," she challenged.

He shook his head and said, "No, *that* I will not do."

And, with that, Kate turned to look at him and said, "Thank you." And she turned and walked out.

"Listen to her," Helena said, in a hoarse whisper. "You brought the bloody cops in here. She already talked to an officer. You didn't have to raise this all up again."

"Of course I did," he said, his voice rising, hoping Louisa heard this part, "and I'd do it again if I found that there was a problem. You don't know the first thing about this," he said. "So don't even try to tell me what to do. I acted in the best interests of Louisa. Can you say the same thing?"

And, with that, he turned and walked out, ignoring her. When he got to the car, he stopped, took a look up at the house on a sigh. "Do you hear the sound of the breaking of a very old friendship?"

"Well, if something is wrong, she'll forgive you. And, if not, I'm sorry. It obviously wasn't meant to be."

He looked at her in surprise. "Is it that easy for you?"

"Well, part of the issue is, who was your friendship with?" she asked quietly. "Was it with him or with her?"

"With him of course."

"And he's gone," she said. "So outside of being there for moral support, I don't know if that relationship is something you could have continued anyway. You said you didn't have very much to do with her in the last few years."

"I didn't have much to do with *them*," he corrected thoughtfully. "And you're right. I didn't, and I certainly hadn't thought about what I would do and not do, should David die," he said. "It's all just happened. There hasn't been any adjustment period."

She nodded. "I get that," she said. "I really do, and I'm sorry if this line of questioning has hurt your relationship with Louisa. Generally that's not what happens, from my experience."

"Then again, what you're saying is, if this breaks up the friendship, then it was time to break it up anyway?"

"Look. I'm not a shrink or anything," she said. "All I can say is that I'm sorry if this in any way contributes to the loss of a friend."

Muttering an expletive under his breath, he got into the vehicle and said, "Hop in. I'll drive you home."

She didn't argue and got in. When they got closer to the area of her apartment, she said, "Drop me anywhere. I'm heading back to the office." He looked at her in surprise. She shrugged. "Just because that job is done doesn't mean anything else is," she said. "I still have a ton of work pending, and I don't have time to let it all slide."

"Slide?"

"All I can tell you is that she's not the only widow right now, or widower, for that matter," she said. "And I really would like to make sure we don't have any more."

PISSED, SIMON WATCHED as Kate walked up the sidewalk toward the station, hating to see her walk out in the dark alone. He shook his head at his own foolishness, since her martial art skills were probably better than his. But he got out and waited until she was safely inside. Then he stepped back into his vehicle and headed to his place. As he walked into his penthouse apartment, his phone rang. Not thinking, he answered it.

"Hey," Caitlin said.

"Oh," he said, his voice dropping in disgust. "What do you want?"

Her voice sad, she said, "I know you don't have any reason to be nice to me, but I wanted to tell you that I really appreciate what you did."

"That's nice," he said, tired and fed up. "You also put me through hell before that."

"And I guess that's why I'm apologizing," she said quietly. "I know it's stupid, and I shouldn't have done it, but I was pissed off and upset that you broke up with me."

"Maybe, but you sure as hell shouldn't have played all

those games with my life."

"Right," she said, "big bad you and all that."

"Don't even go there." She was so damn irritating. But then he seemed to have a problem with irritating women because he was certainly fascinated with the very prickly Detective Kate Morgan. "Whatever," he said. "It's water under the bridge, as long as you don't continue your shenanigans."

"No," she said, "I won't." She hesitated and then said, "Are you seeing someone else?"

He stared down at the phone. "We're well past the point of that being any of your business to even ask that question," he said coolly.

"Oh," she said, "I guess I was just wondering if maybe you wanted to go for a coffee or something sometime."

"No," he said, "I do not. I went down that pathway and didn't like the place I ended up."

"No," Caitlin said, "I understand that. I really do. I wasn't a great person. I understand why you broke up with me."

"Yeah, the problem is what you wanted and what I wanted were very different things, and I wasn't about to be controlled," he said quietly.

"But seeing Leonard go missing like that and realizing that it was through my own actions and inability to respect the needs of a seven-year-old, then coming so damn close to not talking to him or not getting him back," she said, "honestly I've changed."

"I'm glad to hear that." And he was sincere in that. If she did change, it would be a good thing because, wow, it was needed. The fact that she was even now apologizing was amazing. "I'm glad you've had a change of heart."

119

"I was really a bitch before, wasn't I?" she said sadly. "I do want you to know that I've changed and for the better, and I have you to thank for that. I won't bother you again."

And, with that, she hung up on him.

CHAPTER 8

Kate Working Late

KATE BURIED HERSELF in work and tried to forget the look on Simon's face—and on Louisa's—when they heard Kate's questions. But they were necessary. Something really strange was going on, and, at the very worst of all this, somebody was quite likely causing people to commit suicide. Kate wasn't even sure what charges the prosecutor would put against this bad actor, and she didn't give a damn as long as she got them to stop. So she was primed to pull an all-nighter.

When Rodney came in the bullpen, she lifted her head. "You staying late too?"

"You busy?" he asked.

"Always," she said. "I talked to the wife of the one male jumper."

"And?"

"The one who had the laptop," she said.

His eyes lit up, understanding. "How did that go?"

"Not very well," she said. "She didn't like the line of questioning at all."

"When do they ever?" he said, with a shrug. "Seems like we're always half-praised and half-hated."

"Feels like a lot more of the hate these days," she said, with a grim smile. And she knew it. She'd seen it when she was out patrolling the streets every day. But, when she got into the homicide unit, it was like everybody wanted answers now, and, when they didn't have them, the detectives got a ton of abuse sometimes.

"Do you think she had anything to do with it?" Rodney asked Kate, sitting at his desk, prepared to stay a while, it seemed.

She shook her head. "No, I don't think so. I think she was clearly traumatized over the loss of her husband, and finding something in his laptop seems to have freaked her out even more. She did say something along the lines that he had been despondent and upset at times. But the reason she had given the laptop to Simon was that she was afraid he was having an affair or something similar."

"Right, like what? His affair broke up, and he was so despondent that he only had his wife left, so he dove off the bridge?" he said, with a quirk of his lips. Rodney was recently divorced, so any comments he made on the status of relationships had to be taken with a grain of salt.

"I'm not exactly sure, but maybe the coroner's office can help," she said. "I need to talk to Dr. Smidge about that. It's quite possible that maybe David had some underlying health condition too."

At that, Rodney nodded. "Good point."

Kate picked up the phone and contacted the coroner. When she couldn't get him, she left a message, saying that she had a question about the suicide and that she needed an in-depth look, if possible. And potentially on all three jumpers that had come in this week. She hung up and carried on with her work.

When the phone rang, she answered, not surprised to hear the coroner on the other end. "So we're both tied to our desks. And they were definite suicides," he said, puzzled. "They jumped off the bridge, hit the water at a horrific force, and drowned."

"Did they drown or did they die from the impact?"

"One of them, the male, broke his neck, but he drowned. Drowning was the cause of death in all three cases, but the injuries were significantly different, depending on where and how they landed. Why do you think there's a suggestion of murder in this? Are you saying somebody picked them up and threw them off the bridge?"

"No," she said, then explained the little bit that she knew. "It's definitely something we're looking into."

"Jesus," he said, "as if the world isn't screwed up enough. Now we have others trying to force people to commit suicide."

"I know. I know," she said. "And I'm sorry. I know you don't need more work."

"It's not your fault," he said. "I'll take another look. We didn't do any autopsies since the cause of death was pretty simple. When the bodies are found like that, jumpers rarely get autopsied."

"Right," she said, "and, in this case, the wife had no idea why he had done what he'd done. But we do have an email proving that somebody was pressuring him to jump or his wife would end up with a bullet in her forehead."

With him muttering still, he rang off, and she sat down to work on her notes. The notes were important, and her file was getting thick and ugly. She grabbed a whiteboard, parked it in front of her, and started putting up everything that she had on the jumpers' cases. The trouble was, she had enough cases to get a second whiteboard.

As she walked past Lilliana, the woman snorted. "And

here I thought you had gone home already. You do like to collect cases that run on."

"I don't know," Kate said. "I'm worried about this one."

"Why is that?" Lilliana asked, coming to stand behind her. "I mean, besides the fact that it's got such a creep factor to it."

"How long has he been doing this?" Kate asked, looking at her teammate. "How long has this asshole been pushing others to commit suicide and for what reason?"

"Often it's just for kicks," Lilliana said. "There was a case of one young woman, down in, uh, … I can't remember what state, but she ordered her boyfriend to get back into the truck to kill himself. He was parked in the garage or something, with the motor running."

"And he was already out and free and clear?"

Lilliana nodded. "He was. But they had text messages of the girlfriend ordering him to get back in the vehicle and complete the job. As if it's what he really wanted."

"Jesus Christ, please tell me that he was at least eighty years old."

Lilliana shook her head. "Nope, I think he was like twenty-one, twenty-two, if that."

The horror of somebody who would actively push somebody to do that instead of stopping him and calling for help just made her heart cry. "People suck," she muttered, and she turned and headed to sit down again at her deck. She studied the boards and then started pulling up reports.

"Now what are you doing?" Lilliana asked, as she parked her hip on the side of Kate's desk.

"Pulling up all the suicides this year for Vancouver and all neighboring cities."

"Oh, Jesus, that should be an interesting number." And

that total number, when it came, was sixty-seven. Lilliana winced at that. Then filtered by drowning, and it dropped to twenty-five. "Good God, that's even worse than I expected." "I know," Kate said. "Now what we need to do is cross-reference these names to the chat sites."

"And you don't think that Forensics is already doing that?" Lilliana asked.

"I just wanted to nudge them a little," Kate said. "The problem is, we need these names, and they won't match up to the emails."

"They never do," Lilliana said. "Notice how everybody uses a strange email address when they're doing something they shouldn't."

"Yep, but still, this list needs to go to Forensics and to Reese." Kate quickly attached it and sent it off, with a note saying, this *Please compare this list of all the suicides this year and see if any of these people showed up in the laptop or on the chat sites.* She had barely sent that off, when she got another phone call from the coroner.

"Outside of a test that I'm sending off to be run, David's healthy, fit, and doesn't appear to be suffering from anything. I checked his medical records, nothing recent at all."

"Good enough," she said. "Sadly I believe you." With that, she hung up, only to have her phone ring again.

"At least you are working late, like we are. And are you kidding, sixty-seven, really?"

"Yeah, sixty-seven," she said, "and that's just this year alone. Twenty-five were by jumping off a bridge."

"Surely you're not expecting anybody to have committed—er, you know—had a hand in this many deaths."

"No, I don't think so," she said, "but, even if it's one other than David's, it's too many."

"All right, I got you," he said. "I can run the names, but you know what emails are like."

"I do," she said. "Do the best you can." And, with that, she hung up, turned to take another look at her boards. Then she printed off the list of names of suicide jumpers this year and added the list to the newest board.

"And that's just this year so far," she said, mostly to herself.

"You may want to take a look back a few years," Lilliana muttered.

"And then I have to take a look at other bridges in the province," she said.

Lilliana looked at her in surprise. "Why hold it to the province? What about other provinces? What about nations? What about globally? Everything on the internet now is global, right?"

She gasped at that. "Oh my God," Kate said. "I wasn't even thinking about that. I was just thinking of our own little city here. And yet this guy, this is what he's doing. He could have coerced or threatened anybody all around the world to do this."

"Particularly in any English-speaking country," Lilliana murmured.

"Crap." Kate sat down and sent off an addendum to the email on the Forensics request, saying that any areas or countries they could locate where this guy may have been active would also be very helpful.

Her contact sent her back an email. *Uh, yeah, okay, we'll get right on that.*

Sarcasm in print didn't come off quite the same, but Kate got the message anyway. The chances of him finding much weren't great, but he could certainly look at other countries and see if this would go anywhere. He'd start with what they had.

Reese walked in, holding out the records for the last five years. Kate cringed when she quickly reviewed the data, as she found over one hundred suicides. Not all were jumpers. That number was in the sixties.

"But that's sixty jumpers over five years, and you've already got twenty-five jumpers so far this year alone." Lilliana frowned.

"So, something is increasing," Reese said, with a nod, "this year being the worst."

"Well, it's been a hell of a year and a half. Doesn't that count as a major factor?" Rodney asked, as he walked in with a fresh cup of coffee.

She lifted her nose, smelled the air, grabbed her oversize mug, and headed to the coffeemaker. It would be a long night. For her team too. At least she'd eaten something and had fueled up enough that she could be here for a while. The trouble was, only so much she could do, even with help. Online chat stuff was full-on BS because they had a department that could run some of it but couldn't access some of these places. She had a log-in. If she found a way to join some of these groups, she could go in with suicide potential herself.

Kate frowned at that, as she turned to Lilliana. "How stupid would this idea be?" And she ran it past her.

"I was wondering about it myself," Lilliana said. "We need somebody inside these chats."

"I'll do it," Reese said. "Is it okay if I use this spare computer, Kate?"

"Sure, have at it."

"I can take a look at some of the sites too," Andy said.

Kate asked, "Why you?" He grinned and said, "I'm often on these chats anyway." She gasped. He shook his head. "Not suicide chats, beautiful."

"Gross, what then? Hump-and-dump chats?" she teased.

He flushed slightly and said, "Hey, you know that it was good for a while."

"Oh, does that mean you remember the girl you slept with last night?"

"Yeah, she's the same one for the last couple weeks," he said, with a big fat smile.

Kate chuckled. "Good for you. I'm glad you got through that nasty stage."

"It did its job," he said.

She watched him as he logged on to his computer. "Should you be doing that from the work computer?"

"Not only am I doing it from the work computer," he said, "but I'll also track it."

She looked at him with added respect. "Didn't know you had the skills. I'm working on it myself," she said, "but it's one thing to get into the dark web, yet it's another thing entirely to hide your tracks on something like this."

"Yeah, but, in this case, not only do we have to hide the tracks," Reese piped up from the side, "but we have to keep track of our tracks as well."

Kate shook her head at that. "It's a spiderweb out there."

"It is. But look here," Reese pointed out. "I've got twelve different chats."

"Twelve?" Kate said, leaning forward, and, sure enough, Reese had found twelve different suicide support groups. "Good God," Kate said. "Wait. I have the names that match a couple of the addresses." She walked over to her board, pulled off the copy and the little black book that she had and brought both back to Reese.

The analyst looked at it and said, "Three of those are here. Let me go in and take a look."

"Can you though?" Kate asked.

"No, probably not tonight," Reese said. "I can request to join them at least."

"What happens if they let you in?"

"Then I'll probably get a list of rules, and then they'll wait and see what I do."

"Interesting," Kate murmured. "So administrators are on these?"

"There usually is one," Reese said, "if not a couple. Depending on how many people are on the chats. In the loops themselves, there could be anywhere up to five or six administrators. If you've got hundreds or even thousands of people on one particular loop, you could have a lot more, and it could be segregated into subloops."

"Right," Kate agreed. "I've seen that many times."

Reese nodded. "Exactly. This is just the dark web."

"Well, let me know what you find."

"I'm still applying," she said, with a laugh. "Go sit down and do something useful."

"Wouldn't that be nice?" Kate said, staring at her computer. She brought up the email with Louisa's photo and stared at her. "Where did he get that picture from, I wonder?"

"Good point. Does David have photos on his phone?" Lilliana asked.

"Did his phone come in with him?" Kate asked, turning to Lilliana, who hopped up and walked over and printed off the report of what items came in with David.

"His cell phone, yes, but it's dead."

"Of course it is. I wonder if I can get a copy of this and ask his wife where he might have gotten it from."

"Minus the bullet hole?" Lilliana asked drily.

"Yeah, I was thinking I could maybe cut it off." She put it into a free editing program, cut it off just below the bullet hole, and then attached it to an email to the wife, Louisa, with a quick question. Kate got a response a few minutes later, saying, *No idea. I've never seen that photo before.*

Kate frowned and said, "So does that mean somebody's been tracking her?"

"Well, if you think about it," Lilliana said, "part of the actual fear in all of this would be for somebody to know who your wife is."

Kate looked at her team member and said, "Bingo. Nobody on the chats would know that, would they? So somebody had to have tracked down David's real name, found his wife, took a picture of her, and attached it to an email address that may or may not have been public knowledge either."

"In other words, a hacker," Lilliana said.

Rodney turned, looked at her, and said, "Unfortunately way too many of those guys are out there."

She nodded. "Particularly, if they'll do this, they have decent skills."

Rodney started a list for the profile, printing off one for Kate. "You'll have to talk to the shrink again."

"I only got five minutes with him last time. Once he connected the dots, I honestly think I was more of a specimen to put under a microscope than anything else."

Lilliana laughed and laughed. "Well, you did get the last one fired."

"Actually she got put in jail," Rodney said, with a big

grin.

"It's not my fault Yolynda was keeping pedophiles' secrets," Kate stated. "Just think. She could have saved all those kids."

"Not sure if she could have saved them because I think a lot of the conversations between her and her brothers came after the fact, but she could have certainly stopped their vile long ago."

"And it's true that it was the same family who abused Simon, huh?" Lilliana asked.

Kate nodded her head. "And I can assure you, that's not a subject we talk about."

"Nope. But I would like to know more about his psychic gifts."

"Not me," she said. "I just hope that conversation never comes up again."

"But he helped you with that pedophile case."

"He might have," she said, "and I might have gotten there on my own too."

"But maybe not in time to save Leonard," Rodney added.

"I would like to think so," she snapped. Then she groaned. "Sorry, sore subject and I'm tired." She looked at the photo of Louisa again. "I wonder if she would have any idea when the picture was taken, like if she could remember when she wore that shirt."

She quickly called Louisa and said, "I get that you have never seen that photo before, but you're wearing a particular shirt. Do you have any idea how often you would have worn that or when you might have worn it last?"

"It's relatively new," she said. "I just bought it a couple weeks ago, and I wore it on a hike with David," she said quietly, and then the tears started. "We went shopping. We went out for lunch, and, when we came back here, we were talking with the neighbors for a bit, and I was wearing it."

She wondered if David's house wasn't probably the easiest location to grab that photo. If somebody was watching the house, then, *hmm* ... "Okay, that's a help. Thank you."

"Why would somebody take that photo?" Louisa asked, puzzled.

"I'm not sure," Kate said. "That's what we're trying to figure out. It was in David's email inbox."

"Weird," Louisa said. "Well, I mean, unless somebody knew of me ..." And then she stopped, gasped, and said, "Somebody wasn't trying to put an idea in his head that I was having an affair, were they?"

"No, I don't think that was it at all," Kate quickly reassured her.

"Oh, good," Louisa gasped. "I would absolutely hate for anything like that to have happened. He's always been my life."

"I'm sure he knew that."

"Well, if he did," Louisa said quietly, "why didn't it matter then?"

That was a hell of a note to end the call on because Kate had absolutely no idea how to respond.

Simon's Wee Hours of Saturday Morning

SIMON WOKE IN the night—really the wee hours of early morning—with the same voice going on and on in his head.

Do it. Do it. Go ahead and do it.

Simon remained quiet, trying to let the voice wander through his consciousness. He wanted to slam the door to his mind and to lock it on the other side and to find a way to shut out intruders like this. Something was almost mocking, reminiscent of a teenage bully in high school, pushing you to do something you didn't want to do on a dare, knowing that everybody was watching. And, if you didn't do it, you would get picked on for the rest of the school year. Yet, if you did do it and failed, it would be just as freaking bad.

Do it, the voice said, with that hated insinuation that suggested the person on the other end of these words was totally capable of doing whatever it was.

On a hunch, Simon asked, "Do what?"

The voice stopped for a second and said, *Do it*, and then it was gone.

Simon was in bed, quiet, his heart slamming against his chest. He looked at the room around him. "Grandmother, what the hell did you get me into?"

It had been her abilities that had sent him as far away from this world as he had been. There'd been nothing fun about it for her either. She'd been mocked and teased. People laughed; others would cross the street to get away from her, all because of her witchy abilities. And yet his grandmother had been a wonderful woman with a heart of solid gold. Nobody had appreciated the things she had done for the community or for the individuals she had helped. And even those she had helped the most had a hard time seeing her publicly. Because the others would ostracize them as well. And it was all about community back then; it would have been all about keeping his grandmother away from the community.

"Assholes," he muttered under his breath, as he tried to go back to sleep.

Only sleep was the furthest thing from his mind. As he

lay here, he wondered who the hell the voice belonged to. It sounded different every time, different, yet somehow the same. Similar and yet something was off, almost—and then he stopped, not knowing how to describe it. Finally giving up, he rose and had a shower, then sat down with a fresh pot of coffee to do some paperwork.

As he sat in his favorite chair overlooking the view, he saw the sunrise. He smiled; it always helped to restore his faith in humanity, although humanity had nothing to do with that sun. It was all about Mother Nature, and, sure enough, humanity was doing as much to drive her into the ground as it could. He settled back, wondering just how bad things would get before people would take note of the environment and do something about it. When it was almost seven o'clock, his phone rang, and he looked at it in surprise. "Louisa? Are you okay?"

"Yes," she said, her voice hesitant. "I'm making arrangements for David's funeral."

"Ah, I'm sorry," he said. "If there's anything I can do to help—"

"That's why I'm calling. I spoke with the detective yesterday, and she said something about a photo of me in an email."

"And?" he asked, cautiously putting his pen down and picking up his coffee to take a sip. He wondered what she was calling about and how much Kate had told her.

"Well, you remember my friend who was here when you came by?" she said. "She didn't seem to think that the police had any right to take the laptop."

"Didn't have any right?" he said. "Well, for one, I told you that they needed it, and you were in agreement with that."

"But they didn't have a warrant, did they?"

He frowned, confused. "Well, they didn't need a warrant," he said, "because we gave it to them."

"But maybe we shouldn't have," she said in a rush.

"What are you afraid of?" he asked. "Do you really think David did something wrong?"

"No," she cried out. "Why would you even say that?"

"Because I don't understand why you're acting the way you are," he asked in confusion.

"I just feel like I want the laptop," she said.

"You know you're getting it back, right?" There was silence at the other end. Unsure if she understood fully, he continued. "They needed it in order to get whatever forensic information they can for their case, but they're giving it back to you."

"With everything on it?" she asked.

"Yes, of course," he said.

"Well, when can I get it back?"

"I don't know," he said. "You'd have to ask Kate that."

"Oh," she said, her voice changing. "I didn't think she would let me have it."

"Well, she will as soon as she can," he said.

"Can? What do you mean by can?"

"Louisa, I don't understand. All they're trying to do is get information to help clarify David's death."

"Yes, I get that, but I don't want this to become public knowledge."

"You mean, that he committed suicide?"

"Yes, of course," she said.

"And how will the police having the laptop impact that?"

"I don't know," she said, "but I just started to get really

worried about it, and I don't think David would like them to have it."

"Well, in this case, it's not his decision. They already have it, and I don't know how much longer they'll need to keep it."

"I don't understand why they need to keep it at all."

"And I don't understand why there's a problem. It's not like you don't have your own computer."

"You shouldn't have taken it from me," she said, getting bolder in her wording.

"Taken it from you?" he said, shaking his head. "I'm not sure what's going on, but you were in full agreement with the police checking out everything to do with his death."

"I know," she said, "and then I got to thinking."

He frowned. "Is this your *friend* interfering again?"

"Maybe, but she had a couple good points."

"And what was that?"

"What if they find something that'll mar his reputation?"

"I think you need to watch out for possibly well-meaning friends who are feeding you unfounded fears. Don't let them add to your worries with nonexistent problems. David's dead. I don't think the police will find anything that'll make much difference or mar his reputation in any way."

"Well, it will to me," she cried out passionately.

"Are you saying you'd want to keep whatever happened to your husband a secret?"

"Maybe," she said, her voice getting hesitant again, as if she didn't know how to answer.

Simon knew that from the tone of her voice it was more because it wasn't a question that she had thought to ask her friend, so now she didn't have a planned answer to give. "Do you want me to talk to Helena?"

"No," she said in a rush. "She didn't want anything to do with any of this."

"And yet she's pressuring you to get the laptop back before the police are done with it. Helena obviously thinks badly of the police and is trying to get you to do the same thing. And you do realize that wanting the laptop back before the police check out all information about David's death just raises suspicions and may make the investigation take longer?"

Silence. "Suspicion of what?" she said, her voice rising, "I didn't do anything."

"No, but now you're acting weird," he said bluntly. "I understand concern. I understand the fact that, from your perspective, as a civilian who knows nothing of how an official investigation works, that there's no reason for them to have it. But having given it to them voluntarily and not having any viable reason why they can't have it to investigate the death of your husband," he said, "I think demanding it back will just cause them to look at you sideways."

"Oh," she said.

"After what happened to David, you need to be careful about who and what you believe."

She swallowed loudly. "How long do you think they need his computer?"

"Hopefully not very long," he said. "Why don't you simply call and ask Kate about that, if it will make you feel better? And watch out for those negative thoughts taking over in your mind. That's what David did too. Don't listen to Helena's negativity either. Ask the source. Call Kate and say that there's material on there that you want for his eulogy or something. And ask how soon you can get it back. It's just that simple. Don't let Helena make it into some big conspiracy."

"Oh, that's a great idea," she said in a rush. "Thanks." And, with that, she hung up.

He stared down at his phone, wondering what the hell had just gone on. He didn't know Louisa anywhere near as well as he did David, and apparently—after not knowing that the guy was suicidal—Simon didn't know his friend all that well either. But this just ranked up on a level of bizarre. He shook his head, sent a text to Kate, mentioning that Louisa was looking for the laptop back. And then he put it out of his mind and carried on for the day.

CHAPTER 9

Kate's Saturday Morning

K ATE SAW THE text, wondered at it, shrugged, and carried on, as she walked toward the station. It was a beautiful sunny day and promised to be an absolutely gorgeous afternoon, but, as far as she was concerned, she wouldn't get much chance to enjoy it. She and her team were still interviewing families of other suicide victims, and they had begun this process over the past week. She had copious notes, and what she was trying to figure out was some methodology for finding similarities between them. She'd done a couple cases in note form, bringing out the salient points, and now needed to do the same for the rest of the cases.

When she got in, she found a full pot of coffee. With a grin, she snagged a cup, sat down at her desk, grabbed her notepads, brought up her Excel document, and transferred her summary information into the spreadsheet.

When Rodney sauntered in, a little bit later with a cup of coffee in hand, he looked over at the spreadsheet on her computer screen and winced. "I can't stand those things."

"No," she said, "but at least we can use them for data sorting." He looked at her with a grimace, and she shrugged. "We have so many cases year-to-date, I just couldn't figure out the best way to compare for similarities."

"You know there is a search feature online."

"There is," she said, with a nod, "but, when you consider how much information there is, what if somebody didn't put in some of these points? So then, when you do run a search, it doesn't come up with any of the stuff that you're looking for."

He shook his head. "Looks like a ton of man-hours wasted to me."

"Did you have something else you wanted to do?" she asked, looking at him. "Some other case that we need to work on?"

"We don't need any more cases," he said, with a groan. "We've got too many already."

"Nothing new on the drive-bys though, huh?"

"No," he said, "nothing new anywhere." He tossed down his pencil, looked at her, and asked, "You want me to do some?"

"No, I got this."

Just then, both of their phones rang.

"Uh-oh." She groaned and said, "Here we go."

Both checked their phones, each notified of another drive-by shooting. Racing for their jackets, they headed out.

"I'll drive," he said. Running to his vehicle, they drove straight to the scene. Traffic was on their side, making the trip fast.

Kate stood off to the side, taking it all in. They were on scene earlier than the other shooting cases, in time to see people mingling around, witnesses still crying, the victim on the ground with a sheet atop him. Atop *them*. She stepped up toward Rodney. "This would be a first, if it's the same guy."

He looked at her in surprise.

She pointed. "Look. More than one victim."

Rodney frowned and nodded. "Could have been accidentally caught by the gunfire."

She nodded. "But still, it doubles his kill count, and, in that case, he may want to keep that up." Rodney's gaze narrowed. She shrugged. "Just something to keep in mind."

As they turned and took in the scene of the crime, she studied everything that she could get her mind wrapped around. But it seemed fairly simple: a vehicle drove by, took potshots at a couple guys walking along the road, and took them down. She bent to study the two young men; they were once again healthy, under twenty-five most likely, tall and slim, and looked to be athletic.

She straightened, turned to look at the crowd, separated off the witnesses, and took the first one. By the time she was done with the third, the story was the same. These women had been sitting on a bench on the opposite side of the road, and a vehicle drove by. An old blue-green truck. They heard the shooting but didn't realize it involved people on the far side of the street, until the odd-colored truck was gone. Two men were down. They tried to get across the street, but, because of the shooting, all the traffic had snarled up, and they didn't get there as fast as they'd hoped, but the two guys appeared to be already dead.

One woman looked at Kate with tears in her eyes and said, "I used to be an ER nurse. Nothing's more deadly than bullets in the head."

Kate nodded. "I've seen them a time or two myself," she said quietly. "Can you guys identify anything about the truck?" The three women looked at each other and shook their heads. Kate pressed for more. "Did you see a different colored door? Did you see any dents on the vehicle? Did you see the driver?"

"I didn't see any of that. We were busy with girl talk," she said, motioning at the two women beside her. At that, Kate's eyebrow rose up. "Susie's got a new boyfriend, so we were deep in a discussion about him."

"And, therefore, you didn't notice anything around you? Right, got it."

"It's not like we would have known that he was about to shoot somebody, so that we needed to pay attention," she said in their defense.

"Absolutely," Kate said. "I'm just checking if you saw anything else." She asked a few more questions, like if any of these women happened to recognize anybody within the witnesses, or did they know the victims? Had the truck driven by them earlier? All their answers pretty well came back to reveal they didn't have a clue. They never saw anything.

By the time Kate had gone through the other ten witnesses on her side of the road, she was frustrated because nobody saw anything.

"You might want to check with the ice cream parlor there," said one of the older men, pointing across the road.

She turned, looked at it, and asked, "Why is that?"

"They just had new security cameras installed last week."

Her eyebrows shot up at that. "We'll check it out. Thanks," she said. "It's on our list to do anyway. Do you happen to know why they had cameras installed?"

"They've had a series of break-ins," he said. "I know that they were pretty upset because they couldn't seem to get anywhere with the police on them."

"Right," she said; of course it would be something like that. "It's not always easy to solve break-ins, even with the cameras."

He nodded. "That's what I understand. Makes it pretty damn hard when there is no deterrent to crime around here. It's not like there's any penalty."

She looked at him and said, "Well, we're trying our best to stop it, but we still need people to step up and to share what they saw, when there is a problem."

He nodded. "All I can tell you is, they've got cameras now, so you should check it out."

"Will do," she said. "Thanks." As she headed over to the opposite side of the road, where the victims were, Rodney walked toward her.

He shook his head. "How is it that something like this can happen, and nobody sees anything?"

"Because it happened so fast," she said, "at least according to everybody I talked to."

He nodded in agreement with that, as nobody saw anything, except that it was an older blue-green truck. "One actually said *aqua*."

"I get it," she said, "but none of mine could identify any damage to the truck or anything about the driver."

"One said he had a baseball cap pulled way down. At least he saw that much, which goes along with what we knew already."

"But maybe we'll get something from the cameras. I'm interested in knowing if it was deliberate that he shot two this time, or was it just an accident, or was he just firing, and he really didn't give a damn?"

"In the past he has cared, it seemed," Rodney said. "So this one is potentially very different."

"Exactly. He is getting more careless, or this was more impulse, or he knew somebody caught sight of him and decided these two would make a perfect target."

Rodney frowned, as he nodded.

"Nobody seemed to see him a second time around either," she mentioned. "I asked the three women who had been sitting there for quite a while. They didn't see the truck come by earlier."

"Doesn't mean he didn't though," Rodney said. "It just means that they didn't see him if he did."

She had to agree with that.

At the ice cream parlor, she managed to get copies of the street cam video sent to her email. Knowing she would be more successful with a computer than her phone, she walked over to Rodney and said, "If we're done here, I'll head back to the station. I've got the video feed coming, sent from the ice cream parlor."

He nodded and asked, "Are you okay to take a bus?"

She glanced around at a bus coming up now and said, "Sure, that one will take me to just a couple blocks away. What will you do?"

He said, "I'll see if anybody else has cameras." She hesitated, he waited but when she didn't say anything, he added, "Go on. This is a one-person deal at this point in time."

"Yeah, and you've got wheels," she said, with a smile.

"True enough," he said, "so it's up to you."

Deciding that she would hop the bus, she headed back, wondering at her love of the city buses. It was a nostalgia thing. It just reminded her of better memories of home and growing up. Even later, although she had wheels and drove a lot when she was older, she'd also spent a fair amount of time traveling by bus. As it was, this bus got her near the station pretty fast. When she walked in, Lilliana looked up.

"Is Rodney with you?"

"He's still at the scene, checking for more cameras," she said. "I need to look at a feed sent to my email."

"And they didn't have a monitor?" Lilliana asked in surprise.

"Yeah, but it wasn't that clear, and they weren't sure how to use it. I figured I'd do better by having it sent over, so we could look at it here."

"You know what? You'd think, for all the technology in the world, we'd have better luck with it," Lilliana said.

"Yeah, the better quality images and features involve a lot more money," she murmured. "And they are just out of reach for some of these places."

"I know," Lilliana said. "It's not like everybody is prepared for a break-in."

The feed was waiting for Kate at her desk. Bringing it up, she fast-forwarded to the time in question. The ice cream parlor camera caught most of it; the vehicle drove in front of the camera straight across. The driver was staring at the two guys walking on the street. He didn't even slow down, just pulled up a handgun, rested it against the window frame, and started firing. She replayed it several times, but it looked like he fired six shots before he was out of range. She shook her head at that and replayed it several times more.

The angle wasn't quite right to get the license plate, and a close-up on the driver didn't give her anything more than a baseball cap pulled low. But what she did note was that the shooter had zero hesitation. There was no slowing down and no indecision about it. He lifted a gun; he killed two men, and he kept on going, as if he were just out on a Sunday drive. The absolute normality of it contrasted so shockingly with the shots being fired and the two deaths, as their blood poured all over the sidewalk, and the witnesses started screaming.

But from the driver, nothing.

Logging into the city camera system, she tried to track the truck and did manage to pick it up a little farther along. She immediately contacted Rodney. "Are you coming back anytime soon?"

"I just pulled into the parking lot. Why?"

"Because the video has some decent footage," she said. "Nothing that we'll really identify the driver with, but I'm tracking him through the city traffic, and I could use a hand with that, if you're up for it."

"Coming," he said, "and hot damn if you got something we can track. It's not like we've had anything—up until now."

"Right, we definitely needed a break. What about you? Find anything?" she asked.

"A little bit of footage, nothing identifiable."

"Okay," she said. Before they were done talking, she looked up to see him walking into the office.

He pocketed his phone and said, "Let me grab a coffee, and then we'll sit down and see what we can do."

She nodded. "I've already got him tracked and heading over toward the Lions Gate Bridge."

"In that case," he said, "skip the coffee. I'm here."

And he sat down beside her.

WITHIN SECONDS, BOTH Rodney and Kate had their screens up, tracking the truck on different cameras. With both of them talking back and forth, they tracked the shooter through town and across the Lions Gate Bridge— also known as First Narrows Bridge—over to West Vancouver.

"Shit," he said, "we have to change districts."

She quickly moved to shift to cameras in another direction, noting the time the truck went over the bridge. But, when they got to the other side, the truck headed into the mall, one of the great big strip malls that ran along the right side of the highway, and they lost him from the view of the cameras. Using as many other cameras as she could, she tracked for hours through the mall area and the highway to see if he ever came back onto the highway.

But searching through twelve hours' worth of film later, using fast-forward mode, backtracking several times, she sat back in defeat. "Well, if he went in there, I don't know how he came out."

"There are exits out the back," Rodney said, shifting. "If you wanted to avoid the cameras, that would be the easiest way to do it."

"Goddammit," she said. "Now what?"

"You realize, in all that time, we never got an ID on his face, and we never got very much on the license plate."

"I took a couple screenshots," she said, shifting to where she had saved them. She pulled them up and showed them to him. "Do you think Forensics could do anything with that?"

He tapped the screen of one and said, "That one is damn close. We might get some of the letters on it."

She immediately sent it off to the guys and gals in Computer Forensics to see if they could enhance it at all. When Stoop called her, saying there wasn't much to go on, Kate heard the doubt in his tone. Tired and frustrated, she snapped at him. "Come on. It's all we've got, and he just killed two more guys today."

"Right, I'm on it," he said.

"I guess you haven't had a chance to look at that laptop, have you?"

He said, "I wouldn't even have gone in that direction with the jumpers, and I get that you think we have nothing going on here. But cases like these drive-by shootings take precedence over suicides."

"Just not much precedence," she said, "please. We need to make sure that these suicides aren't murders."

"You really think they are?"

"This David guy was threatened with pictures of his wife with a bullet hole in her head if he didn't do what he was told."

"Well, crap," he said. "I'm on it."

She hoped so; she just wasn't so sure. It would be tough right now because she also knew that they were swamped. She sat back and looked over at Rodney. "You realize that took hours."

"Yep," he said, "the day is done."

She shook her head. "How the hell is the day done already?"

He got up, reached in his open drawer for his keys and wallet, and said, "I'll see you later."

She nodded. "I guess."

He stopped, looked over at her, and said, "Look. You were here late last night. You've got to go home. You don't get to live here."

She glared. "We're not getting anywhere."

"And until there's something more to do," he said, "we can't do more. Go home. Refresh your brain while you can."

"There really should be a way for me to keep working on this."

"No, there shouldn't be," he said, his tone heartfelt. "Look, partner. You're no good to us when we do need you if you don't get some rest when you can."

She nodded, stood. "Fine."

He laughed. "You're the damnedest one for not wanting to leave the office."

"I just want to catch this guy," she snapped.

"So do I."

As she headed out to the parking lot, she hopped into her vehicle and wondered; then deciding that it was better to go see for herself, she headed across the bridge out to the mall, where they had last seen the shooter's truck. She then drove around to the back, so she could get an idea where the cameras were. But there weren't many, like she had hoped, and she also found not just one or two exits out of the place but several. She noted a road running parallel to the mall in the back that anybody could get on and off of easily.

She groaned. "Okay, you got away this time," she said, "but we're on to you now."

She'd already put out a BOLO for the vehicle. Now she needed a better description and a license plate number. And, for that, she needed the help of the forensic geeks. She slowly drove home. By the time she pulled into her apartment's parking lot, it was that much later. She hopped up the stairs, still full of energy, and considered a workout immediately upon entering her place. She needed a judo session, so she quickly changed, walked down the stairs, and headed over to her judo center.

Kate stepped inside the dojo and could immediately feel the peace taking over. She went through the paces before doing a bout that worked her hard. By the time she was done, she was grinning like a fool, but she was exhausted.

Her sensei smiled, nodded. "That was good for you."

"It was," she said in agreement. "It's hard to imagine how stressful some days can be."

"And always that stress," he said, "comes from within. Stress is basically fear. You must let it go, before it overtakes you."

She stared at him. "I've heard that before."

"Think about why you're stressed."

She shrugged. "I have a case, and I can't catch this guy."

"So where's the fear coming from?"

She snorted. "The fear is that he'll kill again before I can stop him."

He nodded slowly. "The work you do, it's important," he said. "Not everyone can do it, but you must honor that part of you."

She smiled. "I don't even know how much that part of me exists."

"You're doing fine," he said. "Just remember you need stress relief in order to function at your best."

She nodded quietly, then grabbed her bag and headed outside again. As she started to walk home, she thought she caught sight of a big old truck. Not aqua but suspicious nonetheless. She turned, stared at it, then frowned and kept on walking. When it went past her again, she immediately ducked into a doorway, wondering if it could possibly be this suicide guy, proving her theory that he was local. Or the drive-by shooter in a decoy vehicle. Or anyone else from any number of other cases. And... considering how tired she was... maybe it was just her imagination.

And why would either guy be here, stalking her, unless it was a coincidence? And she wasn't terribly big on those. But whoever he was, he wouldn't know where she was—unless of course he'd gone back to the scene of the latest drive-by crime, with his two victims this time, and had then followed her. She swore at that, and, when the truck was gone, raced up to her place and grabbed her laptop.

She sent Rodney a text message. **We didn't check to see if the shooter hung around at the drive-by crime scenes. Because he took off. We tracked that aqua truck for hours.**

"No," she snapped back, phoning him now. "What if he ditched the vehicle and then came back to the crime scene?"

"But you saw it drive all the way across West Vancouver."

"But did you realize that was an hour later?" she asked. "Remember the digital time reads that we were looking at?"

He stopped and swore. "You could be right."

"I am," she said. "I need to get back in there and look at those crime scene photos and that ice cream shop's video to see if we can get anything from somebody who might have been there."

"Well, there'll be a lot of people who were there," he said. "I get that you're really involved in this, but just stay sane over it all. Just like your suicide cases. If it's a murderer, we'll go after him. And don't you worry. We'll get him."

"But will we get him?" she asked quietly, "before he takes out somebody else? And did Andy ever get into the chats?"

"Why ask me? You know where I was all day," he said in exasperation. "Where the hell are you anyway?"

"I'm at home now," she said, "after a judo session."

"Yeah, so everybody else goes home and collapses, but you go work out," he said in disgust. "What the hell are you, superhuman?"

"No, just pissed. Stressed out, pissed off, and damn angry that this guy keeps getting away with this."

"You don't know where the suicide guy is, and this drive-by shooter is a completely different case. Don't get confused here."

"I know. I know. I know. I'm trying not to let them run together in my head, but it's hard when we know that they're all out there, intent on hurting people."

"And that's why we're doing what we're doing," he said calmly. "Just remember that." And, with that, he hung up.

She groaned, got up, and had a shower, her thoughts immediately going to Simon and wondering if she should call him. But she changed her mind, knowing it was much better if she kept a little bit of distance. But, as she came out from the shower, a knock came at her door. Not sure why, she headed for her weapon sitting on the night table, and, with it held behind her back, she walked over to the door and asked who it was.

When Simon answered, she opened the door, and asked, "What are you doing here?"

He looked at her, wrapped only in a towel, his gaze appreciatively moving up and down, and he said, "Are you going to invite me in?"

His voice had dropped deep and husky, his eyes widening, and she could almost smell the pheromones that immediately lit up and turned her bones to molten lava. "Christ," she said.

He stepped inside, shoving her forward gently with his body. "Come on. Invite me inside," he said, and he slammed the door hard.

"You're inside," she whispered.

He looked at her and, when he saw the weapon, one

eyebrow went up. She shook her head. "Are you really that wary?"

"Maybe. I don't know." She took a step back and said, "I need to go get dressed."

"Not for my sake," he said, pulling her into his arms. Lowering his head where their lips barely touched, he whispered, "You never did invite me in."

"I didn't want to be distracted." She placed her handgun on the side table, where her keys rested. "Now," she threw her arms around his neck and whispered, "distract me."

And then she crushed her mouth against his. He picked her up in a motion she wasn't expecting, so smooth and with more power than she had even contemplated he could muster. He carried her through to the bedroom and, without warning, lowered both of them onto the mattress. It wasn't just a coupling, but something hard, fast, and furious, yet incredibly sexy, as he drove her passion to the point where she couldn't do a thing. She was mindless, as he slipped his hands over her body, up and down, caressing, smoothing, and calming. And yet, with every touch, her temperature rose; her cries came out as tiny wails, as he whispered, "Easy, easy, honey."

She shook her head. "No, it can't be easy." She pivoted and shifted, knocking him onto his back, where she quickly divested him of his clothing. "It's only fair," she said, half panting.

"Oh, I agree," he said, as he took off his shirt. In seconds, he had his pants off, but the boxers were a whole different story, with her hands firmly wrapped around his erection. He groaned heavily, and his hips shot upward, and he swore.

She laughed. "Turnabout is fair play."

By the time he got stripped down, there was no time to take off his socks before she was already astride him. He gasped and froze.

She slowly, gingerly lowered herself down his shaft, just a few inches, then she stopped. He glared up at her. She smiled, stretched his arms over his head, and whispered, "See? Turnabout is fair play."

He nodded and pulled a simple but fast maneuver, and suddenly she was the one underneath. As he sat here, poised at the entrance to the heart of her, he whispered, "Exactly. Turnabout is fair play," and, with one hard movement, he plunged deep.

She cried out, her body arching under his onslaught, and, within seconds, exploded.

He chuckled out loud. "Now it's my turn," he said, then drove hard, fast, and so damn deep that she felt it, almost as if she were split inside, and she couldn't stand it; she wanted so much more. By the time he groaned and shuddered above her, she was coming apart at the seams yet again.

When he collapsed beside her, he wrapped her up in his arms, pulled her close, and, when she went to say something, he placed a finger against her lips and whispered, "Later. Much later."

GOOD TIMING ON his part. Simon had hoped that Kate would be home soon but hadn't really expected to catch her fresh from a shower. He expected a bigger argument from her, but obviously something was tormenting her. And, with her in his arms as she curled up beside him, her breath even and deep, he realized she'd fallen asleep. Her guard was down, even if just for a moment.

He loved that about her; she lived in the moment. She gave 100 percent to whatever she focused on. Right now, she was 100 percent asleep, at peace, like the angel she was. He lowered his lips to her temple, kissed her gently, and settled in deeper. He didn't know what the hell he would do with her. The last thing he wanted was a cop in his world, mostly because, well, he already knew what she thought about his psychic ability.

He wondered if she'd ever come up with anything on that number thirteen that still drove through his head. And how was she handling Louisa? That was a whole different problem. Plus he had yet to share the voice urging him to *Do it*, whatever the hell *it* was. By the time he worked his way through it all, he shrugged, realizing he could do nothing about any of it. So he closed his eyes and fell asleep right beside her.

CHAPTER 10

Sunday Morning

K ATE WOKE WITH a start, instantly sitting up, her body
sore and yet thrumming with joy. She sagged back
down onto the bed and noted it was empty, the covers tossed
wildly about. She smiled because, of all the things that she
felt right now, *perfect* topped the description. After a quick
second shower she got dressed, realizing that the apartment
was very cold and empty. Sad that he wasn't still here, she
headed to the kitchen, where she found a fresh pot of coffee
waiting for her with a small note.

Look after yourself.

A tiny heart was drawn beneath it.

"Silly fool," she said affectionately. She couldn't justify
why, but she picked up the little note and tucked it among
her other personal papers. It was foolish and sentimental, but
she wasn't quite ready to throw it out. Shrugging at the
silliness, she sat and had a cup of coffee with her toast and
then a second cup, before heading off to work. She had a
long agenda and not the least of which was to start searching
the crowds to see if she found somebody who was at the
multiple crime scenes—whether for the jumpers or for the
drive-by shootings.

As she headed into work, she reached the same set of
steps while going inside as Rodney. He looked at her, then

raised an eyebrow but didn't say anything. She appreciated that. Because, of course, one of the big jokes had been about her nonexistent sex life. She didn't want to think about the reality that she now was in a relationship, which she would rather keep secret, yet was easily revealed on her face, so too bad; her team would just have to deal with it. She headed into the office and didn't bother grabbing coffee right away, instead bringing up the crime scene photos.

Rodney looked at her and said, "What's the matter, no coffee?"

"I already had a couple cups," she said thoughtfully. "Do we have any video camera footage from the other drive-by shootings?"

"We have one," he said. "I was just pulling it up to see if we could do some cross-referencing." She explained what she was thinking of, and he nodded. "I talked to Owen about it this morning," he said. "It's a good thought, although it doesn't explain why he took off to West Vancouver."

"Well, it does if he thought he was being followed or if he had a reason to go over there or even if he was just trying to distract everybody. We don't even know for sure that he was even driving the truck by then."

"That's true enough," he said. "Here is what we've got on the second shooting."

"And what about the one from three years ago?"

Rodney shook his head. "I'm not sure that we do. Plus I'm not sure it's the same guy either."

"Well, we're pretty sure it's the same vehicle," she said.

"Okay, I'll give you that—or at least a copycat from back then maybe."

"And that's still important too," she said, "because somebody has got to know something. And, if we've got a copycat here, it's even more important because he may not have the same closing-down routine that the other guy did."

"You really think the other guy did more than one at the time?"

"Well, *this* guy is not stopping," she said. "What's the count now? Two shootings in four days?"

"Something like that," he said.

"Any other drive-bys anywhere else?" she asked him. "We need to run a search and see if anything else matches."

"So we better get at all that now."

By lunchtime, Rodney and Kate both sat back, their eyes sore and weary. They had picked up two more recent shootings, and there was even one more shooting from three years ago.

"So," Rodney said to Kate, "you think he just, out of the blue, started up again, only twice as ferociously?"

"That means this guy wasn't around for some reason between the events of three years ago and now."

"If he just got out of jail?" Rodney offered.

"Yeah, that's possible," Kate replied, "or if he, well, depending on why he's doing this, maybe he had cancer or something, and there's a recurrence of it now."

Rodney looked at her with respect. "You know what? That's a valuable point too. If we're thinking that's why he's killing these healthy young males, then seeing the recurrence of an illness that he thought he'd beat could trigger him in a way that set off the same reaction."

"And even more viciously," she murmured.

He nodded. "Agreed. But we still haven't really found much."

"No, we haven't," she said, frowning.

"When searching the videos, to see if our shooter was coming back to the scene of the crime, I'm finding it hard to see anyone standing out in the crowds gathered at the scene. I was looking more for the hat."

"Interesting," she said. "I wasn't. I was taking the hat off, assuming that would be one of the best disguises."

"And yet, if any camera caught him," Rodney said, "he would be caught then."

She frowned and said, "Why don't we switch?"

"What do you mean?"

"Well, I saw all of these ones, and I didn't see anybody show up to all of the recent shootings. Why don't we switch? You take a look at mine, and I'll take a look at yours." Once she started looking, she saw it almost immediately. "Here," she said. "Take a look at this one."

He rolled his desk chair toward her desk, took a look at it, and said, "See? I was looking for the guys with the hats."

She moved over to the closest unmanned computer, switched to the city camera and the video that she was looking for, and finally, after twenty minutes, she said, "Here it is."

He looked at it and whistled. "You know something? I think you're right."

She nodded. "And if he was at two   "

"Then maybe he was at all of them. Yes!" he said, and that started a frenzy of searching. In the middle of it all, her phone rang. She answered absentmindedly. "Yes?"

"It's Louisa," she said. "Did you think any more about the laptop?"

She frowned into the phone. "It's in Forensics," she said. "As soon as I can get the material off it that we need, I can get it back to you."

"In Forensics?" Louisa said nervously. "I don't know what that means."

"It just means that they're the ones who deal with electronics," she said, trying for reassurance. "Simon did tell me that you wanted it back early."

"Yes, yes," she said eagerly. "I do."

"Well, I'm doing the best I can," she said. "Give me a day or so." And, with that, she said, "I'm sorry. I've got to go," and she hung up on the woman.

Rodney looked at her in surprise, "What was that?"

"The wife of the one jumper, David. She wants his laptop back."

"Any particular reason?"

"Something about wanting stuff for the eulogy."

"Well, that would make sense."

"Maybe," she said, "but you know that she handed it over quite freely."

"But maybe she didn't understand how long Forensics needed it."

She shrugged. "Well, they probably got everything off that laptop that they want." And, with that, she picked up the phone and then stopped. "You know what? I put a bunch of stuff on a rush for them over this last week. This is hardly something I can put a rush on as well."

He nodded and said, "You're learning. Remember. We have to be reasonable, and everyone thinks their cases come first, but we also have to have some consideration for people in these departments."

"Meaning, don't ask for a rush if we really don't need it. I get it."

"Exactly."

She nodded. "In that case, I'll let it ride for another day

or so."

"Do that," he said, "and, besides, I can't imagine that she'll get the body back any time soon."

She looked over at him. "I think it's to be released today."

He looked surprised at that. "Why? If we're looking at it as a possible murder, you would think they'd keep it longer."

"Not necessarily," she said. "They've already done what they need to do. Anything we may find at this point is moot—or at least not related to the evidence found on the body."

He nodded. "In that case, maybe she does need it."

She groaned. "I'm heading over there anyway. I'll see how it looks before I ask." With that, she got up and headed to the computer geeks' corner.

When Kate walked in, Bronwyn looked up, and she said, "It's not done."

"Yeah, sorry," Kate said. "I was looking at a couple other things here too."

"Of course you are," she said, with a frown.

"I was just wondering if you could get a better image off this video feed," Kate said. "We found the same guy at two of the drive-by shootings."

At that, her eyebrows shot up, and Bronwyn said, "Let me look at it."

"Where's Stoop?"

"He's on lunch."

"Okay, good," Kate said. "I hate to say it, but that lady is looking to get her husband's laptop back, whenever you guys have everything you need from it and can release it."

"I think we're ..." she said. "Let me talk to Stoop when he gets back."

Kate nodded and asked, "And these photos?"

"We got it," she said. "I'll get it back as soon as I can."

"Thanks, Bronwyn." Kate smiled, then turned and headed out.

Once outside, she stopped in the fresh air and looked around. She was immediately aware of that weird sensation again, as if being followed, and she didn't think she liked it much. But no way to know who or what it was. She looked around carefully, then shrugged and headed back to her office again. As she walked into the bullpen, her cell phone buzzed, and she found a bunch of emails downloaded onto her phone. When she got to her desk, she brought them up on the big screen, then stopped and swore.

"Now what?" Rodney said.

She said, "Another photo."

He looked at her in surprise and said, "What do you mean, another photo?"

She said, "Come here."

The message this time read *You're too slow.* As she moved down the screen, another picture of a bridge and a pair of sparkly sneakers appeared.

"Ah, crap," he said, "this guy again."

"Not only this guy," she said, "but this guy is getting even more active."

"Yeah, buoyed by success," he said. "I really hate this."

Almost automatically, she reached for the phone and checked in with the desk sergeant to see if any reports of suicide had come in overnight. As soon as she heard the reply, she groaned and sat back. "I need the report," she said.

"We haven't gotten an official one in yet," said the officer at the other end.

"Then can you tell me who the attending officers are?"

She quickly wrote down the names, found the contacts, and called the first one on her list. "Did you get called out on a suicide this morning?" she asked, after identifying herself.

"Yes," he said, "I just got the report in, so I can send you the details."

"Oh, good," she said. "So you saw the bulletin then?"

"Yes," he said. "This is a young woman, twenty-three years old. Her name is Pasha, and the last name is something like Niletto."

"Fine," she said. "Do we know anything about her? Any history?"

"No," he said. "I don't know anything, but the divers do have her up though."

"Okay, good enough," she said. "Send me that report as soon as you log it in." She ended the call, slowly looked over at the rest of the team, and, in a grim voice, said, "We have another jumper."

Just then Andy walked back in. She looked up at him and asked, "Did you get anywhere on those chats?"

"Lots of talk," he said. "I've been acting like I'm suicidal, not ready to switch that around to being positive about life yet."

"Well, it was a twenty-three-year-old woman this morning," she said. "And that photo I got—surely from the guy inciting these suicides—was most likely of her sneakers, although I don't have anything to confirm that. They're sending me the report as soon as it's done."

"Good enough," he said. "This is sick."

"Very sick. I'm not impressed at all." She sat back, her fingers thrumming. "Of course Forensics has David's laptop, and they're going through the chats themselves, but I'm not sure they'll find much."

"No, we need this guy to get back online again," Andy said. "I'll check out what's changed, what's different on the chats, and see if I can find out who this asshole is."

"Appreciate it," she said, "and make sure you keep the Forensics guys in the loop."

He laughed. "We already touched base because they were double-checking my ID. So I gave Stoop my ID and explained what I was doing. They laughed because they had it logged already but had forgotten about it."

"Good enough," she said. She looked over at Rodney. "Did you find anything new on our drive-by shooter?"

Rodney shook his head. "Yes ..."

"Why do I hear a *but* coming?" Kate asked.

"Well, I found some old trucks at the impound lot," he said. "A couple are black. One has a shitty paint job, and one is *aqua blue*. I was wondering if you wanted to go have a look."

She bounced to her feet. "Let's go."

He shook his head and said, "You have the energy of ten people this morning. I wish you'd give me some of it."

"Hey, I had a good night," she said blithely, as she sailed on by.

Lilliana whispered in a low voice, "Getting laid is good for you."

Kate snorted at that and kept on going. It was good for her, but it wasn't the fact that she got laid as much as the fact that she had connected with somebody—more than just Simon too, her whole team—and, for the first time in a very long while, she hadn't felt quite so alone. Nothing like the responsibility of all these deaths riding on her shoulders to make her feel like it was just more than she could handle. It's not that she would give up, but some days she wondered if keeping track of all these bad guys was even doable.

Ten minutes later, she and Rodney were at the impound lot, and, as they walked through the front and dealt with the guy attending the lot, he soon had the paperwork in hand on the vehicles they were interested in.

"Do we know what brought this blue one in?" she asked him.

"It was found parked and abandoned over on the west side."

She perked up. "Really? That's definitely the one I want to see first."

As they walked over to where it sat, she stopped, stared, and said, "Huh. I'm not sure it looks like the one we're after though." She stared at the mock-ups she had in her hand.

"It's amazing how hard it is to tell them apart though, isn't it?" Moving closer, the manager said, "That's a similar truck but definitely a different model, … a different year."

She shook her head. "No wonder people can't tell us very much sometimes."

"If you saw this one driving by the one you want," he said, with a smile, "you'd have a hard time telling me what year it was."

She studied the one in front of her and the picture of the one she wanted and said, "I'm somewhat well versed in cars, but I'm certainly not capable of telling these apart, though I'm not sure why."

"Because this one has some parts from the other model year added on," he said. "It's fairly common, especially at the pick-and-pulls, using whatever you can get to put the vehicle back on the road. If it's not quite as pretty as it once was, well, that's just too bad," he said, with a laugh.

She nodded. "Let me take a look at the other two of interest here."

"Have a go at it, as you like," he said. "I've got plenty of others to keep track of. Give a shout if you need anything."

And, with Rodney at her side, they kept going from vehicle to vehicle. "None of them had quite the right dents in the front," she said.

He nodded. "That's what I was thinking, but we do have the VINs, and the license plates are still on two of them, so we've got that for our records."

"But we didn't have to come down here for that," she said. "We could have just pulled the reports."

"Yes, but sometimes seeing this in person is just as good as being out on the streets," he reminded her.

She nodded.

"It was picked up because it was abandoned," he said. "Have we cross-referenced it to any records?"

The guy came back out from his small cubicle, looking for them, and said, "Hey, the one that we looked at first, it's just come back as stolen."

"Of course," she said.

"Well, in this case it's unusual. It was stolen nearly four years ago."

She turned and looked at the manager. "From where?"

"Arbutus Street," he said.

She shook her head, frowning. "Interesting. And no sign of it in all these years?"

"Not until just now."

She laughed. "I wonder what the chances are it was stolen from him again." At that, Rodney looked at her in surprise. She shrugged. "Unless he's ditching the vehicle. What if he came back to it, thinking it would be parked where he left it, only to find out that somebody had stolen it?"

Rodney looked at her and said, "Well, it's a reach."

"We're always reaching," she said comfortably. "It's just a matter of if we're reaching in the right direction or not." She looked over at the officer. "Has anybody asked about this vehicle?"

"No, not yet," he said. "Just you."

She nodded. "Don't release it until I get some forensics gathered, will you?"

He nodded.

"Are you sure you want to do that?" Rodney said. "If we're wrong, that's money down the tubes."

"I know, but it's the only one that even fits."

"But it doesn't fit," he said.

She groaned. "You want me to just let it sit?"

"Considering the money and time?" He just shrugged.

"How will we know if we don't do any tests?"

"Considering that we don't have any evidence that this is even involved in any crime, yeah."

"Well, it depends if Forensics can get those license plates back to me." And, on that note, she phoned and, when she connected with Stoop she said, "What about those images with the license plate?"

"Yeah," he said. "I was just writing up the report for you. I got three letters."

He read them off, and, as she stood at the back of the truck, she turned with a grin and said, "Okay, now we have a good reason. Three of these plate numbers match."

Rodney looked at her in shock. "You're kidding."

She nodded. "They're sending me the report right now."

"Well, in that case," he said, rubbing his hands together, "let's turn this sucker over to Forensics."

SIMON WALKED DOWN one of the alleys, taking a shortcut in the downtown core and heading up around one of the warehouses, when pain slammed into his brain, and he almost fell. Gasping, he reached out his hands to support himself against the brick wall. He tried to slow and to even out his breathing, and soon he could almost straighten up again. As he leaned a shoulder against the wall, trying to control the pain that rushed through him, he heard a voice.

Just do it. Just do it.

He was so damn tired of that voice, that mocking, that he just couldn't handle whatever the hell this was. In his mind he responded, *Back the fuck off!*

But the voice just continued in a chanting jeer. Simon figured the pain was in somebody's head, somebody holding their own head and yelling and screaming at the voice, *Just shut up. Stop, stop, stop,* and then both voices disappeared.

He stared, not sure exactly what was going on, but it was almost enough to make him grab his own head. As he did place his hands on either side of his head, trying to still the pounding inside, he could suddenly see a river below him and somebody's feet standing at the edge of a railing. He screamed at the top of his lungs, "No!"

Then he blacked out.

CHAPTER 11

W HEN THE PHONE rang, Kate wasn't surprised to see it was Simon. "Hey," she said. "How are you doing?"

"I'm fine," he said, but his voice suggested he was anything but.

"Where are you?"

"At the hospital."

She gasped. "What's the matter?"

"Let's just say I had a vision," he said in low tones. "It didn't work out so well for me."

"Ah, crap, I hope it's got nothing to do with me or my cases."

"It's the suicides," he snapped. "Somebody is trying to pressure them into jumping."

"Well, that's what we were thinking, wasn't it?" she asked curiously.

"Yes, but now it's a different case."

"What do you mean?" she asked.

"*Now* I know. God, I mean that I was in her head, as he was yelling at her."

"You saw where she was?" Kate bolted upright.

"Well, I saw the water from the bridge railing through her point of view. I was screaming at her, *No, no!* Hesitated, lost the connection then, so I don't know. I don't know if she jumped or not."

"Maybe it's a good thing you were there. Maybe you stopped it," she said, quietly pacing the big bullpen room, knowing that everybody else was listening in. She stepped out into the hallway. "Are you okay?"

"Yeah, I passed out though. Some kind passerby called an ambulance."

"Jesus, do you want me to come?"

"No," he said, disgust in his voice. "I'm just pissed off that it happened."

"Well, sometimes there's something out there bigger than us."

"Is that you saying that?" he said in a mocking voice.

She winced because she heard the disgust in his voice. "Thank you for telling me," she said quietly. "We're working on this. We really are."

"I know," he said. "If I thought I had anything more to show you, I would."

"Well, if you do find somebody else in this position, let me know as soon as it happens. Maybe you can convince them to not jump."

"I don't know, maybe," he said. "I just wanted to let you know that this guy is active and is really pissing me off."

"Just don't do anything stupid," she warned.

"Says you," he replied. With that, he hung up.

She walked slowly back inside the bullpen and sat down, then grabbed her report and wrote down notes of what he'd said. It was tough. How did they catch somebody who was a phantom voice in Simon's head, yet an obvious voice in somebody else's? Was the manipulator using these promptings to make the depressed people crazy, thinking they had to jump, or was that what the pictures of loved ones with bullet holes in their foreheads were for? It didn't necessarily make sense, unless it was a two-pronged approach, and that stopped her in her tracks. What were the chances that two people were doing this? Jesus, that would be horrible. Surely that couldn't be. She stopped to look back at the latest suicide reports and then wrote down some musings.

"You okay?" Rodney asked.

"Yeah, just some problems."

"Anything we can help with?"

"Not yet," she said in a low voice. "Soon, maybe."

———⚬⚬⚬———

SIMON CONTINUED HIS day, working hard and shutting down the devil voice in his head. As such, Simon went from one of his rehab projects to another, again and again. By the time four o'clock rolled around, he was tired and ever-so-slightly wet from what appeared to be the damp atmosphere around him. The rain was holding off, spitting every once in a while, matching his mood.

That voice saying, *Just do it,* grew louder and louder. Sometimes it seemed to back off; then other times it seemed to punch in hard and fast. It made no sense.

Simon stood in front of the huge building on Hastings and shook his head, trying to regain his focus. "We're behind here. What do you think?" Simon asked his project manager, Simon's tone caustic. "Every day we're behind costs more money."

"I get it," Francis said, "but we're having trouble getting some of the materials we need. A lot of the plumbing supplies didn't show up."

Simon looked at him, his stare flat. "I get it. Not your problem."

"But it is your problem because we can't get the material," the project manager snapped.

Simon nodded. "What's the new ETA?"

"We're fourteen days behind."

Inwardly Simon winced. Because fourteen days was fourteen days of expenses, extra labor, material costs, leases, and interest. The list went on and on, never seemed to quit. "Well, that's your one freebie," he said. "Let's make sure there aren't any others." And, with that, he turned and left, headed to the next place.

As he walked, the irritating Realtor got back to him finally, after complete silence for days.

"Simon, you drive a hard deal," she snapped into the phone.

He stopped and looked up at the gray sky above him, feeling a raindrop hitting his eyebrow he swore.

"What's the matter?" she said in alarm.

"It's a shit day, and I'm not interested in listening to your shit story."

"Not my shit story," she snapped, "the owners."

"Look. Either he takes the deal or he doesn't. I don't care," he said. "It's not a day to push my buttons."

"Wow," she said, "you are having a shit day." An almost conciliatory tone was in her voice, as if to say, *Hey, sorry. Didn't mean to come across so aggressive.*

But Simon wasn't up for it. "All I'm saying is," he said, "that was my offer, and we have nothing to discuss otherwise." With that, he hung up. He really didn't need to listen to her or to them.

He carried on, walking to the next job that he needed to review, only to find that his project manager wasn't there and that his overseer was standing outside the third floor on scaffolding, yelling at somebody. Simon called up at the supervisor on this rehab, who noticed him and came down. It took twenty minutes for him to get on the ground floor, and he looked like he was in a hell of a temper.

"If it isn't good news, I really don't want to hear it," Simon snapped.

"Well, good luck with that," he said. "Half the crew didn't show up today."

"Why is that?" Simon closed his eyes, praying for patience.

"They all belong to the same family, and they're at some bloody festival."

Simon just stared, and William raised both hands in frustration. "What the hell, I don't know," he said. "Nobody told me anything. I came to work—fat, dumb, and happy, expecting to see a full crew on the job—and nobody's here."

"Well, hell," Simon said. "Who were you yelling at up there then?"

"Somebody else on the crew," he said. "I probably shouldn't have yelled at him. He's likely to walk on me too, but right now I couldn't care less."

"I get it," Simon said. "Some days are just like that, aren't they?"

"You're not kidding," he said. "So our progress is nil today. We haven't got much done, but I'm trying to focus those we have here on making some progress on something."

Simon replied, "I know a whole reset on the plumbing was needed here, right?"

"Yeah, and the plumbers are missing today."

"Of course they are. Wiring?"

"They aren't supposed to come in until after the plumbing. They've done 80 percent of it and need to come back in after the plumbers are done and gone."

"And normally that's not an issue."

"It doesn't have to be," he said, "but, in this case, they were in on top of each other."

"And where is my project manager who is supposed to be coordinating all that? Did he go to the festival too?"

"No, sick," he said.

"Got it," Simon replied. "Too sick to see the planning committee?"

"Oh, hell, is that today? Well, I guess I could spend some time at city hall," he said. "You know how much I'll love that."

Simon laughed. "Yeah, but it'll make my day, thinking of you down there, arguing with them." The two men shared a chuckle, and, with that at least easing some of the tension, Simon turned and headed off to his next project. The way things were going today, he should probably just go home and tell them all to take a hike. And, true enough, he got to the next job, just in time to see more chaos happening. "What the hell is going on today?"

"It's a fucking full moon," his project manager said, glaring at the building.

"Well, do you want to go in and show me?"

The tour on this site proved to be just as disappointing and discouraging as the others. Materials didn't arrive; crew didn't show up, and some welds that had been very necessary and should have been up to code had snapped.

Simon just shook his head as he stared upward. "What a shitty day," Simon muttered under his breath. Feeling the weight of all the decisions and the financial burdens of all the things he'd seen today, he looked at his contractor, who shrugged.

"Tomorrow's another day, huh?"

"It needs to be," Simon replied. "It needs to be a damn sight better than today." Taking his leave, he strolled down the street, taking a shortcut and coming out on the far side, where one of his favorite restaurants was located. Just as he went to cross the road, words slammed into his brain.

Just do it.

He shuddered, and, rather than forcing himself across the street, he grabbed a nearby bus stop bench and collapsed. A woman stopped and looked at him, but he just gave her a wave and a half smile, then shuddered as the pain flooded through his system.

He buried his face in both hands, rested his elbows on his knees, and told the world to F-off. *Leave me alone. I don't need this.*

But instead the voice chanted in his mind, *Just do it, just do it, just do it.*

He couldn't even begin to confirm if this was something happening in real time or some hanger-on from some other damn energy, if in the present or from the past. He wished to God he had learned more from his grandmother, but he hadn't. On the contrary, he'd been too busy ignoring it all, stomping it down, and hoping it wouldn't happen again.

Seeing those abused children had been devastating. Saving the one had helped a lot, and putting the entire ring behind bars where they couldn't hurt children anymore had been a supreme ego boost. But more than that had been the sense of finally controlling something and stopping a travesty. Something that he couldn't do before, and nobody had helped him back then.

But now, here, it was happening all over again. Not children but other vulnerable people, in the sense of it being anybody struggling with depression or other mental health issues. At least that's what he'd figured out so far. It didn't mean he was right by any means, but it definitely meant crap was coming down that he didn't have a clue how to deal with.

As he sat on the bench, a bus came and opened its door. He shook his head, and the door shut, and the bus carried on. It took a long moment for Simon to press the taunting voice out of his brain, then give his body the once-over enough to realize he would be okay to get up and to cross the street. Anybody watching him would think he was either drunk or in some medical crisis.

It hurt to think he would come across that way, and it gave him the added impetus to get out of sight of anyone. With every step he took, he got stronger and stronger though, and, by the time he made it around the corner and out of view from everyone, he felt just that much better. He quickly crossed the next block and then the next. By the time he got one more block over to where he wanted to be, he got comfortable again. But, just as he took another step, the voice slammed into the back of his head.

Just do it.

Simon stopped, froze, turned around, and glared at the complete emptiness around him, confirming the voice wasn't anywhere close by but was inside his head, which he knew all along. But it was so hard to stop that instinctive reaction to look around and to tell somebody to shut up. He told it quietly but firmly, *No.*

The voice stopped, fading away into the darkness.

Simon managed a couple more blocks, changing his plans from going to his favorite restaurant to heading straight home. He might be short on food, but he could quickly order something from home, if it came to that. Food was a constant irritation in his life. He liked good restaurants, but, after a long day, like today, he didn't want to go home only to change clothes to go back out again.

Forcibly trying to stay in control, he raced back to his apartment, lifting a hand at the doorman as he headed to the elevator. He felt the pressure, a swelling in his head, as if somebody were pounding on the outside of his brain. By the time he made it inside the front door of his penthouse, the voice slammed against his forehead.

It screamed, *Just do it.*

Simon collapsed to the floor, his mind already consumed with the vision that had overtaken him.

As he looked down at his feet, all he saw was the edge of a metal piece, his hands gripping a rail, and water. Water flowing underneath his feet, as he looked over the railing. He stared at the rushing depths, almost mesmerized. There was pain, and there was fear, yet also a longing for whatever that water offered. Simon stared down, paralyzed, unable to move, terrified, and yet desperate to break free of this image. He screamed in his head, *No, no, no, no.* But whoever it was that he had connected with lifted his head and looked around at the area. Somebody called out in the distance. A vehicle honked. Then someone spoke.

"Hey, are you okay?"

Almost instantly the paralysis eased, and the person stepped back from the bridge.

"Yeah, yeah, I'm fine. Just looking at the rushing water."

It seemed like it was a kid's voice, the timbre between male and female, almost neutral. Simon couldn't tell who it was, and there had been nothing else to help with that. As he viewed the bridge ahead of him, he knew exactly where the kid was. He was on the Lions Gate Bridge. Simon bolted to

179

his feet, even as the person in the vision started to walk away. And, with that, the vision left him.

Exhausted, sweat running down his face and his heart slamming against his ribs in his chest, he tried hard to figure out what the hell he was supposed to do with this. So what? Somebody looked down at the water. Big deal. He heard that voice in the background.

Do it. Do it.

But was that even somebody else, or was that just the person on the bridge? Their own subconscious telling them, *Hey, this is the time. This is what you need to do. This will make it all stop. Just make it all go away.* Did that have any value, or was this just straight fiction?

Groaning and feeling like every step he took had cement weights attached to his feet, Simon walked to his couch and collapsed on top of it. His hands shook, his breath raspy, and his head still boomed. And all he could think about was the scene on Lions Gate Bridge and how he felt a terrible sense that he needed to be there, even while he wondered just what going there would do for anybody.

He didn't want to do anything because that would mean, every time something like this happened, he would feel like he had to go to the scene of the crime. Indeed, he felt an urgent sense of *go, go, go.* Hating what it was trying to say, he managed to stand and to walk to the door, even as he fought the impulse. *No,* came this … his inner sense of knowing. *You have to go.* Shaking his head, he said out loud, "It won't do any good. By the time I get there, it will already be over, or the person will be gone."

Go, go, go.

Groaning, and yet past the point of ignoring it, he took the elevator downstairs, grabbed his vehicle, hopped in, and headed toward Lions Gate Bridge. He parked at a pullout on the shoulder, then got out, locked up the vehicle, and almost raced down to the bridge. As he got onto the pedestrian walkway, he headed in the direction where he thought the person had been standing. Then as he got here, Simon noted it wasn't quite right. He walked over a bit farther and then back again, only to realize he needed to be on the opposite side of the bridge. The traffic was heavy, coming in all directions. Yet there were traffic cams. He pulled out his phone and contacted Kate.

When she answered, her voice was distracted. With his words coming fast and stumbling over each other, his tongue feeling thick, as if he were pushing back another vision, he said, "Can you access the cameras on the Lions Gate Bridge?"

"Simon? Is that you?"

"Yeah," he said, trying to pull himself together. "Can you access the cameras on the Lions Gate Bridge?"

"Yes," she said, "it might take a bit though."

"I need to know if somebody was at the bridge railing about twenty minutes ago." He heard her brain stumbling through the bits and pieces of information and trying to figure it out.

"Why?" she asked.

"Because I think somebody was here, ready to jump," he said quietly. "It came through my head, and this time I was caught in a vision. I saw the bridge. I saw his feet, as he or she looked out at the water," he said. "There was this voice in the background, saying 'just do it' over and over. But, at the same time, there was almost a longing for the water down below."

"Jesus," she said, her voice hushed. "Can you identify

who it was?"

"No," he said, "I only saw the sneakers."

"Girl sneakers, guy sneakers?"

"I don't know," he snapped, his voice rising. "I'm on the bridge now."

"Seriously?"

He heard a chair being pushed back, as she got up. He could almost imagine her walking over to her window, as if staring out in that direction would show him at the bridge. "Yes," he said, "I'm here. I couldn't stop the impulse to come down."

"God," she said. "What are you getting into? The last thing I want is you running around, heading to bridges, because people are committing suicide."

"Do you think I want to be here?" he said in a hard voice; yet, in her background, he heard clicking keys.

"No," she said, "I get it. You don't want to be there, and something's driving you to be there. I just don't want you to become a victim too."

At that, he stopped and frowned. "I don't think that'll happen."

"But you don't know that," she snapped. "I don't know what's going on with you, and I don't know why this is even happening. I know it's not something you want to happen either, but it doesn't seem to matter because it's coming anyway."

"Thanks," he said almost bitterly, "like I need to hear that."

"What you don't need to hear," she said, "is any more voices in your head."

"Well, instead of telling me to not hear what I can't control, why don't you just find out if I'm right and if somebody was here." And, with that, he hung up.

"God," he said, as he stared out at the water, the wind picking up his short hair and spreading it flat against the side of his head. He gave his head a shake, trying to clear the cobwebs in the grip of a vision, still sitting in the periphery of his brain. "I don't know what the hell's going on here," he said, "but it can damn well stop." And, of course, all he could think about was his grandmother's words of warning.

Once you start down this pathway, you can't stop it.

"Grandmother, please tell me that you found a way to stop it."

But he knew that she'd spent a lifetime avoiding people because of these visions. Sometimes she was a huge help, but she paid a high price, a penalty that he didn't want to pay. She'd been ostracized and hated, terrified by so many. She lived the life of a hermit, tormented more and more as time went on by visions that she had less and less control over. He remembered seeing her in her last few days, where the visions were just pouring out of her.

She carried a recorder, keeping track, yet not keeping track at all. He frowned at that, for the first time remembering her recorder. What had happened to it? Maybe she had thrown it out. Maybe when the house had been cleaned out, nobody had seen the value in it and had tossed it. Or maybe somebody had been afraid of what it held and made sure to destroy it.

He stood here, taking several deep gulps of breath, and, when the pain finally eased back and when he could breathe normally and when the pain in his chest wasn't quite so gripping, he slowly turned toward his vehicle.

CHAPTER 12

KATE PLACED HER cell phone down quietly on the desk, staring at it still.

Rodney walked over and said, "You keep looking at your phone these days."

"I need to access the traffic cams on the Lions Gate Bridge," she said abruptly.

"Another jumper?"

"I'm not sure," she said, trying not to say too much because she didn't want to explain. Simon was already tormented by this. The last thing she needed was others weighing in on his potential inability to handle this stress. Or his bizarre messages. Particularly after what had already happened to his friend David. On that note, she checked her watch, remembering that Louisa had asked for the laptop back. She hadn't bugged the Computer Forensics guys and gals for more, but she had asked, and the least she could do was try to get it back for her.

As she waited for access to the traffic cams, she contacted her computer nerds. As soon as the phone was answered, Stoop said, "Yes, I'm done with the laptop."

"Perfect. Anything on that license plate?"

"Yes, we're working on it," he said. "The video isn't 100 percent clear, so we're trying to clean it up."

"Good enough," she said. "That's progress."

"Hey, we'll take any progress we can get at the moment."

"I know," she said. "I'm still working on that whole suicide thing too."

"I can't imagine that's even feasible," he said, "but I get why you don't want to let it go."

"What about those chats and emails?"

"We're still working on that one."

"Okay. I'll check with Andy, since he's our decoy account on the chats."

"Yeah, and make sure he doesn't commit suicide under some of the pressure from these guys."

"Are they that convincing?"

"It's kinda weird," he said. "I've been monitoring a bunch of the chats. So far, it's mostly supportive, but then you get those little passive-aggressive digs, like 'You're just too scared,' or 'You know the world will be happier without you' and that sort of thing. And then that odd follow-up with, 'Hey, I was just kidding' or something of the like."

"Yeah, yet they aren't kidding at all."

"Well, that's the thing, right? I mean, you get these kinds of assholes all the time, and they're everywhere. You just don't expect to see them on a chat like this."

"But then why not?" she said quietly. "When you think about it, assholes are on every loop. Look at every one of the big sites where you can comment on any subject, and you'll find trolls."

"Trolls, trolls, and more trolls," he said. "I was just hoping on a site like this that they would be more supportive."

"But, at first glance, they probably are, aren't they?"

"Yes, exactly. Supportive and teasing and mocking, all at the same time."

"I get it," she said. "I really do. I just wondered if more than one person is making these mocking comments or whether it's really just one person using multiple accounts."

"That's an interesting point too. People do have multiple accounts in various places, so it's possible. I don't know why they would though."

"Because it would appear to represent opinions from more than one person. Often people can shrug off a single negative or differing opinion, but, if there's more than one, it tends to make people stop and think like, 'Are they both right? Am I the one who's wrong?'"

"Jesus," he said, under his breath. "I really don't like your thinking on this thing."

"Like you," she said quietly, "the mind-set comes from time on the job."

"I know," he snapped, "and it all sucks."

"It does, indeed," she said, "but that doesn't mean it's any less valid." And, on that note, she hung up.

She had access to the camera feeds now for the bridge, so she took it back an hour and watched. Several people walked up and down the length of the bridge, but the traffic was heavy, and the cameras were pointed more at the actual traffic than the pedestrians, which is what they were there for, but, at the same time, it was frustrating when she was looking for something specific. The controls gave her a little bit of a Zoom function, plus a Focus feature that she could manipulate, but the bulk of it was not that easy.

If she found something of interest, she could get the tech guys on to it to get her a better image. She watched carefully, as people came and went and as vehicles traveled, and, at one point in time, she did see what looked like a teenager stand at the side of the bridge. Noting what Simon had mentioned, she watched as the teen's hands reached out and gripped the railing and looked over.

But it was a motion that a lot of people would have done. If you're walking along a bridge like that, and you see all that beautiful water underneath, scary water, with the wind blowing the whitecaps, a lot of people would grip the railing and then carefully look over. So, on the surface, it didn't appear to be deadly or threatening or in any way indicative of somebody looking at suicide.

Just then the person jolted, when somebody else called to them. The person lifted a hand, shook his head, and kept on walking. Not sure exactly what was going on with Simon, she kept watching and watching, and by the time another ten minutes had passed, she was about to let it go, when Simon appeared on-screen and raced to the area.

"Well, he's at least being consistent," she muttered.

At that, Rodney came up behind her. "Who's that?"

"Simon," she said quietly.

He looked at her, then at the screen and said, "What's he doing?"

"You wouldn't believe me if I told you."

"Look. After the last scenario I'm not saying that I don't believe. I'm just saying that I have to be convinced each and every time."

"You and me both," she said quietly. She pointed, and they both watched as Simon looked around, looked over, and walked up and down a few times, then raised both hands. Afterward he pulled out his phone. "There he is, calling me," she said.

"Why?"

"Because," she sighed and then said, "he felt as if somebody were there, ready to commit suicide, that he connected with a vision of somebody else, pushing that person to do it."

Rodney pulled up his chair, plunked down beside her, leaned closer, and said, "Seriously?"

She nodded. "He keeps getting these visions. I haven't had a chance to talk to him about this one specifically, but he sounded pretty shaken."

"Oh, I would be too, if that were the case," he said, staring down at the frozen image of Simon, who was almost close enough to determine it was Simon there on the bridge. "He looks a little shocked and shaken right there."

She nodded. "It's happened a couple times."

"Different people?" he asked, looking at her in surprise.

"Yes, but nothing conclusive. Nothing that he could give me and say, *Hey, this person's committing suicide.*"

"Which vision would, of course, be of zero help," Rodney said, leaning back, crossing his arms and frowning at her.

"I don't know that he knows whether these visions are happening at that moment or if he's connecting to something that happened before or if he's seeing something that could still happen."

At that, Rodney's eyebrows shot up, and he pinched his nose and said, "Besides the whole mind-bending concept of somebody connecting to someone thinking about committing suicide, how the hell is it of any help to him or to us if we don't even know if it's current news?"

"Exactly," she said. She motioned at the video feed. "You can see he believes it's current. And, for this vision, he is seeing it currently, just got to the scene ten minutes later. Yet I don't know how to help him determine whether each vision is current."

"Of course not," he said. "Since when have you become some psychic specialist?"

She snorted at that. "I don't know if you know this," she said, "but I had fairly strong feelings about psychics to begin with, and they weren't pleasant."

"Oh?"

She nodded. "My mother married a charlatan, supposedly a psychic. She ended up giving him basically everything she could possibly give him, and he took it and ran."

"I can only imagine the bedtime stories you and Simon have together."

She shot him a fulminating look. "Not happening."

"The bedtime stories or the one about charlatans?"

"Either," she snapped. She got up and said, "How can we get more information on these cases?"

"The suicides?"

"Unless"—she frowned—"he also said something about a feeling of being watched."

"Who said what?"

She shook her head. "Simon. He said something about a sensation of being watched while on the bridge."

"Did he now?"

"I wonder if, like our drive-by shooter, who's hanging around to see the aftermath of his destruction, if our jumper guy is sticking around to see if his actions bear fruit?"

"Please don't tell me that you're talking about him physically pushing these people over."

"No, no, no," she said, but she sat back and looked at him. "But how would he know if it worked? I mean, he sent that email to David. How would he know if David committed suicide?"

"The news, the obituaries?"

"I don't know that Louisa's put in an obit yet, and would the news have identified this jumper?"

"Maybe a random phone call to the wife?"

"Meaning that our inciter must have tracked down who David even was and where he was in order to do something like that."

"But we already knew that he did, otherwise how did he get a picture of David's wife? We can't hack the emails of every other person in the chat, so how could we possibly know if somebody is threatening them?"

"My only thought is if he's *watching*," she said, with a frown. "And that would mean retrieving all the videos of whatever bridge cameras we have available, before and after any jumper. And not only that, this instigator could be a long way away from the bridge. I mean, just think about it. He could be on land, miles away, depending on how good his set of binoculars are."

He looked at her in surprise. "Don't you think he'd want to be a little more up-front and personal with that?"

"Maybe," she said, "I honestly don't know. This is a very remote way to commit murder."

"Well, we can give it a try," he said. And, with that, they split up the three recent suicides they'd identified. She didn't even want to think about the other jumpers this year or the thought of them being manipulated into this.

"And what about your thought on it being two people?" he asked.

"It could be a pair of them," she said, nodding slowly. "Or at least in the encouraging stage. After that, I don't know. Or it could be just the one, using both the taunting emails and the threatening pictures."

"And it's not a psychic thing you're worried about, right? At least not on the part of the perpetrator," he said, tossing her a sideways glance.

"No," she said, looking at him in surprise, "at least, I don't think so."

He nodded. "As long as that's the way we're going. The last thing I want to think about is that you're taking that a step too far and considering that maybe this is somebody psychically causing trouble."

"Can they even do that?" she asked, looking at him.

"Hey, you're the one with the strange friend. Ask him."

"God, I don't want to," she said, with a frown.

"I can't imagine he'd want you to either," Rodney said, with a laugh, "but I was just checking."

With that disquiet in her mind, she started searching the traffic cams, trying to figure out how many people might have even been in the location.

"Do we know when they jumped?" she asked. Starting the evening before, she was on the Second Narrows Bridge, and it didn't have the most ideal placement of cameras. It was great for traffic jams or breakdowns on the bridge, but it wasn't necessarily any good for some of these pedestrian positions. "I wonder if anybody even looks at the cameras to decide this is a great place to jump. That they'd be on the six o'clock news as a cameo or some such thing."

"You know what? For people looking to jump, I doubt they really care where the camera placement is."

"Unless they're really determined to make sure nobody can come and stop them," she muttered. "I mean, serious-ly"—she looked over at him—"if you would jump, would you go just anywhere?"

"Once you are committed to that act, there is no going back, which is why bridges are so popular."

She nodded slowly. "And I get that. However, if you were choosing a public bridge like this, wouldn't you want the cover of darkness?"

"I would imagine that could be true, but what is the problem with that?"

"Well, the problem," she said, "is the cameras."

"Ah. For some reason I think people jump in the daylight," Rodney noted. "Yet I wonder if any studies have been done on that."

With that logic, she hunkered down to take a look. She saw people walking, more than she had expected, which surprised her, but apparently it was a favorite spot for romance too. After they'd looked for hours, finally sitting back, she said, "I can't even see the jumper."

"No?" he said. "Mine's clearer."

She pushed her chair over to his and took a look. When he pointed out where the jumper was, she saw somebody standing there, but it was in the early hours of the morning. "What's that, five o'clock?"

"It's 5:10 a.m., according to the time stamp."

She nodded. "And that makes sense to me, although I'm usually in a positive frame of mind first thing in the morning, so I don't know that I personally would commit suicide at that time."

"If you had a shitty night," he said, "maybe you wake up and want it to stop." He shrugged.

"I can see that." And, with a nod, they kept looking, watching other pedestrians up and down on the bridge. There were definitely some, though most people didn't seem to be aware of what was going on, and others didn't even look. Some seemed to avoid people, as if this whole world we're in meant that they shouldn't have any contact. One couple stopped just past the woman about to jump, and they stood there for a long moment, their arms around each other, talking quietly, and then they kept on walking and didn't even see when the woman went over the bridge. They never turned and looked.

"Jesus, it's as if everybody is blind."

"I don't know if it's that they're blind or whether they're just so focused on themselves and not on other people." Rodney continued. "It's almost like we're geared not to be nosy and taught not to intrude, that we should keep to ourselves. It's a scary world out there. Maybe they ignore it all, unless bullets or bombs are going off. Then that would cause them to turn and look," he said, as if by explanation.

She struggled as she searched through the people. Some were walking and looked to be dressed for work, heading to the other side of the bridge, which would be a hell of a commute, but it wasn't out of the realm. Some people were jogging, and there were cyclists all over the place. "I didn't think," she said, tapping the monitor, "but a cyclist could get there, and faster, to keep an eye on things."

"Sure, but which one?" Rodney asked. "Look at all of them." At that, they watched some more. One stopped and took several photos, as if picking up on a beautiful sunrise. Then he went forward a little bit and took more photos. Even as Rodney went to skip past and go forward again, she said, "Stop. I want to see this guy."

With a careless shrug, Rodney said, "Fine, I don't know that he's got anything to tell us though."

But she watched as he took more photos, and then slowly he would turn to look behind him and take a few more.

"Look at that. See? He's looking at her."

"Looking but doing nothing. But then why would he? Why would he even contemplate that she's about to do something to herself like that?"

Kate frowned and nodded. "It's still pretty upsetting. There, she's taking off her shoes. There she goes." And, as they watched, the guy took another photo, completely unconcerned that she went over the bridge. "Instead of running to help," she cried out, "he took off."

"Help how?" Rodney asked quietly beside her.

"He could have called for help among the others biking, walking the bridge. He could have called the police. He could have looked over the side ..." And she stopped. "God, I don't know. What do you do in a situation like that?"

He said, "Well, 9-1-1 would be a great start, and he was on the phone as he left."

"Right. So he takes off and leaves and maybe calls on his way out but doesn't stay. Why?"

"Maybe he's late for work. Maybe he doesn't want to get involved. And stay for what? She's gone."

Kate groaned. "None of the vehicles stopped either. Did you notice that? The traffic just keeps on going."

"Again, it's early in the morning, and, as soon as you call something like that in," he said, "it can just be a huge traffic jam."

"So everybody's more concerned about themselves than the poor person who just went off the bridge?"

"And we also know what the stats are for anybody who would have survived. Chances are, she was already dead."

"But," she said, looking at him, "there was a chance. Some people have survived."

"One, two, maybe three," he said. "The numbers do not add up in favor of the jumper."

"No, of course not," she said. "That's why it's such a popular spot for people determined to end their lives." There was no bitterness in her voice; it was just a sad acknowledgment of the facts. As she continued to watch, she said, "So, that cyclist took photos, and it'll be almost impossible to identify him."

"Even if we could identify and talk to him, it's not like we can charge him with anything. He might be a shitty human being, if he didn't call for help, but we don't know that. And we also don't know," Rodney reminded her, "what he was looking at, you know? From his angle? Maybe he wasn't even aware that she jumped."

She nodded slowly. "I know. It's so easy to judge, isn't it?"

"Way too easy," he said.

"Check the other feed," she said. "I'm going back to this one and watching it from the beginning to the end." Even adjusting the lighting still didn't reveal anything she needed it to. "It's just too dark," she said in frustration.

"Well, I haven't had a chance to look at this one," he said. "Want to take a run through it?"

She nodded and worked on the third jumper cams. "It'd be nice if something would break somewhere."

"Unfortunately, whatever breaks," he said, "tends to be when something else happens."

She looked up, frowned, and said, "Yeah, and that wouldn't be a good deal for anybody."

"Or any of these other cases we have," he said, pointing to the stack beside them. "I know, and I'm spending a lot of time on this one."

"Do you have any strings to pull on any of the high-priority cases?" Colby asked, as he walked into the room.

"We're waiting on Forensics for most of it." Kate grimaced.

"*Most of it?*" he said. "If that's on *all of it*, then you're clear to do whatever you think is happening with the suicides. But, if you have anything else to pursue on another case that is hot right now, you need to be working on that."

She nodded. "I've covered everything I can right now."

"Okay. Then keep doing what you're doing," Colby said, "and let's hope something breaks somewhere pretty damn soon."

"Exactly my problem," she said, groaning. "It seems like absolutely nothing breaks anywhere, and it's all going the wrong direction."

"It will, at least we hope so," he said, and, with that, he called a meeting, having them all move to an interview room.

Kate sat through the meeting, a typical weekly one, where everybody shared everything happening on the pending cases. Then Colby turned to Kate and said, "Now do you want to give us an update?"

"On what?" she asked in surprise.

"How about why these suicides have you so bothered."

She shrugged. "I think everybody here already knows by now. But we found with David, the second of three suicides that I'm looking into, that he received an email with a picture of his wife with a bullet through her forehead. 'Do it ... or else,' was the message."

"And are we sure that it didn't have anything to do with the rest of his life?"

"No, I'm not sure of anything at this point. Again, Forensics has his laptop, although I am supposed to go collect it, so I can return it to the wife."

"Did they tell you what they found?"

She shook her head. "No, nothing. The coroner did confirm that David was perfectly healthy, wasn't struggling with a major illness, and he wasn't on drugs. There didn't appear to be any alcohol abuse, and, according to his wife, he was perfectly healthy and happy. Yet his laptop shows he was upset that he could not father children."

"True, since he belonged to a suicide chat room," Rodney said.

Owen agreed, nodding his head. "So, nothing about him was perfectly healthy and happy then."

"And that's where it becomes ... difficult." She quickly explained the little bit that they knew.

"And Simon?"

She looked at Colby with a flat look. "What about him?"

He raised an eyebrow and said, "Spill."

She growled. "It's nothing."

"Come on. It's got to be something."

"Nothing we can prove."

"No, but he was also instrumental in that pedophile case."

"The case with the kids, yes," she said, with a nod. "But that doesn't mean it will happen that way again."

Colby crossed his arms over his chest and tapped his foot on the floor, waiting. She just glared back at him.

"You spill it, or I will," Rodney said at her side. She gasped at him. He shook his head. "Sorry, but it's important, and the team needs to know."

"Fine," she snapped, then explained what Simon had said today.

"Seriously?" Colby said, as he stared at her.

She nodded. "Yes, but we don't know if the voice in his head is somebody pushing the victim to jump or if it's the victim's own subconscious, and Simon's tapping into their emotions. But, yes, he saw himself standing on the bridge, overlooking the river, all from the perspective of a jumper. And, when we did a check of the cameras just now"—she pointed at Rodney and herself—"we did see somebody there but not close enough to identify him or her in any way."

"So then," Rodney added, when she fell silent, "we looked at the videos again, trying to see if somebody may have been close enough to watch."

Colby turned his sharp gaze on him. "Watch? As if to see if his actions netted the result he was after?"

Rodney nodded. "Exactly. And Reese and Andy are still haunting the chat rooms and have had several people talk to him, both good and bad, on the suicide loops." Rodney pointed to Andy.

Andy nodded. "It always amazes me. One guy has these mocking comments all the time. Then another one laughs it off."

"Yet you can't take them at face value," Colby said. "People hide who they really are on the internet all the time."

Kate immediately stepped in. "Agreed, and, at the same time, you also can't disregard all the people encouraging you to get help and to be focused and to find something positive in your life to make it all worthwhile." She paused. "Because, as you well know, that can cover a multitude of sins."

Colby nodded. "Forensics hasn't had any luck yet?"

"They are still working on it, as they can," Kate said, "around the other cases, of course."

At that, Andy's phone dinged. He pulled it up casually, took a look, then frowned and said, "I just got a message from somebody on the loop." He left their meeting and headed back to the bullpen.

"How do you know that?" everybody asked, crowding

around him at his computer.

"Because I deliberately left a different email address, so, if they wanted to contact me directly, they could. This guy is making a comment about me needing help. But saying that, in some cases," he read it off, "*in some cases, suicide often comes to mind as being my best option.*"

"So," Rodney said, "he's making it personal, as if you both are in the same boat."

"And, for all we know, he *is* in the same boat," Colby said. "We can't assume that just because somebody messaged him privately that it's the killer."

"No, if there even is one," Kate said quietly, "and I'm not so far gone that I haven't kept that in mind."

"Good," he said. "That's important too."

She nodded. "I get it. I really do. But, in this instance, it's also interesting that somebody reached out beyond the chat."

Andy looked up, nodded, and said, "I'll respond, and we'll see if we can get this chat to keep going."

"I wish we could check the history, but nothing was there."

"You mean, on David's computer?"

"Yes, unless he deleted his." She frowned at that, picked up the phone to contact the computer forensics geeks, "Stoop, Kate here. I'll give you an email name and address." Then she read off the information from Andy's screen.

"Hang on."

She heard Stoop typing in the background, she presumed going through David's emails.

"Well, several are from that email address," he said. "Interesting."

"What it is?"

"Well, it starts off friendly enough but then isn't so friendly."

"That's not the same email address that sent the image of David's wife, right?"

"No," he said, "not at all. But it's another sender who appears to be both sympathetic, yet angry."

"Seems like a lot of these people are in that boat," she wondered.

"Or they're just manipulative," he said sarcastically.

When she looked up, she saw Colby had already left the bullpen. She looked over to Andy, who was busy answering the direct message he had. "Keep an eye on it, will you?" she told Stoop. "On those particular emails, keep track of whatever might be posted and whatever might be coming from those emails and sent to others. He's just contacted Andy here, who set up the suicidal chat persona."

"Now that would be interesting. Does Andy have any family or anybody who could be used to pressure him?"

"He's recently divorced, with kids," she said quietly, turning to look at him. "I don't think any of us really thought of that."

"Well, it might be a good time to," Stoop said. "I don't know what happens if this guy's threats aren't carried out."

"Meaning?"

"Well, the photo of David's wife had a bullet hole in her head," he said. "If David hadn't committed suicide, you've got to wonder if this guy would have followed through with the threat."

"It doesn't bear thinking about," she said, pinching the bridge of her nose, hard.

"No, but we have to. Once you head down this pathway, and people put that thread out there, the question now becomes whether or not they will make it real or if they will just stay hidden and make it a joke. Or, over time, will they become more emboldened by this behavior, until they feel like they can make good on the threat?"

"Exactly," she said.

"All kinds of avenues can happen here," Stoop said. "It's just a matter of which one this guy in particular will do."

"Scary thought," she said.

"They all are. I'll get back to this, and I'll set up some monitoring on these emails. The wife can still have David's laptop though, as we have all this copied over now."

"Perfect, thanks," she said. She hung up and walked over to see Andy still working on the private emails. "That's the same email?"

He shook his head. "No, we're back-and-forth. He's asking me some personal questions."

"Watch what you tell him."

He looked up at her, nodded, and said, "Not my first rodeo."

"I know," she said, "but obviously this guy is good at finding personal information, and you have kids."

At that, he looked up at her, swallowed hard, and nodded. But bent his head back to the job.

She winced, as she walked toward where Owen sat.

"Isn't it sad when doing our jobs threatens our very families?" the very family-oriented Owen said, clearly moved by that consideration.

"We need to catch this guy," she muttered.

"We're on it," Owen said, his tone determined. "Nobody's getting to our families, to our kids."

"I know," she said. "Yet it just feels, … it feels wrong."

"In what way?"

"I don't know. It just feels bad. Maybe that's a better word."

"Somebody pushing others to commit suicide, whether under pressure or for their own purposes, is bad, but, when you start making threats like this to their family, to do something like this, *or else*, preying on somebody who is already having a hard time, just makes it truly horrific," Owen said quietly.

She moved to sit down at her desk by Rodney.

He shook his head. "It's starting to look like he's thinking about it again, like he's got another victim picked out."

"That could easily be the one Simon connected with earlier today," Kate said. "I wonder why he connects with anybody though."

"Well, more to the point," Rodney muttered, "why does Simon connect with *these* people? How can we pinpoint who he's connecting with, why that connection exists, and how can we find these people and save them before they take a jump off a bridge under pressure? Is Simon's connection with suicidal people or just those depressed souls who were already thinking about it?"

"Maybe it's Simon's association with David."

"Maybe. I don't know," Rodney said, "but these are questions we need to get answers for."

"But this stuff," she said, "I mean, I still have trouble even believing that he's connecting with real people."

"Do you think he's making it up?" Rodney asked in surprise.

"No. Yes. I don't know," she said, raising both hands. "I don't know what to believe. I figured these fake psychics talked to dead people to bilk the grieving relations. This is just so bizarre."

"It is," he said, "but we're at the point of no return in terms of believing Simon, as far as our cases go. But for you? It's either believe him or walk away because you'll never have a chance at a true relationship with somebody you don't trust."

"And I don't know if I can trust him," she snapped, glaring at Rodney for bringing it up.

"Why?"

"Is this something we have to discuss now?"

He sat back and looked at her in surprise. "No, we don't," he said. "But, in your heart, you need to know. You need to know where you stand. So, when push comes to shove, when this all blows up in your face, that you have a leg to stand on. As for motivation, you need to know why you are doing this, who you're doing this for, and whether you'll continue to do this."

"And what the hell is *this?*" she snapped.

"Dealing with him on cases," Rodney said quietly. "And, if you can't trust him, why are you even sleeping with him?" With that, he got up and walked out of the bullpen.

Simon's Sunday Night

LYING IN BED that night, alone and wishing to hell he had gotten up and gone to her place, Simon stared up at the ceiling, hating the feeling that he was on the cusp of something major, and yet knowing, if he took the right avenue, it would go better. And, if he took the wrong avenue, it would go worse. Either way it would be tough.

"How the fuck can that be?" he asked, reaching out and scrubbing his face, before rolling over, punching the pillow, and pushing it farther up under his head.

"If I go one direction, it should be good, and the other one should be bad. So how can they both be bad?" It wasn't even so much that they were both bad, but neither would provide the relief he wanted. He suspected that it was highly connected to these visions, which were out of his control. So, when he had absolutely no control over who he connected with, when to connect, how to connect, or what to connect over, why would anybody want anything to do with this? As he lay here, sleep was a long way off. He felt his body drifting deeper and deeper toward sleep. Right there, at the edge of his consciousness, the words *Do it* slammed into his head again.

He groaned, rolled onto his back, and said, "Fuck off." But, of course, it wasn't so easy as that.

Almost instantly he saw the bridge, with the same sneakers, the same hands gripping the railing, and somebody leaning over the edge, staring at the water. It had never occurred to him, but did these people go to their jump-off point time and time again, as if getting up the courage to make the jump? Because, if that were the case, somebody should be monitoring that location on the bridge and getting out there and stopping her.

Her. It felt like a her, but he didn't know. He didn't have any reason to say her or him, but it felt like a her. And that was good enough for him.

He sat up, reached out in his mind, and said, *Don't. Just go home.* But he felt no connection. As if his connection to her and this other voice was on Mute. He thought about it for a long moment and then whispered, "Don't. Just go home."

Trying to use the same tone, the same mentality, and, in a soft whisper, telling her, "Go home. It's fine. Go home."

But she wasn't listening. She leaned farther and farther over the railing. He saw the whitewater churning below. For whatever reason the current was moving off to the left, and waves crashed down on the rocks. It was dark out.

"Go home," Simon said. "Go home," he repeated, trying to be more emphatic, more forceful. Trying in some way to have the ability to change the outcome. Because the thing that really drove him crazy was that he had no way to control this. He was nothing but an observer. If he couldn't do something to change the outcome, how the hell would any of this matter? Why the hell was he going through this to only suffer and watch someone die?

Then he stopped and thought, was it really another person manipulating her, or was it her own psyche whispering, *Do it*? Was he connecting with that part of her, that part that was desperate to end it all? In which case, how was he even supposed to change it? Or was change not an option? That complete helplessness drove him to more questions.

As he lay here, he felt the same water rushing under his feet, the same fear pressing in on him, the sadness welling up from deep inside. He wondered what the hell it was from. He tried to find out, to delve deeper, but there seemed to be a wall. He was only getting to view it, like a movie playing out in front of him, but there was no audio, except that damn voice that said, *Do it.*

If only there was a way to identify her. He sent a text to Kate. **She's there on the bridge right now.**

Expecting a response and not getting one made him angry. Why was he the only one who was worried? It wasn't so much that it was only him, but Kate didn't even believe in what he was doing. Hell, neither did he for that matter. How could he blame Kate for not believing him when he didn't believe it himself? This was just bullshit, all of it. He groaned and got up, heading for a shower, and instead found himself getting dressed. *No, no, no.* But soon he was dressed, grabbing his keys and wallet, heading outside, and grabbing a cab.

For whatever reason, he didn't even want to drive himself, helpless to do anything but follow along. As he got near, he had the driver drop him off at the spot he was looking for, telling him to come back in maybe forty minutes. "I promise I'll make it worth your while."

The cabbie looked at him in surprise and just said, "I don't know. I'll have to loop completely around to pick you up again."

"Go have a coffee and come back."

The guy shrugged and headed over to West Vancouver.

Simon walked along the bridge, looking to see what was going on. He saw a woman walking up ahead. He came quickly up behind her, wondering, worrying, but the woman seemed to be fine. She was just walking ahead, getting more and more nervous when he came closer behind her. He called out to her, "Hey, I'm just walking. I'm not a threat."

She didn't slow down; instead she broke into run and kept running. He couldn't blame her honestly. He was a single guy down on the bridge in the dark. He walked back to where he thought the actual sighting was but couldn't see anything over the water or on the bridge itself. He groaned, smashed his fist on the railing, then turned and headed back to wait for the cabbie.

As he sat on the curb, cursing his impulsiveness that brought him here, his phone rang.

"Where are you?" Kate asked in a peremptory tone.

"I'm down at the bridge."

"Did you see her?"

He felt the worry in her voice. She did care. "No," he said, his tone heavy. "And no sign that she jumped either."

"Well, that's a godsend."

He heard the relief in her voice. For all the reasons that Kate might distrust his ability, she still didn't want that to prevent him from saving a victim. "I'm waiting for the cab to come back around, wondering what the hell I'm even doing," he said bitterly. "It's gorgeous here. Yet all I can see is somebody throwing themselves over. Don't you understand how this haunts me?"

"I do understand, and I'm sorry," she whispered. "I don't know how any of this can happen, how it is happening," she said, "but I know that, for you, it's real, and, for that, I would do anything to help ease this for you."

He believed her; that was the thing. There was absolutely no way not to believe the sincerity in her voice. "Meet me at home," he said, his voice thick.

"I'm already here," she said gently. "So, come on home, and we'll spend some time remembering about the living and less about the dead."

CHAPTER 13

Kate's Monday Morning

K ATE WOKE UP the next morning and looked over to see Simon in bed beside her. She smiled, got up, had a quick shower, dressed, and snuck out of his penthouse apartment. It was the first time she'd ever stayed overnight until time to go to work. As she checked her watch, it was just 7:00 a.m. She made a quick trip home, changed clothes, and then prepped for work. As she left her apartment, she got a text from Simon, with a sad face. She laughed. **Needed fresh clothes for work.**

As she walked into the bullpen, a buzz of activity was going on. She looked at everybody in surprise. "What happened? Did something break?"

"Well, something broke," Owen said. "We found the guy who parked the blue-green truck on the other side of the mall. Parked it illegally, so it was picked up and taken to the impound lot."

"Because someone had stolen it, right?"

The whole team nodded. Owen continued. "And we found the guy who stole it. Only he came into possession of it that same day. He found it off around the corner from the original shooting scene, with the engine running and the keys in it, so he hopped in and took it for a joyride."

"Oh, crap," she said. "The joke's on him, isn't it? Since

it was used in several drive-by shootings."

"He's in Interview One."

She rubbed her hands together. "Now this is good. Who's going in to interview him?"

"Well, it was your deal, so ..." Owen began.

Colby walked in and said, "You and Rodney take it."

She grinned. "You guys just made my day." She raced to the coffee pot, and her luck was holding; there was even coffee. She didn't know what entity was smiling down on her this morning, but, so far, she had managed to get a couple things accomplished without any of the usual headaches.

As she walked in the interview room, with her file and her coffee, Rodney at her side, she looked at the suspect and frowned. He was just a pimply-faced kid, probably hadn't even had his driver's license for much more than a few months. He looked up at her nervously. She dropped the file with more force than necessary, and he jumped.

She snorted. "How long have you had a driver's license?"

He glared at her.

"Cut the bravado," she said, with a wave of her hand. "I can check for myself easily enough, but I would take it as a sign of cooperation if you just tell me."

"Three months," he snapped.

"And so, in the first three months of your professional driving career, you decide to steal a truck?"

He sank lower in his seat. "You don't know that I did it," he said.

"Cameras are all over the city," she said, "so you'd be surprised." She didn't tell him that she had photos of him getting into the vehicle.

"I don't know why," he moaned. "Man, I was—I was just having a lark," he said. "It was just sitting there, and the motor was running. I mean, it was just asking somebody to take it. And it was a pretty damn sweet ride."

"A sweet ride?"

"Those old trucks are gorgeous," he enthused.

"And here I thought you'd be into muscle cars," she said, studying him carefully.

"Nah," he said, with a lip curl, "muscle cars are for the rich white boys."

"And what are you?" she said, with a laugh.

"I'm a poor white boy," he said, with a nod. "Although I don't think I'm exactly all white."

"Meaning?"

"My mom is mixed something or other."

"Something or other. You don't even know what nationality your mom is?"

"Well, I know what she is. She's Canadian, but she's also part Native American and part white. I just don't know what band or tribe or whatever she's from."

"Interesting," she said. "Most kids have a little more knowledge about the heritage of their family than that."

"Well, I haven't seen her in a very long time," he said. "She went off on a drunken bender, and I never saw her again."

"And your dad?"

"He's a mechanic."

"So, you've been driving for a lot longer than your license may suggest."

He nodded. "And I know how to hot-wire, but the thing is, ... I mean, this didn't even need hot-wiring."

"That's because it was a getaway car," she said quietly.

He looked at her, his eyes growing wider. "What do you mean?"

"That truck was used in several drive-by shootings," she said. "And guess whose fingerprints are all over it now?"

He stared at her, as the hammer went down in his brain, and he bolted to his feet. "Holy shit," he said. "I didn't use any guns. I don't even have any. I didn't kill nobody, honest."

"So you say, but you're the one who was driving the vehicle. For all I know, you were part of the team, and you were the driver of the getaway car."

"No," he said, shaking his head. "No way, no way, no way."

"Yeah? So prove it," she said, leaning back, crossing her arms over her chest, completely nonchalant.

The kid looked from her to Rodney and back again. "No, no, no, you see ..." He stopped and said, "How am I supposed to prove I didn't do something?"

"Tell us where you were beforehand, like right before," she said.

"Well, if this guy did the drive-by shooting, wouldn't he have just taken off?"

"He took off, came around the corner, parked, and then walked back, so he could see the chaos he caused."

"Oh, gross, that's, ... that's just cold. Did he hurt somebody?"

"Killed two men. Young, under twenty-five, healthy, fit, complete strangers."

His face blanched. "I didn't have anything to do with it, I swear."

"So you're just a stupid punk who steals trucks?"

"I didn't even mean to do that," he confessed. He raised both hands. "Honest, I didn't."

"Yeah? And so, here we are. You driving a stolen truck,

trying to tell me that you had nothing to do with the drive-
by shooting just a few minutes earlier."

He shook his head at a rapid rate, tears coming to his
eyes, and, with a sinking heart, he appeared not involved,
didn't have anything to do with it. She looked over at
Rodney, who gave an almost imperceptible shrug of his
shoulders.

"Did you see anybody around the truck? Why were you
even in that area?" Rodney asked.

"I was meeting some friends," he said. "There's a, you
know, like a casual pool hall around the corner. It's just an
old building, and we go in there, and, for a couple bucks, we
play pool," he said.

"So you left the pool hall and came out when?"

"I don't know when," he said. "I mean, I lost track of
time as it was. I was on a day off, so I didn't care. I was just
having fun."

"Doing drugs?"

He flushed. "Just a little weed."

"And what about the harder stuff?"

"No, my dad gets really pissed at me and won't let me
work if I do anything hard-core."

"Well, there are a lot of levels between hard-core and
weed."

"No, man, no. I didn't do anything else, just a little
weed. I was just happy."

"Too happy apparently."

He flushed. "Yeah, that might have had something to do
with it. My dad says it makes me different. Like, I've got no
worries, and it'll all be fine."

"Ya think? Now that you hopped into a truck and stole
it while you were on weed, how do you feel?"

"Like I need to reassess," he said, rubbing his face. "I'm in so much shit."

"Well, and then there's your father you have yet to face."

At that, he paled, and his bottom lip trembled. "Is there any way we can … *not* tell him this?"

"I'm pretty sure he's already on the way to the station," Rodney said. "He called, asking why you were being held."

At that, the kid deflated completely. "My old man, … he'll kill me," he said quietly. "That's just all there is to it." But there was no heat, so he wasn't actually in danger; it seemed more a case of having some consequences for his behavior and choices.

"And what do you think?" Rodney asked. "Do you think you deserve it?"

"Yeah, I do, but that ain't gonna make a damn bit of difference. I've already been warned a couple times."

Just then the door opened, and Lilliana looked in and motioned at Rodney to come out. With that, Rodney got up and stepped out of the interview room.

The kid looked at her. "How much shit am I in?"

"Quite a bit," she said.

"But, on the other hand," he said, some wily intelligence showing through, "because of me, you got the truck."

"And, because of you, we didn't get the driver."

At that, his face fell again. "Holy shit. He really killed two guys?"

"This time," she snapped.

"Oh, jeez."

"Now tell me what you saw."

"Honestly I just … I came out of the pool hall, and people were walking around. I just saw this truck sitting there, idling. I checked the door handle and it was unlocked, and it was just one of those things. I didn't even think," he said. "I just hopped in, whistled at what a sweet ride it was, and then," he said, "I closed the door and put it in Drive."

She nodded. "So you didn't see the driver hop out? You didn't see anybody keeping a close eye on the truck? You didn't see anybody walking away from the truck?"

"Well, one guy was walking up the street, when I was looking at the truck, but he didn't turn around or anything. So, I wondered if it was him, but he didn't appear to care."

"That's because he was focused on the chaos he had caused around the corner," she said quietly. "Can you give me a description of him?"

"Not really. Jeans, looked like he wore an old bomber-style jacket but jeans-colored, you know? Just one of those little short things, and he had on a baseball cap."

At that, her heart slammed. "And that would probably be him," she said quietly. "Anything else you can tell me?"

He shook his head. "I just, ... honestly, he just looked like he was striding away. He was in a hurry."

"And it didn't compute that he was in a hurry and that he would be right back?"

"Apparently nothing computed," he said, staring at her, downcast.

Just then, the door opened, and Rodney returned. With him was a big barrel of a man, worry written all across his face. When he saw his son, he breathed a sigh of relief. Then he pulled up the spare chair and sat down. "What the hell is going on?" he asked her.

She sat back, as the man glared at her. "I'm Detective Kate Morgan," she said coolly. "Your son stole a truck."

He looked at her in shock, looked at his son, then back at her, and said, "No fucking way."

Her eyebrows shot up. "Maybe you should ask your son."

He turned, looked at the kid, and said, "Chuck, tell me the truth. What did you do?"

"I stole a truck," he said faintly.

His dad sat back, complete and utter shock and disappointment on his face.

She knew what was about to come. She jumped up and pushed back her chair. "I know you're about to blow," she interjected, "but not on my turf, not on my time."

He looked at her, completely flummoxed, as she cut him off right there. He burst onto his feet, his fist coming up.

"You already got your one free pass," she warned him. "So, if a fist lands on him or me," she said, "I'll take you down and put you in jail, so you can sit in there and cool off."

At that, the kid jumped up and said, "Dad, don't, please don't. Come on. Calm down. I 'fessed up. I didn't really mean to do it," he said, "and it wouldn't probably be such a big deal, but the truck—it was just used in a drive-by shooting, and two guys were killed. That's why it was just sitting there, idling."

At that, his dad looked at him and said, "Holy fuck."

"I know. I know. When I cross the line, I always go way too far. But I didn't know anything about the truck. I had no idea it was being used for that. I didn't know anything about the killing," he said. "I was down at the pool hall with the guys."

"The guys I told you to stay away from."

"Yeah, I know you don't like them, but I don't have any other friends. Everybody else is online, and it's pretty damn hard to meet people these days. I've known these guys for years."

"So, you're sitting there, smoking your weed, and you think it's a damn good idea to hop in somebody else's truck and take off, is that it?"

As far as Kate was concerned, that was a pretty good summation.

The kid slowly nodded his head.

"Oh my God," the dad said. "I've got to get some air." And, with that, he slammed the chair back down again and bolted from the room.

She looked at the kid. "Well, Chuck, I guess you need to sit here for a little bit." And, with that, she got up and walked to the door.

"What will I get charged with?" he asked anxiously.

"Grand theft auto. Isn't that one of the games you like to play?" And, with that, she turned and walked out.

He had said one thing that was right. They had the truck. If he hadn't dumped it where he had, it wouldn't have been picked up, flagged as stolen, and hauled into impound. Still it had been stolen two times now, and it should have a plethora of DNA for them to harvest. So, all in all, still a damn good day.

Simon's Monday Morning

SITTING OVER HIS morning coffee and hoping that Kate's morning was going as well as it could, Simon opened up his laptop and started in on his business dealings. Two minutes in, a headache slammed into his brain. He gasped at the force of it, the pain almost crushing. He grabbed his abdomen, as he bent over. He tried hard to force back whatever this shit was that was trying to push him into a nightmare.

Then, once again, he was staring down at feet, the same damn feet. He shook his head.

"No, no, no, no, not again," he cried out. But the feet were walking. He looked around, trying hard to separate from the vision, but instead he got sucked in deeper and deeper. Once again, he was a visitor in her eyes. He saw a road ahead, dark. Why was it dark? *Ah, wearing sunglasses.* She wiped her eyes, and they were wet. *Shit,* he muttered to himself. He tried to turn her around, tried to get her to go back. But he had nothing there to grab on to. He wanted some way to identify her or something, but he couldn't even see into her mind; all he could do was see out of her eyes. Helpless.

He knew the city well, but, for the life of him, he couldn't place that street. And, even if he could, he couldn't possibly get there in time. He stared out, looking for any clue, but he could only see more when she turned her head, and right now it was basically locked on the sidewalk a couple feet in front of her. And the shoes were just white sneakers, ordinary. And again, nothing to say it was a woman. It's not like she was looking down on her body to determine whether she had breasts or not.

Still he knew she was female.

Frustrated and angry, he tried to tear himself free and failed, but, if he couldn't free himself, could he at least slam himself further into the vision so he could get more information? And, just like that, as if being sucked out of a long tunnel, he snapped out of the vision, until he was sitting here at his kitchen table, shaking and staring around his own penthouse suite, almost in a blind panic.

What the hell just happened? And why? And the really big question: how could he stop it from happening again?

He sat here, his hands cradling the cup of coffee, his throat parched and dry. Probably because her throat was parched and dry. He lifted the cup and took a sip, wondering if, by easing his throat, it would ease hers. It didn't make any sense that it would, but, hell, none of this made any sense. He took several more sips, allowing the warm caffeine to hit his bloodstream and to flow into his stomach, as it calmed him down and warmed him up. Because that had been another part of that vision. She was cold, so very cold.

Too bad he couldn't see her in a mirror or a reflection, a window, anything that would help identify who she was, so he could reach out. Before it was too late. He didn't want to be connected to a woman when she drowned. God, that would be the worst. He remembered his grandmother had said that she had connected with the driver of a car who had committed suicide by slamming over a cliff edge. Only he had taken his wife and kids with him. The fact that Grandmother couldn't do anything about it had tormented her for a long time.

That was not an experience he wanted to count among his most memorable moments.

CHAPTER 14

B Y THE END of the day Kate had several points ticked off her list. The aqua truck was with forensics. Kate had an update on email addresses in the suicide chat rooms. The techs had tracked down two of the suicidal people in those chats, and she would talk to them next. And Andy, who had been playing a person contemplating suicide in the chat rooms, had received several more emails back and forth from the one guy, then received another email from somebody different.

In both cases, the tone had turned from being supportive to being more equitable and playing both sides, like sometimes suicide was a good thing. She shook her head at that, but Andy was pretty excited, feeling like they were getting somewhere, feeling that either one or both of these people would start urging him to do something. The only problem with that was neither of those emails had sent the manipulating photo to David.

The kid who had stolen the truck was in lockup. His dad had left to arrange for bail, but she imagined life at home wouldn't be quite the same. The reality was that this kid would be facing time for this one. It was a first offense, and she didn't know if that would make it a little easier on him or not. But they did have the truck used in the drive-by shootings, and they were now in a position to run all kinds of tests on it.

Although that was limited as well. It had been stolen out of a garage from an old couple's house, and the owner, a male, had since died. His wife, also a senior, was now in a retirement home. The family didn't want the truck back, which was a good thing because it would be tied up with this case for quite a while. But something else the joyriding kid hadn't said anything about was the weapon under the front seat, and that would go against him.

And that was a whole different story. They weren't certain it was the one used in the shooting, questioning the accuracy compared to other weapons, though this could be a backup piece. When the kid had been asked about it, his eyes had grown large, and he'd immediately shaken his head.

"I don't know anything about it. I didn't see any weapon. I don't do guns."

The father had backed that up and said, "The kid can be trouble but mostly stupid trouble," he said. "I've never known him to have anything to do with weapons."

And that was fine and dandy, but it didn't mean that the dad knew everything.

As it was, things were progressing, and Kate was happy with that. The shooter had lost his truck, and now he would be on the hunt for another one. It was too much to hope that he might not get involved in another shooting. Chances were he would take this as another challenge and just carry on. They could hope not, but life didn't always go their direction.

She walked out of the office and headed to her vehicle, still in a good mood. Buoyed by the day of what seemed like a whole pile of checkmarks and boxes being ticked off her list, she headed to the dojo for a workout. She was tired, but it was a good tired. She was stressed, but it was a good feeling, all tied to a lot of accomplishments in her day.

She walked in, quickly changed, stepped out onto the judo floor, and started one of the hardest workouts she'd been through in days. When she was finally done, she stood there sweating freely but with a big happy grin on her face.

"Now," her sensei said, with a laugh, "you look like you could take on the world."

"Some days it feels like I have," she said. "Today was a good day though."

"Good," he said, "you don't get enough of those."

"No," she said, as she nodded in agreement. "Some days there's just no winning. The world out there is an ugly place, and sometimes, ... sometimes that ugliness overshadows everything."

"But it doesn't have to," he reminded her.

As always, his wisdom struck a chord, and, even after she got home, showered, and crashed on her couch, she was still thinking about his words. It didn't have to overshadow everything, but somehow it always seemed to. She lived, ate, and breathed work. And, even with Simon, their relationship, which wasn't a whole lot, was based on his involvement in her cases.

If he hadn't done that, if they didn't share any of that common ground in their worlds, would they still be friends? Or more? She didn't know. She didn't have much in the way of *friends*-friends. She had a couple, although she hadn't seen Becky in a long time. Nor Afton. Then her phone pinged. She frowned at that. It was almost as if somehow— psychically—somebody knew and texted her.

Hey, Stranger. How're things?

She stared at the phone in the dim light. And then, instead of texting, she responded with a phone call. "You know that you're just topping off a good day," Kate said.

"That's good news," her girlfriend, Afton, said.

"And what are you doing?" Kate asked. "Normally I don't hear from you, except for what? Your birthday and what? One other event that I missed."

"I wish I could come for a visit," Afton said, and then her voice turned hesitant. "But it's not possible right now and probably won't be for a while."

Kate stared at the phone in surprise. "You're welcome any time to come for a visit. You know that. I haven't seen you in what, two years?"

"Yeah, I know. I've been living in San Fran for that long."

"You sound depressed. Any particular reason?"

"Because."

"No, no, no, no. We need more than *because*."

"Really? Okay, fine. I broke up with Jared."

"Ouch, like permanent-permanent?"

"Yeah, like permanent-permanent."

"Well, you're welcome to come visit anytime," she said. "Unfortunately I'm always busy though, so, no matter when you come, I'm not sure that staying here with me will even give us much time together."

"Well, on the other hand," Afton said, "you won't be there to bug me, as I tear up every once in a while. Like I said it won't be for awhile though. I'm still getting stuff organized here."

"You can always tear up with me. We'll go get Häagen-Dazs and some wine."

"Now that's my friend," she said on a laugh. "I'll let you know later, when I can get free here."

"Okay, good enough. I'm still at the same place, so it's not a biggie."

At that, she hung up with a smile on her face. She had not seen Afton in at least two years. She had gone down to San Francisco to see her, and they had had a blast. Afton and Jared had seemed great together then. Kate didn't know what the problem was now, and it was obvious that her friend wasn't up to talking about it on the phone, but they'd have time for some girl chats coming up. Hopefully soon.

Then Kate thought about her caseload and about all the problems she was dealing with at work and winced. She was honest when she said she wouldn't be home all that much. But hopefully her friend wouldn't have a problem with it because some of these cases would take an awful lot more than a nine-to-five work schedule. And that wasn't likely to change. In fact, Kate saw it getting worse. So it really didn't matter when Afton got here, just so long as she did.

Kate smiled at the thought of seeing her friend at some later date. Also Kate had gotten off early today, so another checkmark on that good-day thing.

Then she grimaced because she didn't exactly want to share the details of her relationship with Simon with Afton so early on. Or note even later into this relationship, as Kate feared she'd still be full of doubts when it came to Simon. And yet, no doubt over Afton's eventual visit, depending on how long her friend would stay with Kate, Afton and Simon would cross paths.

Even if Kate tried to stop that, chances were it would happen—and likely in a most memorable way. Every time she tried to avoid or to hide from something like that, it seemed to always go wrong. Afton was a great girl and had been working as a sales manager for one of the women's high-end retail stores. Kate had no idea what Afton's plans would be when she got here, but she had family, which also brought up the question: why wasn't she staying with family? Then she thought about Afton's family and winced. Afton always had trouble with them. Some very long-term discord existed with her, involving her brother and her father.

As Kate tried to dredge up the details, she couldn't really tap into them. There was something. She stopped and frowned, as her brain rattled around—until she remembered. Afton's mother had committed suicide.

She swore. That really wasn't a good topic for Kate right now. She didn't want to tiptoe around Afton, if that was the topic of the day with Kate's cases. Frowning a little and feeling some of the high from her day wearing down, she sent a text to her friend. **Still having problems with the family?**

All the usual.

Kate thought about the response and nodded.

Afton quickly texted again. **Second thoughts about me staying with you when I do get to visit?**

She sent another text back, making it very clear. **WTH? No. Just hellishly busy is all. And may get worse the longer I'm on the job.**

Kate smiled. No matter what, she and Afton had been through too much. Afton knew about Kate's mom, and Afton knew about Kate's brother. Hell, Afton had even been there at the time of her brother's disappearance, and all of that just went way back. Kate had lost touch when Afton hit the foster system temporarily, until her father got his life back together, but then Kate and Afton had reconnected as young adults. No way Kate would do anything to jeopardize that friendship. Some things were just too important, and one of those was her two dear friends.

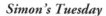

Simon's Tuesday

FUNNY HOW THE changes in his life, especially after that pedophile case, had changed Simon's attitude on friendships. After finding out about the true Yale though, Simon still didn't want to think about all the court cases coming up regarding the pedophiles, Yale included. This discovery about his "friend" made Simon leery about getting to know anybody else. Everybody had history. Everybody had baggage. And Simon knew that Kate had more than most, but so did he.

But now, particularly after Caitlin, Simon had been very leery about getting involved with anybody, male or female, on any level. He had the poker guys he trusted, the people he hired, and not a hell of a lot more than that. And it didn't look like that would change anytime soon. But he did his best to forget about Yale and to put all that pedophile ring ugliness behind him. But it had opened doorways to his own past that he still struggled with. He remembered his whole foster family as being off, but then his whole world had been tainted by his first foster father. So, what did you expect, right?

Simon shook his head and headed out to one of his building projects, hoping for a better day than they'd had this week. He hadn't gone more than a few steps, when he felt that same pressure building in his head, but it was slow this time. He stopped, took several long slow deep breaths, then leaned against the brick wall and tried to forcibly shove it back out of his brain.

He didn't know what it would take, but somehow he

had to get control of this, before it sent him around the bend and made him look like an absolute idiot in the world of business. It seemed like, because this vision was a slow start, he could potentially push it out of his mind and take control of it. Or push it out and keep it out. He wasn't so sure about taking control, but he smiled when the pressure slowly receded again.

"Good," he said, "now keep it that way."

Then he headed over to meet his project manager. Today at least the project manager had a smile on his face. "I presume it's good news today?" Simon asked him.

"Well, let's just say it's not more bad news."

Simon snorted at that. "Since when does no bad news not mean good news?"

"It is what it is," he said. "We do what we need to do."

"I got it. What about the materials?"

"They just arrived at the shipyards."

"Well, that's one good thing. How fast can we get it?"

"The shipyard workers are going on strike. Remember?"

He stared at him and said, "Oh hell no."

"Yeah, oh hell yeah."

"So that smile?"

"Yeah, that smile wasn't a case of we've got good news. It was a case of *we're screwed.*"

Days that started out shitty usually continued that way, and, although Simon did his best to get off that track, it was pretty damn hard.

By the time noon rolled around, Simon was furious, fuming, and ready to fire half a dozen people, including his supply companies. He wasn't sure what the hell was going on or why all of a sudden his supplies were screwed up, but, as days went, this one completely took the cake. By the time he was heading home, tired and frustrated, he wasn't prepared or interested in any more excuses because he had just listened to a mouthful of them all day.

Still, as he walked, he tried to refocus his brain, but he was tired now and weary. His grandmother would say that was a dangerous state, and one always had to guard and protect oneself. He wasn't even sure why now, at this stage of his life, he was hearing some of her more memorable warnings. Because the last thing he wanted was to have anything to do with that world. He could almost hear her voice in the background of his brain, saying, *Should have thought about that earlier then*. As he walked, he knew it was too damn far today for him to return home on foot, so he grabbed a cab and headed back toward his apartment.

Just as he was about to get out of the cab, the force slammed into his head, the words almost indistinct, as someone yelled, *Just do it!*

He stiffened and opened his mouth to retaliate, only to find the cabbie looking at him strangely. Simon pulled cash from his pocket, threw it on the seat, and stumbled his way to the doorman. He reached up, grabbing his head, as the doorman raced to open the door ahead of him.

"Sir, are you okay?"

He nodded but stayed silent, as he stumbled to the elevator.

"Can I do anything for you?"

He gingerly shook his head but didn't bother to answer. There was nothing anybody could do to help right now. If this didn't kill him, it would certainly make people look at him sideways. And he could deal with that, he really could, but, Jesus, this would be a hard one to get through. As soon as he was inside the elevator, he yelled back, "Stop it."

But there was absolutely no way to stop this force slamming through his head. It was like crawling through molasses, yet so painful, but he kept asking it to stop, to go away, and to leave him alone, that it had nothing to do with him.

Entering his living room, he stumbled to the couch, where he collapsed, groaning. Almost with the same force that he hit the couch, as if his mind had opened up, and he heard more. Like a hard step, as somebody's shoe hit a metal surface. And there he was, once again staring down at the river.

The smell of the salt water filled his nostrils, and the breeze ruffled his hair, as the face of this person, whoever this was, stared out at the water around him. Same place, Lions Gate Bridge. He was desperate to pull his phone from his pocket and text Kate, but he couldn't move; he was completely paralyzed and locked into this vision. The fact that he was once again helpless and unable to do anything made him all the more frustrated. And it wasn't even the frustration that was the hardest but the sense of helplessness and hopelessness.

There was also that same confusion, that same focus that the world was better off without her. And again, it was a her. He wasn't sure if it was the same her, but something was vaguely familiar about her, something that made him once again reach for bits and pieces, so he could try to confirm who she was. Why didn't people think in terms of their own names? Why didn't they think in terms of the names of their family or friends? Something. Dates? Places? Something that Simon could lock down and find.

But, of course, she didn't think of any of that. She stared at the water, and the thoughts running through her head were everything from *The world's better off without me* to *Jimmy would be better off without me*. Of course he glommed on to that. But who was Jimmy? Was that a son? Was that a boyfriend, a sibling, or a parent? How could Simon possibly know?

Then came that other voice, that said, *Just do it. Just do it, and get it over with already.*

That could easily be her subconscious pushing her to do something. That part of her that set her on the pathway to get to this bridge, even though it's not what she necessarily wanted to do. Yet it's what she felt she had to do. Like a split in her own consciousness between opposing forces, one pushing her to do it, another pulling back.

He understood bad decisions; hell, he understood all kinds of ugly decisions. But how did one get to the point where these decisions made any sense? He didn't know. How did one make decisions that were just shitty all around? It bothered him a lot, as he sat here, locked in this vision, staring at the beautiful water, because it was beautiful; it really was. There was something absolutely peaceful and still, when looking down at that flowing rush of cold water, and yet something was mystical and magical. It was life. It was true. It was real, but it was also calm and terrifying.

He was being affected by her thoughts. He had never looked at water that way. He'd loved water, but he wanted to be on a sailboat out in the water. He sure as hell didn't want to be floating or even thinking about dropping down into something like that. The force would pull him under in no time, and there must be such a horribly strange feeling when you were stuck between the surface and the bottom of the ocean. It was so easy to get turned around and so easy to not know which way was up. And the farther down, the darker the water got, until it became all-encompassing.

Often people did get turned around, and they didn't know where they were going. It was not an easy thing to deal with. It was also such a weird thought that somebody would willingly want to go deep into the waters, where you didn't know what was underneath you, or what was lying in wait there, or if anything was coming from underneath to grab you. Because a lot of unknowns were in the ocean. It was just as full of predators as anything above the sea.

Simon kept talking to her, sending a message of *Don't, don't.* He then repeatedly gave her a positive message. *This isn't worth it. There's another answer.* But the other answer wasn't exactly coming his way from her. He was getting a million other thoughts, but none of it was helping. He did everything he could to try to push away her thoughts, which overwhelmed him. There had to be another way to get to her. He wished he could lift her arm, but, even as he tried to lift her right arm, she lifted herself, grabbed the railing, gripping it hard.

He called out, "What's your name? Talk to me. Who are you? What is it you want? Why are you doing this? Surely there's another answer. There's always another answer," he cried out, his voice frantic. When she put her foot on the bottom railing and stepped on it, he screamed at her, "No, no, no!"

When she stepped back off again and stood there and stared, he could almost feel the breath in the back of his throat slowly sliding back down again. Maybe, just maybe, she would walk away. He needed her to walk away. Hell, he needed her to walk away and to stay away. Mentally he tried to cut the tie, to cut the channel that had opened up between them.

And not for the first time he wished he knew how to help himself, that he had asked his grandmother for more help, but he'd been so against any of this that he hadn't even gotten the basics.

With sheer determination he mentally slammed a great big steel plate down in the mental tunnel, cutting the connection in half. Almost instantly he felt the cool warmth of his apartment around him. He opened his eyes. "Thank God," he cried out, as he sagged against the couch. He sent a text to Kate. **She's on the bridge. Damn it, I can't stop her. She did step on the railing, but the vision's gone. Sorry.**

CHAPTER 15

Kate's Wednesday Morning

KATE WOKE THE next morning, quiet and controlled, enjoying the peaceful silence of her mind. She couldn't imagine what chaos Simon's mind was in as he dealt with this psychic stuff all the time. She once again looked at his text from late last night.

She hadn't said anything more than **Sorry.**

What was she supposed to say? He was apparently tormented by a connection to a woman who was thinking about committing suicide. It could connect to Kate's jumper cases, but Simon had no details for Kate, like to know who Simon was connecting with, for one thing. Again no physical evidence that it had anything to do with her cases, and it left Kate stuck, not knowing how to handle it.

She also didn't know how to handle Simon. A part of her still didn't want to believe; a part of her still thought it was all gobbledygook. She knew that some of the guys at work wished she would ask for more information, but she had asked, and there wasn't anything to report. That was part of the problem. If this was all real and true and factual, then why the hell wasn't there more information? She understood that some psychics could get more information than others, and it was really not a case of getting better at it, as much as it being *take what you get or leave it.*

It was so frustrating.

She got up, had her shower, and headed into the office.

As she got in, Rodney looked at her. "What? No marital bliss?"

"Why would there be?" she asked, confused.

"Aren't you spending most of your off time with Simon?"

"No, not at the moment," she said. "Both busy."

"You might be busy," he said, "but remember. Our relationships keep us sane and functioning, when the rest of the world goes crazy."

She looked at him in surprise. "I didn't know you cared."

"I'm just a little worried. You're very intense when it comes to this work, and we want to see you last and not burn out."

"I have no plans to burn out," she said, "and your concern is noted."

He laughed. "Noted and ignored from the sounds of it."

"Not so much ignored," she said, with a smile. "Consider it noted. I'm not sure what to do with it or any of this at the moment."

"Or Simon either from the looks of it."

She frowned at him. "Is it that obvious?"

He nodded. "Yes, it is," he said, "and I don't blame you. He can't be an easy person to live with, and to know that he has some information but not enough has got to be frustrating."

"Does he have real information though?" she asked. "I'm still trying to figure that out."

"Ah," he said, with a smile. "You're trying to figure out if he's telling the truth. I would have thought you'd already gotten there by now."

"I already did," she said, "at least on the last case. And I know that he's connected to someone out there who's currently contemplating suicide."

"Maybe the problem is that you do believe it, and you're having trouble with it."

"Don't start psychoanalyzing me," she snapped.

He held up his hands. "Whoa, whoa, whoa," he said. "Time to change the subject."

"Good," she said, glaring at him. "Is there any coffee?"

"I'll hope so," he said, "if this is how you're starting the day."

She shook her head. "Look. I don't know how I feel about all of this. I don't know how I feel about Simon or his somewhat useful information sometimes," she snapped. "I find it to all be a bit much."

"It's absolutely a bit much," he said. "Personally I'm getting more open to it. Remember my grandmother had the sight too? I kinda like this stuff. I think it's cool. I really am fascinated with the fact that any of this information is even accessible because, if it's accessible to somebody, it could be accessible to all kinds of people."

She stopped and stared. "What do you mean by that?"

"Well, I imagine that other people can do what he does too."

"Sure," she said, "charlatans are all over the world."

He rolled his eyes at that.

"All right, all right. It's a defense mechanism, okay?" she admitted. "Basically I just don't know what to believe. It feels like you guys are always pushing me to give you more than I can give you."

"Maybe that's how Simon feels about you too," Rodney

noted. When she almost growled at her partner, he added, "It's not that we want more from you," he said, "but, if Simon had more information, we'd cheerfully take it."

"Even though the information comes from these crazy oblique sources?"

"Yes," he said. "There are no real answers anywhere. Sure, a certain amount are clear, but the vast majority come to us tied up in puzzles of one kind or another. But that's what we do, unravel puzzles, right?"

Walking toward the coffee room to get herself a coffee, she had to ponder his words. Because that was exactly what they did; *putting puzzles together* was a perfect description. Of course that made her feel like shit because she hadn't talked to Simon last night. She'd hoped that he would assume it was all about work, and it was to a certain extent.

But her hesitancy was also about her confusion and about not knowing how to handle Simon and his "gift." He was as much tormented by all of this as she was tormented by the information she couldn't get. And to think that a well of it might be there for him to tap into, but couldn't, drove her crazy, and that just brought her back to wondering how the hell she could even believe this stuff in the first place.

Maybe she was the one who was crazy.

As she walked back into the bullpen, some of the other team members arrived. Lilliana was dressed to the nines. Kate stopped, stared, and whistled. "Good God," she said, "you're always magazine perfect."

Lilliana looked at her in surprise. "Magazine perfect?"

"Yeah," she said. "I wouldn't have a clue how to even begin to dress like that. And I can't imagine doing any work in heels."

"They're not so bad," she said. "I've been wearing them

all my life, so whatever."

"Yeah, for you maybe. I'd get headaches from the altitude," she said, with a sneer.

"Maybe, but, if you weren't so short in the first place, it wouldn't be a problem."

She laughed, and the two women settled into their desks, as Colby walked in.

"We got in a couple reports overnight," he said. "Nothing too bad. You've got a new case downtown on the east side. A body in a Dumpster. Looks like she was an escort. I don't see it as connected to any other case. But, of course, it's up to you guys to figure that out, and we need to get moving on these other cases. I understand that we've made some progress, but we haven't gotten anything we can give to the prosecutor. And believe me. He's chomping at the bit on the drive-by shootings."

"We're getting somewhere on that one," Kate said, "but it's still not anything we have an actual suspect on."

"That's the problem," he said. "We don't have anyone to lock on to, so we don't have anything to give him."

"And you gave him what we had?"

"Oh, yes, he was happy with that. I mean, it's progress. We have the guy who drove off with the vehicle. We have an eyewitness viewing of this guy from the back, which isn't helpful at all, so what the heck are we supposed to do now?"

"I don't know," she snapped. "I wanted to go back to the older woman, who originally owned the vehicle."

"And what will that tell you?" Colby asked her in surprise.

"If she had any idea who stole the vehicle."

The others turned to look at her; she shrugged. "They had to have shown it to somebody at some point. It was kept in their locked garage at home, so who would have known it was there? Could have been a random theft maybe, but it's not exactly a collector's item. It's not something that would have had a GPS on it or some car alarm for sure. But chances are also good that nobody would have known it was even there. So what are the chances that her husband showed it to somebody, and then it went missing, either right away or a little later?"

"Follow it up," Colby said. "And make sure you're checking on the Forensics Division."

"They're all over it," she said. "We're just waiting for the reports."

At that, his lips twitched. "Looking good. We're always waiting on something, aren't we?"

"Forensics usually," she said, with spirit.

He nodded. "I hear you, but I'll talk to the DA anyway." And, with that, he turned and walked back out again.

She looked over at the others and shrugged. "I'm not wrong, am I?"

"No, the backlog is usually Forensics. Like everyone, they're short on budget. We need more people down there, and we're not getting them."

"I think the cities are always short on budgets, aren't they?" Kate asked curiously. "Is this really an issue, or is it an ongoing excuse?"

"I think it really is an issue at this point," Rodney said, stepping up. "I'll come with you to ask the wife about the truck."

"Why is that?"

"Because I like the idea," he said, "and just because the husband may have shown it to somebody doesn't mean the wife knows."

Lilliana added, "Remember too that she's in a home. So just because she might have known something at one time doesn't mean she knows it anymore."

With that warning in the back of her mind, Kate drove this time and took Rodney to the retirement home, which was located in the Locarno area. "Nice area," she said, looking around.

"Yeah, it's really built up in here. We have a lot of really high-end places, but this area being close to the university has always been popular."

"As long as you don't mind hills," she said, as she turned off Eleventh Street and headed down to Tenth.

"Absolutely," he said, as he looked at her in surprise. "You're going up the alleyway?"

"Yeah, I checked online, and the parking is a little on the scarce side," she said, as she parked at the back, and they got out and took a look around. "Looks like a nice little place." The lot was very large, with trees on the side, a nice wooden fence, and lots of little benches.

"Look. A bit of a view too," he said, pointing to the front, which looked out over Locarno Beach.

"Which is lovely," she murmured.

"Thinking about your own retirement?" he said jokingly.

She rolled her eyes at him. "My mother is in a home already," she said.

"We could always transfer her here," he said in serious tone.

"No, she won't be doing with me," she snapped.

"Ouch, ugly childhood."

She looked at him and said, "I'm sure you know my history."

He flushed. "Oh God, I'm sorry. I forgot."

"It is what it is," she said.

"Must have been really tough," he said. "I can't even imagine what it would have been like."

"Most people can't," she said, "and, to a certain extent, that's totally okay. What makes it tough is when it keeps coming back and hitting you every once in a while, and you don't realize just what the impact is."

"You don't get along with her?"

"She still blames me," she said briefly.

He looked at her in surprise.

She shrugged. "It's easier if you can blame somebody else instead of yourself, right?"

"I suppose. But how old were you?" he asked.

"Seven," she said quietly, knowing full well that nobody in this world would believe a seven-year-old except for the parent. But not hers.

"I'm sorry," he said. "I mean, not only did you lose your brother, it sounds like you also lost your mother at the same time."

She cocked her head, as they walked up the front steps. "It's not a bad way of looking at it," she murmured. "I didn't really put the words that way in my head, but it's not bad."

"How could anybody blame you at that age?" he asked, shaking his head. "That just doesn't make sense."

"Like I said, it's much easier to blame somebody else."

He nodded. "And it's still an open case, isn't it?"

"Well, if you mean in the sense that he's never been found, yes," she said. "Open in that it was never solved. But is anybody looking at it besides me? I doubt it. There's not been any news. There hasn't been anything to move forward with. So, in other words, nothing for anybody to go on. But still, every time I hear that a body has turned up for a child gone missing," she said, "it just brings it all back up."

"Which is why the last case would have really gotten to you," he said, nodding. "I'm sorry. We didn't realize how tough it would have been for you."

"It was a long time ago," she said.

"Maybe so, but I'm sure dealing with that pedophile ring didn't help you."

"No, and it didn't help that one of the victims was named Timothy," she said shortly. He looked at her sideways, and she nodded. "Yes, that was my brother's name."

"Talk about pushing some buttons." He winced. "At the same time, we were pretty shitty to you, weren't we?"

She shrugged. "I expected it. It's over with now anyway."

"No," he said, "we were definitely shitty to you."

She laughed. "Whatever. I had my own problems, so I wasn't getting sucked into yours."

"We as a group definitely had a problem," he said. "So it's good that we're all getting along much better now."

"Yeah. It's a good thing," she said cheerfully. "Who has time for all that anyway?"

"Right," he said, shaking his head. He stepped forward, opened the door, and she walked in past him.

"Thanks," she said, with a cheeky grin. As they walked up to the reception desk, Kate identified herself. "Hello, we're here to see Jan Spiller."

The woman looked at her in surprise. "I'll see where she is right now," she said, then got up and walked into the back.

"What do you think she's checking?" Rodney asked her.

"The schedule maybe, who knows. Maybe she's trying to

figure out which resident it is."

When the woman came back, she had a chart. "It looks like she is outside in the backyard."

"I saw a couple ladies sitting off to the side," Kate said, as she turned and studied the big window behind her. "We need to know which one she is, so could somebody take us out there, please?" She used a more informal tone of voice, looking for cooperation instead of trying to make this formal. But, at the same time, she wasn't about to go around talking to several residents trying to find the one they were looking for.

"Yes, of course," she said, "just a moment." She called over an aide, and when the gentleman arrived, she said, "Could you take these two out to meet with Jan Spiller, please?"

He nodded. "Sure, she's outside having tea," he said. "Follow me."

They followed him back outside, and Kate could really appreciate the fact that the residents had lots of fresh air, big open doors, and lots of light. "Are the residents generally happy here?" she asked.

He nodded. "We have very little turnover," he said, "outside of the expected."

At that, she raised an eyebrow in question.

He shrugged. "Most of them leave in an ambulance."

She nodded. "I guess it goes with the age group, doesn't it?"

"It does," he said. "Jan is no problem. She's easy to get along with and always has a friendly smile on her face."

"Good."

"Is there a problem?" he asked hesitantly.

"Nope, not at all," Kate said. "Just need to ask her some

questions."

He nodded. "I hope you don't upset her. She does take a long time to calm down."

"What things would upset her?" Kate asked in surprise.

"It's hard to say but usually her family."

"Oh, that's great," she said. "Because we definitely have some family questions involved."

He winced. "Would you object if I hung around? She might feel better."

"Nope, we're not asking anything private," she said.

"Okay, good. Maybe I'll do that then."

As they approached, he walked up and said, "Hello, Jan. How are you doing today?"

Jan looked up, smiled at him, and said, "Darryl, it's so good to see you. How's the wife doing, dear?"

They had a quick chat that said a lot about how informal and friendly everybody was with each other here. He turned and looked to Kate, who held up her badge, as he said, "These two people are here to ask you a few questions."

Jan turned and looked at the two of them in surprise. "Oh, well, I don't know what possible questions you think you could ask me," she said. "I really don't know anything. What's this all about?"

Kate stepped forward, took one of the other chairs, and pulled it around so she was closer but not intimidatingly so. "We wanted to ask you about your truck that was stolen a while back."

She groaned. "Oh, that old thing," she said. "I can't imagine that it's of any value anymore, and it's been gone for years." She frowned for a moment and said, "I think it's been maybe four or five years. I'm not so good with time anymore, you know?" she said, leaning forward almost conspiratorially.

"You're doing just fine," Kate said, with a chuckle. "And, yes, it was about that time frame. The truck has turned up again, and we're just wondering if you had any idea who might have stolen it."

"I can't imagine why the police would care after all this time," she said almost crossly.

"Well, it's important," Kate explained. "So it was worth the trip to come and see this lovely place and to see if you had any information you could share with us."

"Oh my," she said.

It was almost as if the woman could imagine what budget money was being wasted on this. Kate didn't want to be the one to tell her that the truck had been used in several drive-by shootings. But, as she studied the woman, Kate asked, "Did your husband do a lot of work on it?"

"He was always out there with that thing."

"Did the neighbors come and see it? Did anybody seem particularly interested in it?"

The old woman looked at her in surprise. "You're not thinking one of our friends stole it, are you?"

"I just wondered how anybody would even have known it was there, since it was always in the garage."

At that, the older woman frowned. "I know he wasn't sure when it had gone missing because he hadn't been out there for a while. He was pretty upset about the whole thing though."

"I can imagine," she said gently. "Guys and their cars, right?"

"Sometimes I thought it was more important to him than I was," she said, with a laugh. "He spent an awful lot of time with that thing."

"I think a lot of guys feel that way about vehicles," Kate said, smiling.

The other woman nodded. "Isn't that the truth. And, yes, he worked on it all the time with a bunch of friends. Some came and went. A couple people seemed interested in it, and they would come over sometimes."

"Did anybody ever take it for a drive?"

She shook her head. "No. He would never let anybody drive it. One guy wanted to buy it off him, and he wasn't having anything to do with it."

"And I don't suppose you have any idea who that was," she said in a dry tone.

Jan shook her head. "No, I can't imagine. He was a fairly young guy, and he came back several times, but George always said no. He said that the guy wasn't old enough to appreciate such a beauty. Because, of course, when it was the best thing in your life—or certainly a favorite hobby—you wanted to be sure they go to someone sure to look after it."

"And you don't remember who he was, right? How about where he lived or what he did for a job?"

"Oh, he was a mechanic," she said. "It's one of the reasons I didn't understand why my husband wouldn't sell it. We could have used the money too," she said in exasperation. "But he was always very single-minded when it came to keeping that vehicle."

"I'm sure he was. Do you know where this guy worked?"

"Well, I just said he was a mechanic," she said.

"No, no, I realize that," Kate said. "I just wondered if you knew what shop he might have worked at."

Jan frowned as she thought, and her foot tapped the concrete patio. Kate wasn't sure if it was impatience or if it was trying to get her brain to kick in and to give her the answers she was looking for. "You know what? I think it was the one just around the corner."

"Just around the corner?"

"Yeah," she said, "we lived on Sixteenth in the Arbutus area," she said, "and there was a shop just around the corner from there. I know my husband used to go talk with him every once in a while."

"And that's probably when he asked to buy it one more time," she said, with a smile.

"Maybe, but I can't be sure."

"I can. We'll go check it out," she muttered.

The older woman looked at her. "I won't be very impressed if he's the one who stole it. My husband was devastated."

"I'm sure he was," she said. "I'll let you know."

"Do that please," she said. "Yes, please do that. Too bad we couldn't have solved this before my husband's death."

"I agree," she said. "It would have saved us all a lot of trouble."

And, with that, the older woman gave her a confused look and then turned to Darryl. "I think I'd like to go in now."

"Of course you can," he said. He shifted her chair back, so she could get up easier, and looked at Kate and Rodney. "If that'll be all?" he asked pointedly.

She nodded. "If need be, we'll come back," she said, "but hopefully we won't have to bother her again."

"Well, it was nice seeing you," Jan said, with a smile and a wave. And then she allowed Darryl to give her a hand getting back inside again.

As the two detectives walked around the side of the building to return to the parking lot, Kate looked over at

Rodney. "You were awfully quiet in there."

"I have found," he said, "that older people tend to do better speaking with one person and one person only. It stops them from getting too confused, when the questioning can get a little more difficult."

"I don't know that the questions were difficult," she said, "but trying to loosen things up and to jog up the bits and pieces of the memories we need can be hard."

"Exactly," he said. "But she did pretty well. I was quite surprised. She seems to have all her faculties."

Kate said, "And I'm sure there were a lot of neighbors who knew about the truck, so that might be something we should follow up on too. I didn't see anything in the original theft report about that. Did anybody follow up with the neighbors when it was originally stolen?"

"I'm not sure," he said, "but it's worth a quick check again. It's funny how time has a way of loosening tongues."

She nodded because it was very true. Sometimes people couldn't remember anything, and sometimes they felt safer after a long period of time had elapsed and could speak the truth. "Why don't we do that now?" she asked. She checked her watch and just then a message came from Simon. She frowned at that. "Uh-oh. Simon is telling me *thirteen* again." She shook her head. "He seems to be way off the mark. I can't make any sense of what *thirteen* has to do with anything."

"Or," Rodney said, "maybe it's not that he's way off the mark. Maybe we're just not in a position to get the information yet."

She shrugged. "Either way it's not helpful."

"Aren't you in a fine mood today."

"I'm frustrated, fed up, and I want these cases to close."

"Well, I get you there," he said. "You haven't been on the team long enough to understand how many cases we never get closed at all."

"That's very depressing," she said. "How do you stay positive if you can't close any of these? If you can't capture any of the criminals who are making life miserable?"

"We get just enough to keep ourselves happy."

"It sucks," she said, not pulling any punches.

He laughed. "Absolutely it does. Obviously we do our best for each and every one, but you have to understand and accept that not every case is closable."

"Every case *is* closable," she said, with a snap to her tone. "It just might take a little more work."

"Well, I'm glad to have you as part of the team," he said comfortably. "If nothing else, you'll keep us all pushing harder."

"I don't think it's a matter of not having pushed hard enough," she said, immediately feeling bad for making that suggestion. "I think it's more just a case of a fresh set of eyes and maybe a little more interest in some of these cases versus others," she said. "These drive-by shootings will drive me crazy. The fact that he went quiet for a few years is enough to really get me."

"Did anybody check recent parolees?" he asked suddenly.

She looked over at him, frowned, and said, "I did, but nothing popped. A relationship could easily be why he stopped. Although it often happens that when they get into a relationship with another person, their need to do whatever it is that they're doing stops. Until they get angry over a breakup or something, and they start all over again."

He shook his head. "I just don't get that mentality."

"Whether we get it or not doesn't change the fact that it's there," she said.

"Agreed," he said.

With that, they pulled up to their destination. The house had been sold the year after her husband's death. As they got out, they went and checked with the neighbors on either side. There were only six houses on this block, with a corner store at the end. They checked with everybody, talked with whoever they could. Two of the people remembered the older couple; one remembered the truck.

"He was always playing with that thing. He'd spend every Sunday out there, tinkering around with it."

"Did you go over and talk to him about it?"

The neighbor, who couldn't have been more than fifty, nodded. "Yeah, my dad was a tinkerer too," he said. "So it brought back memories every time I went over with a cup of coffee in my hand, just to see what George was up to."

"What was he up to?" Rodney asked curiously. "I'm not a car junkie myself, so I never really understood what they did."

The other gentleman laughed. "Sometimes he was just cleaning it. Sometimes he was changing the oil because it had been parked too long. Sometimes it was, you know, just brushing up on the lugs on the wheels. Sometimes he was tweaking away under the hood." He shook his head. "He always just seemed happy doing it."

"And what about other people? Did he often do this alone, or were there people who would come over and visit, besides you?"

"A couple of us used to hang around there. I think it was more a little like a men's coffee-shop atmosphere that gave us an excuse to visit for a few minutes and to get out of the house, you know?"

From inside the house a woman's laughing voice called out, "I heard that."

He grinned. "A couple younger kids hung around every once in a while, but they just had no concept of the value a truck like that had for him."

"Did anybody ever try to buy it from him?"

"Sure, one kid from the mechanic's shop around the corner used to come by. I mean, I call him a kid, but he was probably twenty-seven, twenty-eight back then. He really wanted it. I think he also thought it should go cheap, and that's where the discussion ended. Of course, old man George would never sell it cheap. This truck was the love of his life," he said, with a big smile.

"Got it," Kate said, with an understanding nod. "And, of course, for the youngster," she said, with emphasis, "it would have been something cheap because it was old and something he could fix up."

"Exactly, but George never did sell it."

"Did they ever argue about it?"

He shook his head. "Not that I know of, although the kid was a little bit more emphatic about wanting it than he should have been."

"And what about selling it? Did George ever look seriously at selling it?"

"No, I don't think so. I don't think he was at all interested in going that route. I know, when it was stolen, he was devastated, and that was hard on everybody. He was pretty upset."

"And nobody saw anything? Nobody heard anything?"

"That was the odd thing because that truck, when you started it up, made a huge vrooming sound," he said. "I mean, the carburetor system on it was huge. I'm pretty sure he had some straight-pipe modification in there because, when it turned on, it was noisy. So I don't know how the thief got it out of the garage without half the neighborhood noticing."

"Now that is an interesting point," she said, staring at him. "How could they have gotten it out of there, without the owners hearing it?"

"Well, George was definitely short on hearing," he said, "but you've got to consider that his wife should have heard it."

"Yes, absolutely," she frowned, as she thought about it and looked across the street to where the house was. The garage was right there at the side of the road. "I suppose somebody could have put the truck in Neutral, and they could have rolled it out into the street a couple houses down before starting it up," she said.

He nodded. "It's possible. I also figured that, if somebody knew anything about trucks, they might have done something about that noisy muffler before stealing it."

"Most likely they would have," she said, with a nod. She turned, smiled at the guy, and said, "I don't suppose you know who the kid was who wanted to buy it?"

"Not by name. Only that he worked at the mechanic's shop."

"Does he still?"

"I don't believe so, no," he said, frowning. "But I'm not exactly sure. I don't go to that one."

"Any particular reason why?" she asked.

"Nope," he said, "it just wasn't my choice."

She nodded at that and said, "Thanks very much for your time."

When they got back into the vehicle, she drove forward and headed to the mechanic's shop.

Rodney nodded. "Let me talk to him."

"Oh, why this time?"

"Just because," he said, with a grin, "sometimes you make me feel like I'm slacking."

"You talked to a couple of the neighbors," she protested.

"I did, but, for some reason, sometimes the guys at gas stations and mechanic yards treat women differently."

With that, she hopped out, slammed the door shut, and said, "Well, we'll fix that right now."

He groaned. "Just joking."

"I got it," she said. "Let's go take a look."

As they walked in, the owner of the shop came out to talk to them, wiping at his hands with a grease rag. She pulled her badge, and he just nodded, didn't show a positive or a negative response in any way. But he did turn and talk to Rodney. "What's up? What can I do for you?"

"You had a kid working here for you a couple, three or four years back, in his late twenties or so."

"I've only had three guys over the last four or five years, and only one of them has left, and that happened to be the youngest of the group," he said. "Everybody else who works for me is forty plus."

"What was his name?"

"Tex," he said, "Tex Rambler. What's this got to do with him?"

"We're looking into the theft of an old teal blue truck from just around the corner here."

"Well, I don't know about him stealing the rig, but he was certainly fixated on that one. He tried to buy it off the old guy several times."

"And yet the old guy never sold it, but it was stolen not very long afterward," she said.

"I know," he said. "Tex worked for me at the time, but then he left maybe four or five months later. I never saw any sign of the truck in all that time."

"But then why would he?" Rodney said. "That would just let it out that he'd been the one to steal it."

"He could have told me that he'd bought it though," the owner argued.

"Do you have a forwarding address for him?"

"*Um*," he thought about it and said, "let me go check. I'm not sure if I do or not."

"What about his last paycheck?" Rodney asked.

"He picked it up," he said. "He said he would go to another shop, one that had more business. Things here weren't all that busy at the time, so he wasn't getting as many hours as he needed."

"Which is a good reason for moving on," Rodney said. "Times are tough in some places."

"They've been tough in a lot of places," he said, with a frown. "You do your best, but you can't force people to come to you just because you need them to."

"No, of course not," he said.

"So, let me go on in and take a look. I'll be back in a minute."

They followed him to the edge of the office, where they could stop and look around. One of the guys was standing off to the side, looking at them. She walked over and asked, "Hey, remember Tex who used to work here? Have you got any idea where he is now?"

"Probably at home," he said. "That kid is freaking lazy."

"No, he's not at home," the other guy said. "He got in

trouble a while back. I thought he left."

"What trouble?" Kate asked.

"I think he nicked something from somebody, but I could be wrong."

"Interesting," she murmured. "*Something*," she said, "as in car parts?"

He looked over at the boss and nodded. "He was let go from here because of that. So, I'm not sure if he ended up getting a reference and going on to another place or not."

"Yet, the boss didn't mention that," she said quietly.

"He didn't want to ruin the kid's life."

"Maybe not, but it reflects on his character. We're looking into the theft of an old truck from around the corner here."

Both of the guys snorted at that. "That was like three or four years ago, wasn't it?"

She nodded. "Yeah, it was. Maybe he was generally a pretty good kid, but maybe he had big plans. He may have had ambitions, and he probably wanted to do things. And the money just wasn't there to do them, I suppose."

"Hey, the hours were all over the place," he said. "We were lucky to get through that time. Things have improved a lot."

"Could it be because you're splitting the hours with one less guy?"

He nodded. "Can't argue with that."

She frowned, as she looked around. "Any idea where he lives?"

"Nope," he said, "I'm not even sure he's still around here."

"Good enough," she said, with a nod. "Thanks." With that, she walked back over just as the boss man came out.

He said, "This is all I have for a forwarding address."

"Why didn't you tell us that you had trouble here with Tex over stolen parts?"

He flushed. "I didn't have any proof," he said, "and we couldn't square it off when everybody here has access to everything, and I just got the wrong vibe off it. I wouldn't go ruin the kid's life when I didn't know for sure."

"I get it," she said, "but it would have been nice if you'd at least given us a bit of a heads-up on that."

"Again, I don't know anything for certain," he said, "and what if you went after this kid, but he hadn't really taken anything?"

"And what if he did steal that truck?" she snapped.

"So, it's an old truck, whatever," he said. "It's hardly like it's a major deal."

Rodney turned, looked at him, and said, "Except for the fact that it's now been used in at least three very recent drive-by shootings with a death toll of four people. How do you think it looks now?"

Simon's Wednesday

SIMON WASN'T SURE what to say to this poor woman in his visions. But today he'd stayed home, the pain racking through him as the vision kept coming back again and again. The more he fought it, the harder it was for him to get rid of. He didn't understand, couldn't fight it, and couldn't do anything about it.

But if something didn't happen soon, he would have a breakdown. Or at least everybody else would think he was having a breakdown. For his part he just wanted to let loose with a screaming fit and start ranting and raving to get this to stop. But nothing he did helped. He got up and walked over to a picture of his grandmother.

"Surely this isn't what my life will be like," he muttered. He sat back down on the chair, grabbed a pen, and started writing down all the details. If the only way to get out of this was to solve it, then he needed Kate to listen to him, and he needed this to provide enough information that she could do something with it. That seemed to be where the problem was. All he was getting were impressions, but what impressions though?

Lions Gate Bridge? Check.

Early morning, late evening, check.

White sneakers, check.

Seems to be female, check.

Hearing other voices in her head, check.

But it could easily be her own subconscious or some part of her telling her that life wasn't worth living. He couldn't guarantee that it was another person, like him; that's not what he was saying at all. But it's like this other part of her was saying it was better for her to do this, and she was fighting it. There was part of her that didn't believe it, and that part desperately wanted to have this all go away.

He was rooting for that part to win, if it meant finding a solution other than jumping. The last thing he wanted was to have anything to do with somebody jumping. Even worse, he didn't want to be connected to her when she did it. The helplessness he felt already made him feel like life wasn't worth living sometimes.

He remembered the feeling with the boys from the pedophile case, knowing that he could do nothing but watch them and see the stupid rooms where they were being held or that black-and-white vision of a little man walking under the stupid lamppost. Simon had yet to even tell Kate that he was still seeing that one. He hoped they were just residual tidbits. Simon had nobody to call for help, nobody to ask, and his grandmother was long gone. And, damn it, at this point in time he wished he'd never even gone down this passageway. How was he supposed to function in real life? He was a businessman, with responsibilities and people depending on him. And here he was incapacitated because he was caught up in something that he couldn't even begin to describe to other people.

He got up and made himself a very hot rich espresso, then sat back down again. "Kill myself with coffee, huh," he said, shaking his head. When his phone rang, he looked down to see it was one of his foremen. He answered it and dealt with another series of problems that were starting to get to him today. Finally realizing that he couldn't do anything more, he got up, changed into jeans, grabbed his jacket, and went outside. There he grabbed an Uber and got off at the Lions Gate Bridge.

It was hard to explain that compelling drive in order to be here, just in case she might show up at some point in time. Surely she would come, but he couldn't spend his whole time, sitting here, wondering and waiting, and how would he tell Kate that's what he was doing? She'd asked him to leave it alone if he could, saying that she was working on it. But he also knew this wasn't the only case she was working on. There were other cases, other things going on in her world, cases he had no connection to, nothing that led him in any direction. But this was something. And now he was sitting at the end of the bridge, looking up and down the walkway, wondering what the hell was going on and if this poor woman would even show, as he just waited.

He didn't have long to wait. Several other people walked up and down the bridge. He walked all the way across to the other side, which took twenty-five damn minutes, then slowly walked back again. The wind picked up, as it crossed the harbor and slammed into the bridge and kept on going. He looked over the side a couple times and swore because the water churned with an ominous presence down below. He noted a couple standing there, looking over at the water.

The woman smiled at him. "It's a beautiful day, isn't it?" she yelled over the wind.

He nodded. "Stormy and crazy."

"It is." At that, she said, "We've never been to Vancouver before. We were told that this was one of the prettiest spots."

"Well, it is," he said in surprise. "It's a popular tourist spot."

"Yes," she said, turning sad. "But we just heard that an awful lot of suicides were here." He looked at her in alarm, and she laughed. "I'm a journalist. I'm just here to contemplate what it would take for somebody to do something like that."

He shook his head. "I have no idea," he said. "Not my wheelhouse."

"Good," she said. "I saw you walking up and down the bridge here."

He looked at her in surprise; she was worried he was dealing with something difficult in his life. "Yeah, not me," he said, with a smile. "I've got too many businesses and people depending on me to take an exit like that."

"Not to mention the fact that there's so much else in life to live for," her partner said.

"That too," he said. "And, besides, I have a special lady

in my life. We're not exactly a done deal, but I sure wouldn't ruin it by cutting the opportunity short."

The other man laughed. "Isn't that the truth? Anyway, have a good day." And, with that, the couple walked on past, and Simon headed back toward his side of the bridge.

Another police station division was on the other side of West Vancouver, which wasn't related to the Vancouver police. Obviously they worked together, but he wondered if maybe the suicides on the other end of the bridge went to them. He texted Kate and asked that.

She texted back right away. **I've pulled thirteen suicides in the entire Lower Mainland on jumpers alone.**

"Ouch," he murmured to himself, as he stared at that number, thirteen. Jesus! Surely that wasn't all about the same thing. No way that could be. Surely not. But the thought was just horrifying and mind-boggling. Were that many people unhappy? Another text came in.

That's multiple bridges, not just this area.

Reading that detail brought a sigh of relief. **Still way too high.**

It is. It's been much higher this year.

And why?

Still working on that.

Her responses were pointed, but she was talking to him.

He smiled at that and pocketed his phone. As he walked back, he thought he saw a young woman standing along the edge opposite him. His footsteps slowed. He didn't know if it was the same one he'd seen before because he was too far away. As he slowly walked toward her, she looked at him nervously and then took several steps toward shore. He just stopped in place and looked over, but there was no way to cross traffic to get to the other side.

DALE MAYER

He just smiled at her from a distance. "Hey," he said, "I'm not a threat." She frowned at that. He immediately knew that was hardly the best wording. He shrugged. "I'm just walking up to the hill there."

She nodded and said, "Sorry, I—it's an instinctive reaction."

"I get it," he said, as he approached slowly. "I just talked to a young couple over there. They're here for the first time in Vancouver, and she's a journalist, looking at doing an article on the suicides off the bridge."

She winced. "To even think like that," she said, shaking her head.

"Depressing, isn't it?"

"It is," she muttered and looked over at the water.

"Have you ever thought about it?"

"What? No," she said, but her words came too fast, ... were too instant. And her voice was raised and nervous.

He smiled gently. "That's good," he said, desperate to memorize her features, hoping to get a picture of her face somehow. He brought out his phone and took a picture of the bridge around them. "Do you mind?"

She frowned and looked at him nervously. "Okay, that's fine," he said, and he took several all around for the view and of the bridge around them. When she relaxed a little bit, he turned, and, with stealth, took several photos of her face. Enough that maybe, if he were lucky, she could be identified.

He walked around her and said, "I really hope you don't ever consider it."

"No, of course not," she said. "That would be foolish."

"I don't know about foolish," he muttered, "but there is help if you need it." Her next words broke his heart, and he wasn't sure what to do.

"Sometimes there is no help available."

At that, he stopped, but when he turned back to look at her, she was already walking away. "Hey, look," he yelled. "If you need help, I can help."

She just lifted a hand and waved and kept on going. He wasn't sure if she was trying to get away from him or just trying to get away from her life. Either way it wasn't long before she picked up the pace and started to run. He was hesitant, not sure if he should go after her, since that would just make her run faster and would terrify her even more. As for himself, he sent the photos to Kate.

"This woman on the bridge," he said in a voicemail, "she's not wearing the same sneakers, but she looked like suicide was on her mind."

As he walked back up the hill, Kate called him. "I can't chase down everybody who's walking on a bridge," she said quietly.

"I know. I know that," he said. "Just something was so weird about her. Something needy."

"Did you try to talk to her?"

"I did, but she got nervous. She wouldn't let me take her photo, and then she got even more nervous and just took off."

"Well, if you think about it, why wouldn't she? You're a stranger. You're on a bridge, and you're talking suicide."

"I know," he said in frustration. "It's a shit deal all the way around."

"She didn't look the way you thought she would, or she wasn't wearing the clothes that you thought?"

"Not the person that I knew," he said quietly. "I just—" And he stopped, not sure what to say.

"Well, I'll see what I can do with her picture," she said,

"but that's all I can promise."

"Thank you," he said. As he hung up and pocketed his phone, he turned to look back. The young woman had stopped at the far end of the bridge, but she turned to look at him. He lifted a hand, and she turned and walked away. And, of course, that's all it was, replaying Kate's words in his mind. He was a male; they were on a bridge. It was dark, overcast. It was windy, and, although it was still early in the morning, an ominous feeling was here, almost like she wanted to come back in his direction, and he was stopping her because he was standing there.

He probably *was* stopping her, so he turned and headed back up and called for a ride. He didn't know what the hell today would bring. He didn't know if he'd helped her or hurt her, but, on second thought, he pulled out a business card, lifted it up so she saw it, even though she was walking slowly toward him. Finding a rock to hold it with, he placed the card on the ground and then turned and walked away.

Maybe she'd call.

Maybe she wouldn't.

CHAPTER 16

Kate's Wednesday Evening

WALKING INTO HER apartment after yet another judo session, Kate wearily dropped her bag on the floor and closed the door behind her. Almost immediately a horrible premonition washed over her.

She stopped, pulled her weapon from her bag, and silently moved through her apartment. And yet found nothing. Frowning, she checked everything that she could and then stepped back into the same spot, where she'd felt whatever it was that was so wrong. It was the first time she'd ever felt anything like that, and she didn't know what it was or where it was coming from. As she stood here, the same horrible feeling met her again. She pulled out her phone, but she saw no new text; there was nothing. She immediately sent Simon a message. **Are you okay?**

When she got no answer, she was hardly surprised. There were often minutes to hours between their texts. And, of course, she couldn't expect him to jump on the phone immediately. But, as she walked into the kitchen to get a glass of water, the feeling grew worse and worse and worse.

Finally she quickly changed into jeans and a T-shirt, grabbed her purse, threw on a light jacket, and snatched her keys. And she stepped outside, she felt such a sense of urgency that just wouldn't quit. She raced to her vehicle and drove straight over to Simon's apartment. No point in questioning her motivation or the destination.

As she got in his apartment building, she walked toward the doorman. As soon as she reached him, she asked, "Have you seen Simon today?"

He nodded. "Yes, he went up not too long ago."

She nodded and said, "Call and tell him I'm here, will you?"

When he hesitated, she pulled out her badge and gave him a hard look. "I'm not taking no for an answer."

He swallowed, stepped back over to the counter, and she raced for the elevator.

"Is there a problem?" he asked, as if suddenly realizing the speed of her actions.

"Yes," she snapped. "Now do what I say."

With that, she bolted into the elevator and started punching buttons. It was damn frustrating when she had to wait for it to get anywhere. But finally she was cleared for the top floor, and, as she walked into his living room, she called out, "Simon, you here?"

But there was only silence. She raced through the living room to his bedroom. And there she found him fully dressed, collapsed at the end of his bed. He looked at her, and she saw recognition in his pain-filled eyes.

She dropped down beside him. "Jesus, what's wrong?" she asked.

He opened his mouth to speak and then clenched his eyes shut.

"I'll get an ambulance for you," she cried out. She bolted to her feet but couldn't move as his hand had locked on her wrist, and he stared at her. "No." His tone was firm, hard even.

She sank back down beside him, her arms around him, trying to ease him back up fully on the bed, so that he could crash there.

"What's the matter?" she cried out. She tested his forehead for a fever and checked his body over but found no visible injuries. "If you're hurt, why not the hospital?"

And with the last of his breath, he whispered, "Psychic."

She felt part of her revolting at the idea. And it was all she could do to not step back and to reject everything he was saying—or at least everything she thought he was saying. Keeping her counsel to herself, she shifted him gently on the bed and quickly took off his shoes, eased up his belt and shirt, and pulled a blanket over him.

As she sat on the bedside beside him, she whispered, "How long has this been going on?"

"Not long," he whispered back.

"Can you pull out of it?" This was her only acknowledgment that *something*—definitely beyond the scope of what most people would say was *normal*—was happening here.

"Trying," he whispered back. And then his body went stiff and rigid.

She stared in shock, as he trembled in reaction to something. She cried out, "Simon! What's going on? Break free." And she tried to shake him out of it. When that didn't work, she winced and hauled back with her right hand and smacked him as hard as she could, followed by an almost audible *pop* in the air and then a groan from Simon. When she checked him over, he lay here, his body slowly calming, and his breath slowly balancing out.

When he opened his eyes and looked at her, she whispered, "Sorry," with a question in her tone.

His lips quirked. "No," he said. "This time is about the only time I've ever been grateful for getting smacked."

She shook her hand, feeling the weight of her slap. "Can't say that it was an easy thing to do either. Are you back?"

His gaze narrowed with interest. "Interesting phraseology."

"Look. I don't know any of this stuff," she said in frustration, "and whatever I just saw? I'm not sure I want to either."

"Hey, neither do I," he groaned. "I'm blaming Grandmother for this."

"Is that fair?" she asked, tilting her head sideways. "I don't think she's around to defend herself."

"Not only is she not around," he said, "she warned me ahead of time, and I didn't listen."

"Ah, so you're the one who's to blame."

He winced. "If you want to put it that way, then yeah."

"Is there any other way?"

"She told me"—he paused—"and I'm saying it clearly," he said, as if the effort to speak were still hard for him, "that, if I ever started down this road, there was no going back."

"So why the hell would you start down this road?" she asked, staring at him, puzzled.

He blinked; as far as he was concerned, she already knew the answers.

She narrowed her gaze, thought about the little she knew, and then she nodded. "The children."

He nodded slowly. "I couldn't let the children keep getting hurt," he said quietly.

She sat back with a sigh, staring down at the man who had more principles than she'd expected and more honor than she could have hoped for. "I'm glad you did."

His lips twitched again. "Maybe," he said, "but not when I'm caught in something like this."

"You're out now though, right?" she asked in alarm.

He nodded. "I am out now."

"Well, thank God for that," she muttered. She got up and said, "How about I put on coffee?"

"Yeah, how about it."

And, with that, she bolted safely to freedom.

In the kitchen, she made coffee, her mind going over the scene, and she'd never seen anything like it. It was a bit hard for her to even stomach any of this. And yet, at the same time, was it his fault? Did he have anything to do with any of this, or was he as much of a victim to the circumstances as she was? She'd always considered herself honest and yet a pragmatist. So what was that feeling that sent her racing to his side?

Did that mean she was a psychic, like he was? Did that mean that she was *connected* or whatever else one might want to use for strange terminology? Was it her intuition? She would consider that she had a strong intuitive sense. Most cops believed in that much. Did that mean she was supernatural psychic weird? No, it didn't because she was used to it because that was something that she considered normal in her professional world.

While the coffee hissed behind her, she walked over and stared out the window, still not quite ready to go back in there and to deal with whatever answers and questions would arise. Could he stop it from happening again? What did he need to do to make this go away, and could she have any relationship with somebody who had these episodes? Was there a medical reason? A medical solution?

Could he learn to control it, or would he always be at the whim and the mercy of this?

Questions she'd never thought to even have to ask, yet those questions sat right between them. Part of her wanted to turn and to walk right out of that apartment and never come back. Another part of her was fascinated, intrigued, and terrified. Conflicted, she had no idea how to handle this.

———

A TRIP TO the bathroom, a cold washcloth to his face, a hard glare into the mirror, telling himself to buck up and to deal with this, and Simon turned and headed out of the bathroom. He wasn't surprised that she hadn't come back into the bedroom. When he saw her standing in front of the big living room window, he had to admit to being somewhat surprised that she was still here. "I thought you'd left," he said, his voice unintentionally harsh.

She slowly turned, looked at him, and said, "A part of me wishes I had."

He tried to hold back the wince, but, the one thing about Kate was, she was direct, and he really appreciated that. There was a lot to be said for finding out the truth. "Why didn't you?"

"I don't know," she said. "I don't have an answer for you. I don't know what's going on. I don't understand, and I don't like anything I don't understand. It's a scary thought to think that you can connect to people, other people around the world, that you might have information that's not even possible for anybody to know. It's not logical. It's not reasonable. It's nothing that I've ever prided myself on in terms of truth and facts. I said it borders on fiction and so much more of the garbage in life that I've heard from other people—particularly my stepfather—that I just don't even know what to say, and yet the truth is irrefutable when I see you in the middle of something like this."

"And yet what am I in the middle of?" he asked. "I don't know how it looks because I'm on the inside."

"It's scary as hell," she snapped. "You're like completely catatonic. I was this close"—and she held up her fingers pinched together—"to calling an ambulance. Only because you were capable of objecting did I stop. And even then, I had to question my better judgment. What the hell is going on?"

"I'm not sure," he said, "but I think"—he took a long slow deep breath—"you have to reserve judgment on this." At that, her eyebrows shot up. He nodded. "I get it. I've asked you to suspend belief on a lot of things, and it's really pushing your buttons."

"You think?" she said sarcastically. "Tell me what happened, please."

"I think," he said, "that I'm connected to a woman. The same woman," he said, "and I don't understand why her, but I presume there's a reason for it. I think she is looking to commit suicide, and I think she's really torn about it. And I keep getting sent back to the bridge, where she stands, looking down at the water, contemplating her options."

"And why are you connected to her, or why is she connected to you? Why would whatever, whoever is doing this, care about her, and what the hell are you supposed to do about it? You don't even know who she is." She spun and looked at him, her lips tight. "Or did you get an ID?"

"No," he said, "I sent you the photographs."

Her mouth opened. "Seriously, is that the woman?"

He stopped, frowned, and said, "I don't know."

"Okay, hang on a minute. What do you mean, *you don't know?*"

"A part of me says yes, but I haven't confirmed it," he said immediately. "And yet I think it's her."

"Think?" She stared at him in astonishment. "I can hardly track down this woman on just this. Imagine a public plea for help to identify her and then to find out that it's not her and, even worse, to have ruined her life by intimating that she might be suicidal."

"I know. I can only give you what I feel, what I see, when I'm looking out of her eyes," he said. "I get it, and it's crazy, and it's stupid, and I don't know what I'm supposed to do about it." She sagged down into the couch and dropped her face into her hands. He walked over, sat down beside her, and said, "On the other hand, I'm really happy that you came."

"And what the hell does that say about me?" she said, turning to look at him, her face still resting in her hands. "What the hell does it say that I walked into my apartment after my judo session and *knew* something was wrong. I knew something was wrong. I didn't know what. I first did a search of my place, thinking I might have had an intruder because I had that weird sense of something supremely wrong. Instinct said that I needed to defend myself first and foremost, and then I realized that it wasn't me. It was you."

He stared at her in shock.

"And I came racing over here, used my badge to pull authority over your doorman to get up here, to get inside your apartment, and to find you in some sort of catatonic state, completely helpless. What the hell does that say about me?"

He reached over, picked up the one hand that wasn't

supporting her head, brought it to his lips, where he kissed her gently, and whispered, "You won't like my answer."

She stared at him, her gaze hard. "And what would that be?"

"That you're psychic?"

She bolted to her feet and paced around the room. Obviously not the answer she wanted to hear, and he could understand because it was her inherent disbelief in this whole process that caused her so much trouble. "I don't know what it is," he said, "but I'm grateful."

"But you would have been fine, right?" When he didn't answer, she pressed heavier.

"I don't know," he said. "I was connected, but I don't know how it works." He shrugged. "It's my first time to experience this—fully. I don't know. I've tried to snap free, and I did manage to one time. I couldn't snap free this time." He stopped, frowned, and looked out the window. "It's almost like I can see that water again right now. But I don't feel that she's there. I feel that, for her, this is her end result, and it's just a matter of the timing."

"Do you feel that she's being pressured?"

He nodded. "Yes, she's for sure pressured, but I don't know if she's doing the pushing. For all I know, she's conflicted, and one part of her is saying, *Do this*, and the other part is saying, *Don't do this*."

"I think every suicide victim is torn, and mental arguments like that one are part of the norm," she murmured, as she looked over at him.

"All I can tell you is, when I came home, I got sucked into this vision, and that's where I was stuck. I couldn't get out. I couldn't get in."

"Do you know why?"

Part of Simon's worry was, if he was connected to this person, and then she died, what would happen to him? "You're looking for a reassurance, and I don't have it to give. I can only follow this plan, this program. I don't know the rules of the game. I don't know the borders and the boundaries of human behavior here. I don't understand how the psychic energy works. I don't understand why I'm picking up on her and only her. I'm learning as I go. As for uncertainties? Blocking it completely? That's the one thing I guarantee you that I can't give you."

At that, she turned and walked out of the apartment, leaving him alone.

CHAPTER 17

Kate's Thursday Morning

KATE WALKED INTO the station the next morning, exhausted, frustrated, angry, and depressed. Even though she'd given herself a bolstering talk this morning, she knew her expression would tell the rest of her team the reality of her rough night.

Rodney got up and said, "Hey, let me grab you a coffee."

She looked at him in surprise and then nodded, without saying anything. She sat down at her desk and turned on her computer.

In the background, Lilliana quietly asked, "Are you okay?"

She lifted her thumb up and said, "I'm just peachy."

Obviously from her tone of voice, Kate wasn't peachy at all, but it was also fair warning to everybody to stay the hell away, that she was dealing. The problem was, she didn't know exactly what she was dealing with. This was too stupid, too sad, and too extreme for anyone to even begin to help her.

"Well, if you want good news," Lilliana said, "we've got an address for your Tex guy."

Kate spun in her chair, looked at Lilliana, and said, "Seriously?"

"Yes," she said, "but what we don't have is any a motive.

Did you consider that?"

She shook her head. "No, one of the two guys at the station said that he'd gotten into trouble for stealing something."

"Interesting. Any idea what he took?"

"It wasn't proven, but they alluded to car parts. But, if he did that there, maybe he did it somewhere else. We need to track him down and see what his next place of work was."

"We have nothing on record after that garage," Lilliana said.

"Doesn't mean he didn't work for somebody. He could have been working for cash under the table."

"Yes, but we don't have anything where his social insurance number was used."

"Right," Kate said thoughtfully. "Well, I'm up for having a talk with him. See what the hell he knows." Kate looked over at Rodney.

He nodded, as he came back with coffee. "You want to have a little coffee and go then?"

Kate said, "Yeah, I need to check in with Forensics and deal with emails, and then we'll go," she said, reaching for the coffee. "And thanks for this. I need it today."

As Rodney sat at his own desk, running through his emails, he asked, "Problems in paradise?"

"No, not necessarily," she said quietly. "It's just he's different. Comes with baggage."

He looked over and said, "Can he read minds?" The question just seemed to burst out of him.

She stared at him in shock. "Jesus, I hope not," she said, with a half laugh.

"Hey, it's just a thought," he said. "Can you imagine living with that?"

"No," she said, "I can't." By the time she'd gone through her email, Kate reached for the phone and called Forensics. "Anything on the truck?"

"Lots of DNA, nothing in the database," said Bronwyn on the other end. "We're still working on it."

"What about the suicide emails?"

"Yeah, now that's an interesting one," Bronwyn said. "We have a couple email addresses that we think we can work through the system."

"Sounds good," Kate said. "If you can run that down, it would be great. I really would like a chance to talk to somebody."

"Ah, that's still not a crime in Canada."

"Suicide is not a crime, but aiding and abetting it is," she said.

"You're not thinking these are assisted suicides, are you?"

"No, not physically, but, if they're being threatened, and it's presented as *suicide or else*, that's a problem."

"*Hmm*," Bronwyn murmured, "the prosecutors would have a heyday with that."

"Absolutely, but I want to stop this guy. And, if we can find out how many chats he's dealing with, it would help."

"Well, we've locked it down to thirteen."

"What does that mean though, thirteen *what*?"

"I'm saying, thirteen that he's had success with."

Kate froze and stared at the phone. "Success with what?"

"It looks like thirteen of the people he's talked to have committed suicide."

"Jesus," Kate said, sitting back and looking over at the others in her team. Immediately aware that something was happening, the others turned toward her. "So you're saying that this guy, through the chat, had communications with thirteen people who followed through and committed suicide."

"He had communications with a lot more people than that," Bronwyn said. "But thirteen of them committed suicide. And we don't have a private personal email that we can check to see if they did something off chat. This is just what we found through the online chats," she said. "I highly suspect that, if we could track down that private email address, we could get more information."

"What about the emails you got from David's laptop?"

"That's the one we're working on right now," she said. "We're close, really close."

"So, we're thinking that he may have thirteen victims?" Kate said.

"Depending on how you want to phrase it, yes," Bronwyn said. "Based on the tone of the chats, I'd say he's had a hand in at least thirteen."

"And are they all local?"

"The thirteen are. As for everybody else, I have no idea. You'll have to do some running around online and through other jurisdictions to answer that question."

"So he could be doing this globally too."

"These chats are local," Bronwyn said, "specifically for the Vancouver Lower Mainland, although there are branches for Surrey, Burnaby, Langley, Chilliwack." She paused. "We haven't gone through all of those yet."

"Fine," Kate said. "Can you send me the names of everybody who it looks like he's contacted?" With that agreed to, she hung up and hopped to her feet. Looking around at the team, she said, "That jumper scenario—"

"The one with the threatening note?" Lilliana asked.

"Yeah, they tracked an email address down on the chats,

and they feel that, through various chats, this guy has had communication with thirteen confirmed jumpers in the Lower Mainland." At that point she had their full attention.

"And he's pushing people to commit suicide?"

"That's why I'm asking for copies of all the chat records," she said, "but, according to Bronwyn in Forensics, yes. What we don't know is whether there are also any private emails. Of course we expect there to be but Forensics doesn't have a handle on any private DM addresses. That's something we need to contact the relatives for, to see if we can get a hold of their laptops."

Lilliana nodded slowly. "Why does that number sound familiar?"

Rodney stood and looked at Kate. "Thirteen."

She stared at him, puzzled.

He said, "Check your phone."

"What do you mean?"

"What was that number Simon texted you again?"

She stared at them, the color fading from her cheeks, before she whispered, "Thirteen. He keeps telling me *thirteen*."

"Jesus," Lilliana said. "We need to have a talk with him."

"I'll talk to him later," Kate said, shoving it down deep inside. "Only so much I can deal with at once. We're waiting on Forensics for this lead now, so let's go talk to Tex, our possible drive-by shooter. By the way, ballistics matched our current shooting with the one from three years ago." And, with that, she led the way out the door.

Rodney raced to catch up with her. "That's got to be what the thirteen is."

She nodded, but she didn't say anything.

"Will you ask him about it?"

"No," she said, "not right now."

"Trouble in paradise," he said. "I knew it."

"The only problem in paradise," she said, "is being with a psychic, who is very tormented by his visions."

At that, Rodney winced. "You know what? I can see that. Do you want to be the one on the other end of these crazy phone calls or these crazy messages?"

"No," she snapped. "I really don't."

He nodded. "Okay, so let's park that for now. Clearly you're pretty good at compartmentalizing, and let's focus on this kid and the shootings. What the hell would be his motive? Because, you know, that's what kept me awake in the night. I don't understand why somebody would want anything to do with these drive-by shootings."

"It's a hands-off way of getting payback, but we don't know payback from what or from who," she said. "But sometimes motives seem awfully thin."

"Meaning that a motive may not be enough for you and me but seems to be enough to trigger the perp?"

"Yes," she said, with a shrug. "When you think about it, you know, we're all different people. We don't understand how people can do some of this twisted-up shit that they're doing, but *they* do. And, as long as we have enough proof to explain it to the DA, then it doesn't really matter what we think of it. We're doing our job anyway."

He nodded. "I get it," he said. "We're doing our job, even when we don't necessarily understand it."

"Maybe you should drive," she muttered.

"Yeah, you think?" he said, as he walked over to his car. "Sounds like a good idea."

With that, he unlocked the vehicle, and she got in on the passenger side. She pulled up the address that they had been given. "Interesting. East Hastings."

"Yeah, so he may not have a ton of money coming in," he said, "but maybe he's got a job."

"There was something about him being lazy, remember?" she said, studying the traffic, as they headed toward an old apartment building. As they got out and looked around, she said, "This doesn't say *wealthy* or *decent job*. This says *rundown, out of luck*, and *having a tough time with life*."

"And that could be part of the shooter's motivation," Rodney said.

"Meaning that you think he's getting money for these hits?" She looked at him in surprise.

"No, that's not what I meant at all." He frowned. "Are you thinking these are pros?"

"No," she said, "not at all. It was your comment about the money aspect. I'm wondering if he's just angry about his lot in life. Like maybe he feels like the world owes him or maybe there is some connection that we haven't found yet between him and the victims."

Rodney replied, "So far, we haven't found any connection. Not schools, not religious groups, not online chats, nothing. Nothing that connects the victims and nobody in common who would allow us to connect to him. But now that we have a name, we can carry on and see if he's involved with them somehow. At the moment, we're just talking to the one next puzzle piece we have to work with. That's all this detective work is. But, in the best of times, you track down every lead, and you chase down each piece of information and hope that, at the end of the day, you've gathered up enough information and puzzle pieces that go together in a coherent pattern, and then you find your suspect."

"Agreed," she said. "Some days that's easier to do than

others."

He laughed. "Yeah, some days it seems like we just make it more confusing instead of less. That's where persistence comes in. Our job is not for everyone."

"No," she said; then she chuckled. "But I wouldn't have it any other way."

As they knocked on the apartment, there was no answer. They knocked again and then waited. They heard an odd shuffling sound inside. They shared a look, and Rodney whispered, "I'll go to the other hallway there."

She nodded and knocked again. Still no answer. She stealthily walked to the opposite staircase. With each of them at either end of the hallway, they sat here and waited. They waited a good forty-five minutes. Finally their patience was rewarded when the door opened, and a younger male stuck his head out slowly, checking in both directions. When it seemed clear, he got out, closed the door quietly, and headed down the hallway toward Kate's position.

He walked with a limp, and it was obvious that his arm was injured too. Although neither injury looked new. She frowned at that thought. When he got closer to her, she stepped out in front of him. "Hi, Tex."

He froze, then looked at her in absolute terror and said, "Who are you? What do you want?" His voice revealed his stress level and came out in a high-pitched squeak.

She pulled out her badge and said, "Well, we want to talk to you."

He squealed, turned, and bolted right into Rodney's arms.

Quickly subdued, still standing in the hallway, Tex turned as she approached him. "Why did you run, Tex?"

He shook his head. "I had nothing to do with it."

"Nothing to do with what?"

"Whatever you want me for," he said. "I can't do nothing, see? I'm injured."

"Well, I can see that you're injured. What happened?"

"Some guys beat me up a while ago," he said in a resentful voice.

"Was this about three to four years ago? Because you stole from them?"

He stared at her and then shrugged. "Maybe, but they didn't have to do this to me," he snapped. "I was just trying to get ahead."

"And I gather they didn't appreciate you getting ahead at their expense."

"No," he said, "but they crippled me."

"I'm sorry to hear that," she said. "I guess they really didn't like you stealing their stuff."

He shook his head. "No," he said, "but they didn't have to do this. I would have given the shit back."

"I wonder though," she said, looking at him. "Maybe they'd dealt with a bunch of people who made them believe you wouldn't."

"Maybe," he said, staring at her, "but you can see this has got nothing to do with me."

"Yeah, what's got nothing to do with you?"

He looked at her and shrugged.

"Know anything about drive-by shootings?"

He looked to his left, down at the floor, then gave her a one-arm shrug.

"Interesting," she murmured. "What about the truck?"

"What truck?" he asked, widening his eyes innocently.

But she wasn't fooled, since she'd seen the furtive dart to the left. "You know the truck. The one that we just picked up that got stolen from you, from where it was parked downtown. After you got out and left it running and headed back to look at the chaos you'd created."

He shook his head repeatedly. "I don't know what you're talking about."

"Well, we'll see about that," she said, with a half smile. "It's motive I'm still looking at, but I think I just found it." She glanced over at her partner. "Do you get it?"

"Yeah, I think I do."

She looked at Tex. "It would have been nice if you'd had a good reason for killing those particular people though. You didn't have to just grab those guys and shoot them because they were everything you weren't, because you couldn't pay back the guys who did this to you."

He stared at her resentfully. "They were healthy. They were fit. They were strong. They were in their prime. Not like a beaten-up cripple, whose best days were past him." He puffed up and tried to take a step forward but tripped, his left leg quite lame.

She could almost see him crumbling in front of her.

"And this is as good as it gets," he yelled, then simmered down. "After three years of surgeries which some rich do-gooder doc paid for. I should have killed him too."

"All those young men you killed, it wasn't their fault that you are crippled," she said quietly. "And to even think about killing a Good Samaritan doctor is sick. None of these people harmed you."

"Maybe not, but they would have," he said on a snarl. "They were the same, ... arrogant. The same guys who never give anybody a fair shake or a hand up. They were just takers."

"So, because you didn't know who your victims were,

you made that negative assessment and killed them on the spot, even though they were just walking down the street."

He shrugged. "Why not?" he said. "I could do that. And it felt pretty damn decent."

"Yeah," she said, looking at him, "and how do you think being in prison in the physical condition you're in will feel?"

He stared at her in shock; then he shook his head. "No, no, no, no. They'll kill me."

She shrugged. "They might. I guess it depends on if you keep up your interesting ways of taking your problems out on the rest of the world. Yeah, it's terrible you were hurt, and it was shitty, but you know what? A part of me says you probably brought it on yourself because you stole from them. They didn't need to do what they did to you, but you didn't need to turn around and kill all those innocent men, all because you couldn't confront the guys who crippled you. There was no need for that."

"There sure as hell was," he snapped. "They were assholes. Every last one of them was an asshole."

"You didn't even know who these guys were, and you killed them anyway," she said, staring at him like a bug. "You'd never met them and never had anything to do with them."

"I didn't need to," he said. "You can tell who they are just by the way they walk. No way you can miss that kind."

"That kind?" Rodney asked.

"Yeah," Tex snapped. "That arrogance, that *I own the world* attitude. That alpha male stride," he sneered. "But I taught them, didn't I?"

"I don't know," she said, suddenly tired of the whole damn thing. "I'm not sure you taught them anything. They're dead, and their families will forever wonder why and what they could have done to save them," she said. "You couldn't even give them that with a reasonable explanation, just that you were angry at the world," she said quietly. "But we'll be taking you down to the station now, so you won't have to worry about it anymore."

"I'm still not sorry," he snapped. "Those people were bad."

"Which ones?" she asked. "The guys who beat you up three or four years ago, or the innocent ones you murdered?"

At that, he didn't have another word to say.

Simon's Thursday Morning

SIMON WASN'T SURE whether it was worth trying to go to work today or not. But he didn't want to appear weak or to even show weakness to himself in any way because that would allow him to sit here and to take another day off, and that was just not acceptable. He still had a life, and he had to make sure he honored that; otherwise he would succumb to these psychic seizures even more often. The more you dove into the avoidance, the more it would take over.

No way he could allow something this all-encompassing, this incapacitating to have that much freedom in his life. The damage would be irreparable, and, even now, he didn't know what to do about Kate. Last night had been a hell of a talk and a hell of a psychic session, and the fact that she had been the one to find him was both good and bad. Good in that she was all action, and not only had she listened to his plea about not contacting the hospital but she had chosen that as a rational decision. One that she wasn't comfortable with, but she had made it, and it had been for the best at the time.

She'd also seen him at his weakest, something he was not

comfortable with. And something he really didn't want to have to admit to himself, but, when it was staring him in the face, how could he not? He didn't even know if she would ever even speak to him again because that one session had been way too far afield for her. Hell, it had been the same for him, but he didn't get the option of walking away or ignoring it.

There wouldn't be any of that *close your eyes and pretend it never happened* scenario for him. Life wasn't that easy, and it wasn't that generous. He'd been in too many situations where he'd been forced to shut up and to deal, and this appeared to be another one. On that note, he got out of bed after a shitty night for all. At least he presumed Kate hadn't had a good night because he sure as hell hadn't.

He'd thought about contacting her many times since she left last night but held off, deciding to just leave it and to see what she ended up doing. Later he could always try to talk her out of whatever plan she was making. Only so much he could do right now, and it was always better to deal with things face-to-face. How did one explain any of this shit over a damn text anyway?

He got dressed, choosing something a little more casual. He smiled as he pulled on jeans and boots, then grabbed a blazer.

With that, he pocketed his watch and his keys and headed downstairs.

The doorman, Harry, was there. "Good morning, sir."

Simon nodded and kept on going.

"Sir?"

He stopped, looked at Harry, and asked, "What?"

"Was it okay that I let her up last night?"

Simon heard the anxiousness in the man's voice because,

even though Simon was the one dealing with these issues, he couldn't forget that there was a ripple effect too. Not only was Kate affected, so was Harry.

"You did the right thing. Thanks, Harry." At that, he watched the relief wash over the other man's face. Of course his livelihood was dependent on his job, and his job was dependent on keeping the privacy and protection of the residents. "Thanks again," Simon said, with a lifted hand, and he walked out.

There'd been that impulse to explain, something he'd promised himself he'd never do. Besides, how would he ever explain anything like this anyway? It was beyond explanation. He left it at that because he could say what he wanted to say until he was blue in the face, but that didn't mean that anybody would believe him. Particularly not Kate and that hurt even more.

With a groan, he parked her firmly out of his brain, then sending a quiet all-encompassing message to the forces that be to shut up and to stay out of his world today, he set about trying to get control of the chaos that had overtaken his business in the last few days. But first he would start with coffee, finding his favorite vendor.

By the time he'd finished that coffee, plus two more during a couple site visits, followed by the lunch special from one of his favorite little restaurants around the corner from one of the building rehabs he was doing, he started to feel better and more in control. It was much easier to put the night's events behind him, as time and distance worked to make things more equitable.

As he said goodbye to the foreman at the end of the day, realizing it was ten after five, Simon turned and set out for a long walk home. Somehow he'd ended up down at the end of Hastings Street, not very far away from Stanley Park, which of course led to where the Lions Gate Bridge was located. He frowned at that, since it was still quite a distance, but he shook his head; it was a bad idea, and he needed to stay away at all costs. He'd had enough of this crap. Enough of whatever the hell you wanted to call it, but his feet were doing something all on their own, and they kept walking toward Stanley Park.

"You idiots," he shouted down at his feet, attracting the attention of people passing by. He shrugged and presumed to carry on, even though he was now forcibly trying to change the direction his feet were taking him. And, when he had zero control over this, and he couldn't make his feet do anything else, he got seriously worried.

"This isn't happening," he said in a hard whisper. "Stop it. This isn't the way life is. I don't know what the hell's going on, but knock it off." More than a few people were looking at him now. He groaned and shut his mouth. At the same time, he pulled out his phone. Stared at it. Kate would probably be off work already, yet there wasn't anything official she could do to help him. Almost as if she somehow knew he was in trouble again, his phone rang.

"Where are you?" she asked quietly.

"I'm on my way to Stanley Park," he said, his voice tight.

"Why?" she cried out. "You need to let this go."

"Do you think I have a choice?" he asked, his voice hard. "I could tell you something right now," he said, "but you won't believe it. So don't even bother calling me. I'll let you know if and when it's over."

And, with that, he hung up. Finally, just letting his feet do the walking, he muttered out loud, "It'd be a hell of a lot faster if we took a cab." And dammit if a cab didn't pull up right beside him. He looked at the guy in shock.

"Hey, where you headed? Can I give you a lift?"

"You mean, can I pay you to drive me a little farther?"

He shrugged. "I took you to Lions Gate Bridge a while ago," he said. "I figured, at the pace you're going, you're probably heading to the same place."

He stared at him, vaguely remembering the cabbie's face, and then shrugged. "Yeah, that's exactly where I'm going."

He got into the back seat, and the guy said, "You must really love that place."

"Yeah, that's one way to describe it," he muttered.

"You're not suicidal or anything, are you?"

He looked at him in shock. "Why would you even say that?"

"I don't know," he said. "Just some weird shit going on these days."

"Like what?"

"Like the fact that I intended to drive right past you because of the last time, and instead I stopped, without even thinking about it."

"Yeah," Simon muttered, "weird shit, indeed." He sat in the back, as the cab zipped through the next few blocks.

When the cabbie pulled off to the side, he said, "No charge for this one."

Simon hopped out, and the cab took off like there was a fire burning deep within. And there probably was because Simon was pretty damn sure that poor guy had no idea what he was being called to do either, but there had to be something, some reason why everything was lining up this way.

Just then, Kate called. "I'm confused," she said, the minute he answered.

"So am I," he said. "And I can't really explain it."

"I get that you're connected to this person—"

"That's not the word for it. If I could just—" And then he stopped himself. What was the point of trying to explain when no explanation would work?

"Tell me," she cried out. "I want to understand."

There was sincerity in her voice, something he could recognize even through the craziness of his feet moving him forward. "Well, let me tell you. It's not even necessarily my connection right now, but my feet are moving me in the direction of that bridge, whether I want to go there or not."

There was a moment of silence. "Your feet?"

"Yes, as in, I can't turn and go another direction. Believe me. I've tried." His voice sped up as the words tumbled out, and he explained what had happened since he finished work for the day and when he got picked up by the cab. He hesitated, then said, "You wouldn't believe it, but, just as I was thinking that a taxi would be faster, a taxi pulled up. The driver was the same taxi guy who drove me there the other night," he said. "He dropped me off at the same place with no charge and sped away as if he were scared."

"Well, I imagine he probably was," she said quietly. "I'm coming to you."

"Yeah, do that," he said. "Maybe it'll be easier." With that, he hung up the phone, and, instead of letting his feet do the walking, he took charge, picked up the pace, and ran as fast as he could toward the same spot. Only as he got on the bridge, his stride strong and sure, his boots clicking on the metal of the bridge, could he see a young woman up at the same spot. He called out instinctively, "Mali."

She turned and looked at him in shock, then bolted. This time he didn't hesitate, and he ran as fast as he could, trying to catch her. But she had just that much of a head start. When he got to the far side of the bridge, he was winded, and he saw that she was slowing down too.

She stopped, then turned and looked at him. "Why are you following me?" she asked, her voice broken, and tears streaming down her face.

He stopped, as she reached for the railing at the bridge.

"I want to help you," he cried out. "I don't want you to jump."

She stared at him. "How did you know I would jump?"

"I don't know," he said. "I can't really answer that, but please, please don't jump."

"You don't understand," she said brokenly.

"Yes, I do," he said. "I understand. I understand a lot."

"No, you can't. Nobody can," she said, crying hard. She looked at him suspiciously. "How did you know my name?"

"I don't know," he said, raising both hands. "I know that makes no sense and isn't something you want to hear, but I really don't know. It's just—it was the voice that called out to me."

"A voice?" She looked at him, confused.

Simon probably sounded like a crazy man. "Please tell me why. Why do you think you need to jump?" he asked, taking a step closer.

As soon as he took that step, she backed up a step. "Don't come any closer," she cried out.

"I'm not planning on it," he said. "Honest, I just want to keep you safe."

"And throw me over."

He stared at her in surprise. "No, not at all."

"What do you mean?" She started to bawl right in front of him, a breakdown happening, as she sat cross-legged on the bridge.

But the minute he went to take a step closer, she started to get to her feet again. "Stop," he said, "I'm not coming to hurt you."

She still sobbed, but it was obvious she didn't trust him at all.

"But I don't know what's going on," he said. "I just want to help."

"Don't you understand? Nobody can help."

"That's not true. Somebody can."

"No," she whispered, "nobody can."

"But why?"

"It's too late. It's gone too far," she said. "I can't live with this."

"Tell me what it is you can't live with."

She whispered, "You don't understand."

"No, I don't," he said. "I really don't."

And then another voice spoke in her head, or his head—somebody's head. Or maybe it was in the air around him, flying on a breeze. He had no fucking idea, but it whispered, "*Do it.*"

"No, don't do it," he cried out instantly.

She looked at him. "Did you hear that voice?" she stared.

"Shit," he said. "I know I'll sound absolutely crazy, but is a voice telling you to *do it?*"

"My voice always tells me to do it," she said bitterly.

He nodded. "And I had that same voice in my head."

She slowly got to her feet. "Are you suicidal too?"

"Sometimes," he admitted. "I've been there. I've been to that edge."

"But you've never gone over."

"Well, I'm still here," he said, with a wry smile.

"You are," she said, studying him, clearly confused.

"I don't get it. Are you in that same chat?" He was fishing for answers, looking for anything that would help her loosen up.

"Lots of them," she said. "Sometimes it really helps."

"It does really help sometimes," he said, very careful with his wording, not wanting to send her off in the wrong direction. "But sometimes it doesn't help."

"No, of course not," she said. "Nobody has the answers. Nobody can make that decision for you."

"Did anybody ever email you?"

She turned slowly, and, with her voice hard, she said, "Was it you?"

"No," he said immediately, "it's not me."

"Then how do you know about an email?" she asked, her voice turning ugly, as she glared at him. "You said it would be over if I did this. You said it would be finished."

"That's not true. It wasn't me." But she didn't believe him. He saw it in her eyes.

"I don't know," she said, and this time instead of going over, she backed away. "You told me that it would be finished and that nobody would know."

"I didn't tell you anything,"

"Are you going back on your word?" she cried out.

In her confusion, she now thought that he was going back on whatever it was that this stupid email writer had said to her.

"Listen. I work with the police," he said, not even realizing what he'd said, until she froze and stared at him. "It's true," he said. "We know that somebody is trying to convince people to jump off the bridge."

She looked at him, her gaze going around her. "Other

people?"

And that's when his heart broke, and he whispered, "Yes, sweetie, other people and you."

She shook her head. "You can only know that if you know what's in the email."

"I don't know what's in your email, but I know somebody else who jumped a few days ago, a friend of mine," he said, his hand going to his heart. "He left behind a wife who loved him dearly, but, for whatever reason, he believed that her life would be better if he did this."

"But that's what they say, isn't it?" she said, sounding broken again.

But such distrust was in her voice, in her face, he knew he had to be beyond careful. "I get it," he said quietly. "I really do, but this guy isn't trying to help you. It's his own perverse sense of satisfaction and making people do what he wants them to do. He's a puppeteer, and he's pulling your strings."

"I know," she said. "I've known that all along. But I can't stop him."

"What do you mean, you can't stop him?"

She shook her head. "You really don't know. You're just fishing."

"Help me to understand," he said quietly. "Please."

She shook her head. "I can't." She suddenly moved to the bridge, her hands on the railing.

"Dear God, please don't jump."

She looked at him. "Why do you care?" she asked in bewilderment. "Why do you even care?"

"I do care," he said. "I care a lot."

"But why? What difference does it make?"

"You know what? I've had some things in life that were

pretty shitty too," he said. "I've had some reasons to want to take that short walk off a bridge myself," he said, "but I haven't yet."

"*Yet*," she pounced.

"And I won't," he said, "because I've worked hard to find balance in my life and to find a reason to live."

"It doesn't matter how much reason you have," she said, "you still don't get it. I don't have a choice."

"That's not true," he said. "Please don't believe his lies. It's not true."

She started to back away from the bridge. As long as she kept going in that direction, he was okay with it. "Please go home and rethink all this," he said quietly.

In the background he heard Kate.

"Simon, is that you?"

He reached up a hand and said, "See? She's the police."

"The police," Mali gasped, then turned and looked at Kate, coming up behind him. But in a reaction that he hadn't expected, she said, "God, I have to get out of here." And, with that, she turned and bolted.

He tried to run across, but she darted into the traffic. Even as he tried to get across, a huge bus came up, and he saw a vehicle on the other side stop to give her a lift.

He cried out, "No, no, no."

At that, Kate reached his side, panting from her race across the bridge. "What the hell is going on?"

He pointed and said, "Did you see the woman I was talking to?"

"Well, I saw someone, yes. Why?"

"It's her," he said. "It's her."

"Who's her?" she asked quietly. "Come on. Let's get some clarity here. Who are you talking about?"

"It's the woman who I'm connected to."

She turned and looked down the road. "She's gone."

"Yeah, I think she would have jumped tonight."

"Well, it sounds like you got her to stop."

"No, all I got was more confusion and no answers. I need to know who she is, although I do know something."

"What's that?"

"I know her first name—or at least a nickname. *Mali.* When I called out, 'Mali, don't,' she asked how I knew her name."

"Mali," Kate said, as if turning the name over and over again in her mind. "Yeah, do you know her?"

"I don't know her."

But, at that, Kate stopped, frowned, and pulled out her phone. When somebody answered on the other end, she spoke quickly. "Check that email address list we were talking about, will you? See if a Mali is on it."

"Can you spell that?"

"No, I have no idea how to spell it. Just run through whatever options there are."

"Yeah, yeah, give me ten minutes."

She put her phone back in her pocket and said, "I feel like there was an email address with a Mali in it."

Simon stared at her. "You mean, we can track her?"

"I have no idea. That could be a nickname. We need more than that."

"Can you get her image off the bridge cameras?"

"Yes, and I can do facial recognition, and we have those other photos you took too."

"But will that help?"

"Not necessarily. We'll run it through the DMV and see if we come up with anything," she said. "Come on. Let's get you home." He stopped, and she asked, "Do you really think she'll come back tonight?"

He frowned, then shook his head. "No." He looked down at his feet, gave them a good shake, and said, "My feet say it's okay to go home."

She looked at him, and he shrugged. "I know. I get it. Trust me. I already know what that looks like, and I also know what it feels like," he said, "so don't even start with me."

She nodded quietly and said, "Okay, fine. I get it. Let's get you home."

CHAPTER 18

A ND, WITH THAT, they got into her car. "Do you really think they'll find her?" Simon asked.

"Maybe," Kate said.

He looked at her and said, "I'm really sorry about last night."

Surprised, she stared at him and said, "It wasn't your fault."

That was the very first time she had really acknowledged that it was something beyond his control.

"I don't know what to do about it," she said. "It's something beyond my experience. It's beyond the norm for me. I'm not sure how I feel about any of it."

"Good enough," he said, and he just relaxed into the seat beside her.

"It was kind of a day as it was," she said. "We caught the drive-by shooter, who was killing healthy guys because he was crippled." With a shake of her head, "I'll never understand people. Then I thought we had a hot lead on this case, and we may still. Just have to wait." she said. "The frustration just continues."

"That's part of your world, isn't it?" he asked.

"It is," she said. "Unfortunately it gets to be a little too much sometimes."

"And you've got a double set of cases going on here."

"Oh, don't forget the giant stack of other cases on my desk as well," she said. "But, when things are hot, you've got to move and take advantage of it. You've got to stay on top of things. Otherwise you lose the threads and the momentum, you know? Then the trail goes cold, and people get away with all kinds of shit."

"Sounds like you're always juggling priorities."

"Exactly, so right now, the top priority is tracking down this girl. How did she look to you?"

"Distraught, upset, like nobody in the world understands, and, although I kept saying there was another answer, she kept telling me there wasn't."

"Well, I'm not sure in that suicidal mind-set anybody ever believes that some of these things can have a solution that's equitable for everyone," she said quietly. "So, even though you were telling her that, she's probably thinking you don't know anything, you don't really understand, and you've never been there."

"Yet I have been there," he admitted quietly.

She gave him a half smile and said, "So have I."

He looked at her in surprise and then nodded in understanding. "We're a pair, aren't we?"

"Well, we're a pair all right," she said. "A pair of what I'm not sure." Her phone rang again. She hit Speaker and said, "What have you got, Bronwyn?"

"I've got a name and an address. Her name is Mali Turner. And the name that she was using in the emails was Mali."

"Interesting name. Okay," she said. "I'm heading across the bridge into West Vancouver right now. I'll stop in and take a look."

"The address we have on file puts her just off Cypress

Street, close to Burrard Street Bridge."

"Good enough. I'll head there now." As soon as she got on the other side of the bridge, she made the series of turns she needed to head back over again. Once turned around, she said to Simon, "I'll head over and talk to her."

"I'm coming," he said. She shook her head, and he said, "Don't even go there. You know that she wouldn't recognize you, and it's likely to scare her."

"Oh," she said. "What'll she do if she's scared?"

"I don't know, but do you really want to find out?"

She winced at that. "You're not a cop."

"No, but I'm a concerned citizen who's already spoken to her. You know that, if anybody will get her to open up, it'll be me."

"You've already terrified her," she said. "You could also be the final straw."

"She has to get to a bridge first."

"No. There are a lot of ways to commit suicide. For all you know, she's been contemplating several, and you're about to push her to make a final choice."

"That's a horrible thought," he said.

"I know, but we need to get to the bottom of this, and we need to find answers fast." And, with that, she pulled up in front of an apartment building. She looked at it and said, "She's on the third floor, so we need to make sure she doesn't get a chance to jump out of any windows."

"Third floor is all about paralyzing yourself. I don't know that it's a guaranteed suicide. And we don't know that she's actually suicidal either. I got the sense that she thinks it's her only choice," Simon replied.

"Well, let's go have a talk with her. Maybe we can change her mind," she said.

With that, she shut off the engine and hopped out.

——— ⁓⁓ ———

SIMON DIDN'T KNOW if Kate realized that she had said *we*, but he wasn't giving her a chance to backtrack. As soon as they got into the apartment building and up to the third floor, they walked to her door and knocked. Almost immediately there was a call out.

"Who is it?" Mali said.

Kate looked over at Simon, then shrugged and said, "It's the police. I just have a couple questions for you."

First came a shocked gasp, and then the door opened, but the chain was still up on the other side.

At that, Kate held up her badge, so the woman saw it. "May we come in and talk to you, please?"

"What about?" she said nervously.

"Inside would be easier," she said firmly. So many people were used to authority, and unless they had been brought up in a system that loved to buck it, most people would open the door. And, in this case, that's exactly what Mali did.

She shut the door, removed the chain, and pulled it open. When she saw Simon there, she paled and stared at him in shock. "How did you find me?" she whispered in horror.

At that, Simon stepped forward, and Kate closed the door behind them.

"First off," Kate said, "Simon did find you on the bridge. He's very concerned that you stay healthy and sane and don't take a chance on another bridge. Second, we believe that you're being pressured to commit suicide. Is that true?"

Mali stared, her gaze going from Simon to Kate and

back again. "Yes, but how did you know?"

"Because you're not the first one."

At that, the young woman collapsed in the closest chair. "What do you mean?" she asked, her gaze darting from one to the other.

"As I was trying to explain to you," Simon said, "a friend of mine was pressured into committing suicide. In his case he was told that his wife would be murdered or found dead with a bullet hole in her head if he didn't go through with it."

She stared at him in horror. "Oh my God, that's terrible."

"Which is why he ended up jumping. He was already potentially partially suicidal to some degree," he said. "I didn't know about it but he was on forums where there was a support group."

"Yeah, support group," she said, with a wry smile.

"Some of them are supportive, and some of them aren't, it seems."

"Exactly."

"And did you encounter somebody like that too?"

"Yeah," she said, "but it wasn't about killing my spouse."

"What were you being blackmailed about then?"

"My younger sister died," she said painfully. "She choked to death. But he says he has the medical file to prove that I murdered her. And that, if I don't jump, he would release that information to the police."

"Well, first things first," Kate said, in her usual blunt way. "Did you?"

The woman looked dazed, as she lifted her gaze to her. "Did I what?"

"Did you kill your sister?"

"No, of course not. She did choke."

"So why would you worry about it?"

"Because of my parents," she said. "They're already torn apart by all this, and for them to even have that come up as a possibility would destroy them," she said simply.

"Would they not believe your version?"

"They would, but I don't know that everybody around them would. They've always been very leery about the public and what people say. Even back then when it happened," she said, "people looked at them sideways, and they felt they were being judged for not having been good parents. If it even came out in a rumor that I had killed her, I know that they would suffer terribly," she whispered.

"And yet that isn't a good reason for killing yourself," Simon said. "And, if you think about it, if your parents have any suspicion that her death was deliberate in any way, by killing yourself, you would essentially appear to be proving your guilt had driven you to suicide."

She stared at Simon in shock. "But I wouldn't do that normally."

"But where are your parents at mentally? Would they understand that?" he asked quietly. "This guy is trying to manipulate you."

She nodded slowly. "I know. I know," she said. "It started off friendly, and then it turned not-so-friendly. He was my friend, and I talked to him way too much, like, over the last year or so. I didn't even see it coming. Then, all of a sudden, he seemed less friendly and more ominous. Then he started to say I wasn't a good person, and it would be better off if I wasn't around in the world. He said my parents would be better off, and it was too bad the wrong sister had died," she said, tears pouring down her cheeks. "And he's asking why I did it, but I'd told him clearly that I didn't do it, but he wasn't listening." By now she was openly sobbing.

Kate crouched in front of her. "Do you know who this person is?"

"No, just someone from the chat."

"But, in all that talking, did he ever email you?"

She nodded. "Yes, he had this file and pictures. I don't know," she said. "It's on my laptop. Every time I come in, I see it, and it makes me just want to head back out to the bridge again."

"The bridge won't make this go away," Simon said firmly. "And not only will the bridge not make it go away, it would cause so much more trauma for your family, and so much more guilt that they couldn't help you because they were so tied up in grief over your sister."

She stared at him and said, "I know that," her voice barely above a whisper. "But I didn't know how to stop it."

"We'll help you stop it," Kate said firmly. "But first I need you to promise that you won't commit suicide. I need a commitment that you won't listen to this guy and that you will not follow through."

"But what if he follows through?" she asked painfully.

"Then we'll explain it to your parents," she said, her voice firm. "This morbid pressure about suicide has to end."

Mali looked at her and slowly sagged into the chair, and she nodded.

"Now I need your permission to access your laptop," Kate said.

Mali made a hand motion to where it sat on the coffee table. "Go ahead," she said. "I'll never forget those emails or his words," she said, "but I sure as hell want to." And, with that, she burst into tears.

Simon gathered her in his arms, sat down with her, and let her cry. He felt the tears in the back of his own eyes burning. He looked over at Kate and said, "We need to get on this now."

But she was already at the laptop, studying it. She pulled out her phone and called Forensics. With her on the phone, he just held Mali in his arms and rocked her gently.

"I didn't know what to do," Mali blubbered. "I was so scared every time you showed up."

"And I'm afraid," he said, "that I wasn't the only one."

She stared, shifted back, and asked, "Were you there every time?"

"How many times is *every time?*"

"Seven or eight."

He stared and shook his head. "No, just the last couple. Though I guess I don't even know if they were the last two."

She frowned. "Was somebody else there?"

"That's what I was just going to ask you. Did you ever see anybody else?"

"Yes," she said, "there was another man."

"I'm afraid it was him," Simon said quietly. "I'm afraid that looking wasn't enough anymore. And then it was all about wanting to see it in action."

"That's terrible," she said in horror. "It's so terrible."

"I know," he said. "I get it."

By then, Kate hopped to her feet, snatched up the laptop, and said, "I need you to sign a receipt for this. I'm taking this to the office." And, with that done, she said to Simon, "I've got to go."

He nodded, stood, and asked Mali, "Will you be okay?"

Mali smiled and said, "Yes," she said. "I will now. And I promise I won't jump."

"Good," he said. And then rolling his eyes, he asked, "Did you happen to keep my card?"

She nodded.

"So use it. You can text me or call me anytime. We'll get to the bottom of this. I need you to trust that we're working for you now."

"Yes," she said, "I do." And, with a shaky breath, she gave him a hug and said, "Thank you."

He nodded, then smiled and looked back at Kate. "Okay, let's go."

And, with that, they left.

CHAPTER 19

ALTHOUGH IT WAS late, after she dropped Simon off, Kate raced back into the station. She caught Rodney, coming out the door.

"What's the matter?" he asked. "I was just leaving."

She took a long slow deep breath. "The case with the suicides," she said, "we just managed to speak with the woman who has been tormenting Simon."

His eyebrows shot up. "She didn't jump?"

She shook her head. "No, but now I have her laptop. She's being pressured to jump, blackmailed in a way. He's threatening to unleash a false rumor that she murdered her younger sister, who choked to death, according to the autopsy report. But the idea that such a terrible lie would be made known, exposing her as a murderer," she said, "was too much. She worries it would kill her parents, who are already struggling so hard over the loss of her sister. She's already weak and vulnerable and was easily victimized."

Rodney said, "Wow, that's a terrible move."

"This may match with the last picture the instigator sent me, with the unisex tennis shoes," she said. "Better than that, she said that every time she's been on the bridge, it's like this guy was watching her."

"Do you believe it?" Rodney asked.

"I don't know," she said, "but I want to see if I can verify anything. I do have a record of when she was on the bridge."

"Ah," he said, "I can run through the video cameras to confirm that and see if we can pick out this guy."

"Perfect," she said, "because, if we can get this guy tonight, maybe we can stop another person from dying."

"That's huge that you managed to find and to talk to her," he said.

"I know," she said. "It was driving Simon absolutely batty."

"Well, then that's another victim who might be saved through all this psychic stuff."

She shot Rodney a sharp look, but he was already headed to the computers and turning on all the monitors.

As Colby walked in, he asked, "I was just about to leave. What's going on? You guys look like something's breaking."

She quickly explained, and he stared at her. "You know that this guy could be watching her from a long way off."

"That's possible," she said, then hesitated. "But how would that be? How would he know what she's doing?"

"Well, that's what I mean," he said. "What if he's tracking her somehow? What if he's tracking her phone or—" He stopped, frowned, and said, "What if he's just doing simple surveillance outside her house. Maybe he sends a message and pushes her, then manages to be outside her place and watches. Maybe that's part of the thrill for him. If he can't actually kill somebody, he can do it by remote control."

She winced at that phrase because that was a horrible thought. Of course that's what he had been doing. He'd been pushing other people to kill themselves, which gave him satisfaction somehow. "I don't know," she said, "but we'll need to see what we've got for cameras around her place." She quickly punched in the address she'd just come from and said, "We've got several video cameras in the area. Both street cameras and the parking lot."

"Start with the parking lot," Colby said. "It'll be the same vehicle every time."

"Yeah, but they'll all be the same vehicle," she muttered. "They'll live there."

"Then run them and eliminate all the license plates registered to that address. Hang on," he said. "I'll bring over one of the computer forensic techs to help you." With that, he disappeared.

When Kate turned around ten minutes later, Bronwyn was walking in. "Wow," Kate said. "When you get pulled, you get pulled. I'm so glad you're here. We just had a break on the jumpers, and I need help on the street cams. We're trying to see if the same vehicle was there on the nights that Mali went to the bridge. He knows somehow that she's there, and he's got to be following her, is there waiting for her, or he has some other way to track her."

"Meaning, she thinks she's being followed."

"Not exactly. It's not that she thinks she's being followed per se, but she feels like she's being watched."

"Interesting," Bronwyn muttered. "Let me take a look."

It was a systematically slow and laborious process as they went through the dates and times in question. Not until the fourth visit at the bridge by Mali did Kate find something. "I've got this little red truck that comes and goes," she said, tapping the screen. "I swear I've seen it time and time again. Can you get me the address on that license plate?" she asked the analyst.

When Kate reeled it off, Bronwyn ran it through and brought it up on the screen. "It's not registered at the apartment, and here's the driver's license on that person."

There, on the screen, was the driver's license of the person in the red truck.

"Look at that. We've got a Kenneth Walker." Kate punched in his address and said, "He has an address near the university."

"That's a long way for him to go for something like this," Bronwyn said, shooting that down.

"He takes his time, and he sets it up though. He's local enough to go to any of these places and watch."

"Do you think the watching is the main part?" Bronwyn asked.

"No, I think concluding this is. He may not know if his victims have all done what he asked them to do, but I think, in this case, he can check the obituaries, check with the police, or something."

"And we won't really get a handle on that until we do more investigation. And, of course, time is at a premium."

"Okay," Colby said, "but you've got this girl safe, right?"

Kate frowned. "Initially she wouldn't let us come in, and she didn't want anybody with her," she said, "but she was definitely in a different mind-set once we talked."

"Of course, but she's vulnerable though"—Colby arched one eyebrow—"and, if this guy got to her somehow …"

Kate added, "I thought for sure she'd be okay because now she seemed to be quite aware that this online stalker's targeting multiple people, and we were on to him."

"Maybe," Bronwyn said, doubt evidently in her tone.

Kate pulled out her phone and sent Simon a text. When there was no answer, she frowned and said, "Crap, now Simon isn't answering."

"Simon?" Bronwyn asked.

Kate didn't even bother with a reply but looked over at Rodney and saw he was busy screening video too. "Rodney, have you seen a little red truck anywhere around the bridge?"

"Yeah," he said, "it's often in the pull out."

"Interesting," she muttered. "What we need to know is if this guy's a camera buff or something."

"I'm pulling everything I can on him," Bronwyn said. "He's got a couple parking tickets and a speeding ticket out in Richmond."

"When was that?" Kate asked.

Bronwyn looked at her and said, "Is there a date you're interested in?"

Kate brought up her spreadsheets and said, "Well, there was a jumper in that area on the seventeenth."

"Okay, let me check." Bronwyn whistled. "And that's when he got the ticket."

"Wow, seriously?"

"Yeah, so we can place him in the same area on that date too."

"Yeah," Kate said. "You know what? We might have someone here as a viable suspect. I sure hope so. This has been driving me nuts."

"Well, not just you, although you're the only one who thought it was a problem."

"No, Simon did," she said. "He's the one who pushed me in that direction."

"Oh," Bronwyn said, "*that* Simon."

Kate glared at her. "What does that mean?"

Bronwyn raised her hands. "Nothing," she said, "but it sounds like this guy will be a huge help in closing cases."

"Trouble is, he doesn't get to pick the cases," Kate said, "so just because he says it's a case, that doesn't mean that we're all that concerned."

"I guess that's the problem with this one, isn't it? They were all jumpers, and suicide isn't considered a crime."

"But aiding and abetting is."

"But is that what this is?" Bronwyn asked.

"Come on," Rodney said beside her. "That makes me think of assisted suicide. This is something entirely different."

"Oh no, that's true. Maybe just call him a stalker for now. I don't even know what charge we'll be looking at here—manslaughter, homicide, what?"

"It would be manslaughter or homicide most likely, no hands-on," Rodney offered, "yet inciting to commit suicide through threats."

"Yeah"—Kate shook her head—"the prosecutors will have a heyday with it."

"Give them something solid, and they'll go to bat for you. But, if we don't, they'll be cursing your name."

Kate winced at that because it was true. "Still, we've got to do what we can do," she said. "These people are being tortured into hurling themselves off a bridge."

"Well, I got a little bit more for you," Bronwyn said. "Kenneth Walker has never been married. His parents are local Vancouverites, as are his grandparents. He's currently"—she clicked on a few pages—"alone. He had a twin brother."

"Oh," Kate said, turning to look at Bronwyn, "that can often confuse DNA."

"Not in this case. He committed suicide."

"Jesus. How long ago?"

"About eighteen months ago."

She stopped and stared. "His brother committed suicide.

That is no coincidence."

Bronwyn groaned. "This is awful, but what's the motive there anyway?"

"Well, the problem is, we have to look into whether or not he's responsible for the brother's suicide," Rodney said. "That's the first place to start, and maybe it was the trigger."

"Maybe because his brother is gone, so he wants other people to go too?" Bronwyn asked. "I don't get that."

"Or maybe, *If I can't have my brother, no one can have you either?*" Kate suggested.

"God only knows," Rodney said, "but you can bet your ass something will be there. The problem will be prying it out of him to get that motive. And that motive will be very important."

"It'll be there," Bronwyn said. "We just don't always know what the hell it'll be. Or how crazy these guys are. Most of the time they don't explain anything, and we have to figure it out."

"Yeah," Kate said. "Like the drive-by guy. But now that we have an address, we need to go talk to this Kenneth Walker guy pronto." She pulled out her phone and said, "I wish Simon would answer."

"Any reason he wouldn't?"

She shrugged. "I don't know. I mean, he doesn't take his phone in the shower, and he's had a hell of a long day, so that would be one option."

"And what would be the worst option?" Rodney asked, standing up beside her.

"Is that the damn woman has connected with him again, and she's on her way to the bridge," she said quietly.

At that, Bronwyn winced and said, "I don't want to be him."

"Neither do I," Kate said. "It's hard enough being me without all that baggage." Kate phoned him again and got nothing. "We can't wait, Rodney. Let's go find this guy."

"If he's even home."

"Okay, well, if he's not," she said, "we'll go to the bridge because you can bet that he's out checking on one of his subjects."

"You think he's done this more than once?" Bronwyn asked.

"Oh hell yes, I know so," she said, "at least I'm hoping it's only one guy. We know that David was targeted as well."

"The guy's laptop I've been looking into," Bronwyn said, looking up.

Kate nodded. "Yes."

"And that is a friend of Simon's, which would explain how and why he ended up connected to this case then. There's almost always a personal connection," Rodney said in a knowing tone.

"Maybe," Kate said, "I don't know the details on something like that."

"Well, think about it because chances are good that's why this is all coming down now. You may need to rein Simon back in again. If he finds out that this guy is responsible for his friend's death, can you really trust how he'll react?"

She thought about that, as she raced out to the car, because the answer was no. Rodney was at her heels. Of course she didn't trust how Simon would react. She had no idea how he would react under all this pressure. But it was something she couldn't deal with right now, since she couldn't even get him on the phone.

With Rodney driving, they pulled up to University

Boulevard and into the residential area, before the entrance to the university.

"Is this the place?" Kate asked.

"Yeah. I got a text from Bronwyn. Walker's mother was a professor and died recently."

"What did she teach?"

"Psychology or something, and she was counselor, specializing in suicide and grief."

Kate shook her head at that. "What the hell? We just keep getting suicides popping up all over the place in this mess."

"That's good," Rodney said. "That brings us a lot of connections here."

"I know. I know," she said. "I just feel like we're not in time."

"In time for what?"

She shook her head and raced up the stairs of a beautiful townhome. She knocked on the door and heard only a hollowness behind it. She looked over at Rodney. "Okay, he's not home. Do you see the red truck anywhere? What do you want to bet he's not here?"

Then one of the neighbors popped out and said, "Hey, if you looking for him, he left about an hour ago."

"Did he?" she said. "I guess you don't really know where he went though, huh?"

"Well, honestly, ever since his mom took her life, he's been pretty morose. Depressed, you know? I told him to get some help, and he just shrugged and said nobody really understood. I hope you find him," he said. "He's a really nice guy."

"Did you say his mother committed suicide?" she asked, incredulous.

"Yeah, I thought that's what he said."

She nodded slowly. "Okay, I'd heard it was his brother."

"Apparently, well, his brother did too, and I think it was too much for his mom. Anyway, that's all I can tell you."

"Do you know how long he's lived here?"

"A while I think, but I don't really know."

"Interesting," she said. "I'm surprised he's still here."

"She didn't quite do the job. ... That was the problem. She was in the hospital for quite a while, with a broken neck, but she didn't survive."

"Thanks." Kate turned and bolted down the stairs.

Leaving the guy staring after them blindly, Rodney caught up with her and said, "What the hell did that just do?"

"That's the trigger. She was fine, and then she wasn't. As in, there was hope that she would pull through, but then she died. What do you want to bet she died when we've got the first one going through this cycle?"

"Wait, but he's been on this kick for years online."

"Yes, he's been on the chats for years, and he was really positive, remember? And then it turned not so positive."

"So you're saying that he soured."

"He soured, and then he ended up turning into this version of himself, dealing with his own grief, his own problems, and probably feeling like nothing was worth it. And that absolutely everything would go wrong. But instead of going alone and taking his own life, he would make sure that he took the others with him."

"So you think that he is suicidal now?" He swore. "Nothing from Simon?"

"No," she snapped. "I'll try him again."

As he drove down toward the bridge, Rodney said, "You

know that we could be heading to the wrong bridge."

"I know," she said. "I know. I know. I know. I can only tell you what I feel."

He looked at her, raising his eyebrows.

She shrugged. "Don't even start with me."

"Hey, maybe some of Simon's sixth sense is rubbing off on you. We could have the best damn department in the place."

"Too often it's likely to be the wrong path, or the timing would be all wrong—or the interpretation," she snapped.

"I forgot how negative you were," he said, with the chuckle.

"How could you?" she said. "It's still me."

"Well, there's that."

She tried Simon again and let it just ring. Mentally she sent out a message. *Dear God, please don't. Don't be heading back down there.*

But, in her heart of hearts, she knew that's exactly where he was. She looked over at Rodney. "Drive," she said. "Drive as if a life depends on it because, in this case, I'm pretty sure it does."

———— ✤ ————

SIMON STARED FOR the tenth time at the phone, knowing it would be Kate. But he didn't dare stop, he was already on his way back down to Lions Gate Bridge, his heart slamming against his chest and his feet moving on their own accord. He had called Mali several times, but she wasn't answering. He kept sending her texts, as he raced toward the bridge.

Stay home, Mali.

Please, just stay home.

Don't do this.

But he knew that she was out there, that she was running for the bridge. And, dear God, this time it would be bad. When he finally couldn't stand it anymore, he phoned Kate. "She's back at the bridge," he said in a rush. "I'm almost there."

"So are we," she said, "because the guy we were after, he's not home."

"You think he's down there too?" he said in alarm. "Oh, God. I wouldn't be at all surprised. This is crunch time. I don't know where he's hiding or what he's done in order to get her there. But chances are, he's got some final push, and it'll be happening right now."

"We have to stop this guy before he goes underground or jumps himself. Both his brother and mother committed suicide."

"No argument there," he said. "And that could trigger anyone."

"Have you got any connection to her at all?"

"Nothing more than my feet racing in that direction," he said in a dry tone. "I feel terrible about this. I thought she was safe."

"I did too," Kate said. "So either she didn't tell us everything, or he found another way to get to her."

"Yeah, I suspect it's both," he said.

"Did it ever occur to you that it's possible she killed her sister?"

"I don't know," he said. "I couldn't even begin to tell you."

"I know," she said. "It's disconcerting to consider that he could have something like that on her."

"How would he know though? That's the question."

"I don't know. Maybe he haunts the newspapers. Maybe

he's haunting the suicide support groups and then researches them. Maybe he befriends them to gain their confidence and finds out their secrets, then uses it against them."

"Of course," Simon said instantly, "this is what he's doing. Somehow, somewhere along the line Mali must have confessed something to him, either that she's afraid she might have done something or that she's such a terrible person and needs to die because she did do something."

"But of course that doesn't mean that she did."

"No," he said, "we all know what that mind-set is like. How far away are you?"

"We're at least fifteen minutes out," she said. "How about you?"

"I'm heading toward the bridge now."

"Can you see her?" she asked evenly.

"No, not yet, and it's getting damn dark out here."

"What about anybody else?" she said. "Any lights or anything?"

"Nothing, just the traffic," he said. "Never a shortage of that. I'll let you know as soon as I see something." With that, he hung up, and, all on their own volition, his feet started to run. He swore. "If you keep doing this," he roared into the darkness, "I'll need proper running shoes!"

He was in his loafers, not exactly the best thing for speed. He was fit and in good shape, but he hadn't expected to sprint for a mile. By the time he hit the center of the bridge, he was wondering what the hell was going on. Because there was no slowing down, and his feet kept him running and running and running. Finally they came to a dead stop. He froze and looked at the railing. A man and a woman stood there, but they were arguing. He wanted to approach because something was ever-so-slightly familiar about her face, but he wasn't exactly sure if it was Mali.

Underneath the bridge, he saw scaffolding. He frowned at that. He knew that the city was doing a lot of work on the bridge, topside and underneath, but did anybody realize what was going on? He wondered if he could get down there. Any way for him to get below where Mali stood. Could he stop her, or, if she jumped, could he help her?

He studied the construction work and pulled out his phone, calling Kate. "Work's being done on the bridge."

"There's always work being done on the bridge," she said. "So what?"

"It's in same area where they are."

"They?"

"I think it's Mali, and a guy's with her."

"Oh, *great*." Kate thought out loud. "I could get ahold of the construction crews, the city workers, and see just what the plan was and what was down there. Maybe they could get a helicopter here."

At that point, Simon also noted that a lot of work had been going on right where he stood. He'd seen part of it before, but he'd been on the other side of the bridge. This time he was on the right side of the bridge for a change, where the scaffolding was underneath. They must have been doing some reinforcement work or maybe even just a paint job; he didn't know.

He slipped over the side and made it onto the scaffolding, where the safety rail part of it had already been ripped off. Had some kids done that? It should never have been left open like this. Yet, since the scaffolding was closer to the water, the wind kept slamming one portion of it against the bridge, banging it over and over again. Simon crept his way down until he was as close as he could be, beneath where

Mali stood with the man. The cold wind had a bite to it. Add in the growing darkness and the lonely spot, … talk about unnerving. He heard them arguing.

"You need to do this. You know that," he said in that soothing tone.

"Oh, God, I don't want to call my parents," she said. "Please don't make me."

"But I'm not making you do anything," he said, with that horrible snarky voice that Simon had heard time and time again. "This is all you. It's got nothing to do with me."

She started to cry louder and louder.

The man said, "You know it's important."

While he was under here, Simon saw some netting, which secured the portion of the bridge where they were at, probably for the workers, along with security ropes and leads. Everything was nicely tied up under the bridge for safekeeping, until the workers returned the next day. Simon quickly grabbed a safety line and put it on.

Just then, when his phone rang, he swore because the sound was horribly loud. He snatched his phone and whispered, "What?"

"A night crew is coming on right now."

"They're supposed to be here twenty-four hours a day. Yet they haven't been any time I've been down here."

"They've had a ton of breakdowns, and some of their safety gear was missing," she said. "But a crew is on its way right now."

"Well, I'm standing right below the pier, and I'm hooked up to one of the security lines that's here."

"What?" she shouted. "Are you serious? What the hell?"

"Exactly," he said. "*What the hell* is right." She was only echoing this sentiment on repeat in his head.

"Did you see all that construction before?"

"I did, I just didn't think too much of it, as it's on the opposite side of the bridge," he said, peering upward in the gloom. "They're arguing really badly."

"We're about eight minutes out."

"I'm not sure we have eight minutes," he said. "I've stayed out of sight, and I'm of two minds, wondering whether I should try to break up the fight or not." Looking at the scaffolding all around the side of the bridge, he said, "I think I could get up there quite easily."

"You stay where you are," she said in a hard voice.

"Yeah, right, like that'll work." And, with that, he pocketed his phone. With the safety line still attached, he climbed from the scaffold onto the lip on the outside of the bridge. Almost immediately the woman turned, looked at him, and shrieked.

He held up his hands. "Hey, sorry, just doing traffic work." Simon hoped that Mali didn't recognize him, thinking that might just freak her out even more. She wrapped her coat around herself and tried to back away, but her companion grabbed her and held her close, saying, "It's okay. Calm down. He's just leaving."

Simon smiled. "Well, not quite," he said. "What are you two doing here?"

Mali looked at the man beside her and said, "We were just leaving."

The man shrugged and said, "Yeah, sure, we can come back again."

As they headed off, as if to walk away, Simon heard her saying, "I don't want to."

"Well, if it's not tonight, we have to come back tomorrow apparently."

"No," she said. "I won't."

Simon called out, "Hey, is there a problem?"

The woman looked up and started to walk toward him, but the other guy grabbed her and said, "No, no problem at all," he said, "just having a little disagreement, that's all. Young love and all."

"If you say so," Simon said. He addressed the woman. "Look. If you're in trouble, just come in my direction. You know me."

She looked at him through the poor light and said, "Simon?"

He nodded. "Yes, it's me," he said. "You don't have to stay here with that guy."

She looked at Simon, to the other guy, then back again, tried to step toward Simon, but the man grabbed her.

"Do you know who he is?" Simon asked.

"Yes," she said, "he's the one who's been sending the emails."

At that, a hand was slapped over her mouth, and she was jerked backward. "Don't you say a fucking word," the man said. "Don't say anything at all."

She groaned, struggling, but Simon couldn't even hear a word.

He walked along the lip on the outside of the bridge, getting closer to them, and said, "Come on, Mali. Come over here to me."

"She's not going anywhere," the man said, as he pulled her closer to the railing.

Simon said, "Hey, hey, hey, don't you even think about throwing her over." He was still on the outside of the railing, and he shuffled closer and closer, trying not to think about the cold inky churning water below. As he got nearer, the other man pulled back.

"You can't keep going." The guy laughed. "It looks like your safety line will only take you so far."

That was very true. Simon was almost about out of rope here and knew he would have to decide if he would unhook himself and jump over onto the main portion of the bridge.

At that, the guy picked up Mali—making her scream in panic, fighting her attacker—and held her on top of the railing.

"You know, up until now," Simon said, "I wasn't even sure what charges they would file against you, but the minute you drop her off that bridge, it's murder one."

"What the hell do you know?" he sneered. "It wasn't premeditated."

"Well, that's not quite true," Simon said, "considering all the emails you've been sending to the people on the chat groups."

"What are you talking about?" he said in shock. "And what do you even know about it?"

"Oh, let's see. I know that you're blackmailing these people into committing suicide. Thirteen times now, isn't it? Mali here would be fourteen."

The guy just stared at him, shocked. "Who the hell are you?"

"Someone who cares about your victims," he said quietly, "but I don't really give a shit about you."

At that, the other man sneered. "You can't say anything about me," he said. "You know nothing about me."

"I know that your twin died. I know that your mother's dead," he said, thankful Kate had shared that information moments ago.

The guy just stared at him in shock. "No, no, no," he

said, "no way you could know any of that." Nervously he climbed a little bit higher, still holding Mali in his arms. She was frantic, trying to grab onto the railing.

Simon was almost close enough to snatch her out of his arms. "I do know that," Simon said. "What I don't know is whether you helped your mother and your brother die or if this is something you came up with afterward."

"What difference does it make?" he said. "I'm all alone."

"Of course you are, and being alone is not the easiest place to be, but you sure as hell didn't have to make other families suffer by losing loved ones they care about."

"Nobody in her family cares about her," he snarled. "She's better off dead."

"I don't believe that for a minute," Simon said.

Mali was crying and screaming hysterically. By now traffic had backed up around them, as people stopped. Others honked and tried to weave around them because nobody wanted to get stopped on a bridge. Of course not everybody saw what was happening either.

In the distance, he heard sirens coming. "Oh, the cops are here," Simon said. "What will you do now?"

He just laughed.

"Don't you drop her—" Simon said, and, with that, the man tossed her off. Screaming, she went over.

Simon lunged forward and grabbed Mali by the leg, just as the laughing man threw her off. Her weight sent Simon flying off the bridge, knowing that, when they hit the end of the rope, the snap on his grip would be horrific. They plummeted down, and the safety harness jerked hard, but he hung on to her.

Mali screamed, as the rope came to the end of its line abruptly. They were dangling upside down, but she was safe.

She reached out, grabbing for his hand, pulling herself up, until she was wrapped around him, both dangling upside down.

He held on to her and whispered, "Just stop moving. We'll get help. See? Look."

"My God," she buried her face for a moment, then looked up at the deranged man on the bridge. "You're nuts," she yelled. "I didn't kill my sister," she said.

"You did," the man said. "You said you did. The world is better off without you, you know that."

"No," she said, bawling her eyes out. "It isn't. It isn't."

As Simon held her tight, he looked up at the would-be killer and asked, "And your mother?"

"What about her? She was weak. All she cared about was the fact that my brother was gone," he said, leaning over and laughing at them. Then he held up something that glinted in the bridge light.

The fucking animal had a knife.

"He was always the favorite."

"That's not true," she whispered, her breathing labored, still in Simon's arms. "He told me that his brother committed suicide, and that ever since then he'd been lost. And his mother finally came around to seeing that life was better if she wasn't here because she was responsible for his suicide."

That made sense. Simon's arms started to tremble. Where the hell was Kate? He couldn't hold Mali for much longer. Then how long would it take for a knife to cut this line …

"Police! Hands up."

CHAPTER 20

K ENNETH WALKER STARED at Kate and swore. "I'm not going down with them," he said, as he held the knife over the rope.

"That won't cut through in one fell swoop either," Kate said, her voice calm and controlled. "Do you really think they make safety lines out of twine?"

He stared at her and said, "I'm not going down for this."

From below Kate heard a woman yelling.

"Why don't *you* jump? You just wanted me to jump because you were too chicken, too scared to do it yourself."

He yelled down, "Shut up. I'm out of here. I'm not jumping, so just shut the fuck up."

"You've been trying to get the courage to jump yourself, to end your pain." Mali cried out. "You're the one who loved your twin. You're the one who missed him so badly that you couldn't go on without him, but you couldn't do it. You didn't have the strength or the confidence to do it. You spent all your time making other people feel bad, driving them to commit suicide, when it was really you who wanted to die. What is it you've been saying to me? *Just do it.*"

"Step away from the bridge and put the knife down," Kate told Walker.

The man suddenly held up his hands. "Okay. Okay, don't shoot." He dropped the knife, grabbed the railing, and jumped off.

It was hard to see in the darkening evening; Kate raced to the railing, but she hadn't heard even an audible splash. Kate looked frantically in the water below. There was no sign of him. The black water churned endlessly below. As she raced to Simon, he spoke to the construction crew.

Simon said, "Pretty damn sloppy that you left all this out here but a good thing for us."

Hearing an odd sound, she watched the construction crew winch up an exhausted Simon and Mali. By the time they reached the safety of the bridge deck, traffic was stopped in both directions, plus cops and an ambulance had arrived. Rodney stood at her side.

"None of this gear should have been left here," Simon said quietly, standing on the ledge of the bridge, hanging on, while Mali still clung to him.

"It wasn't supposed to be," the foreman said, "but we ended up with a problem with one of the crew. He had to go get medical attention fast, and we didn't have anybody to guard this. What a shit show."

"Yeah, you're not kidding," Simon said, as the construction guy helped Mali back onto the bridge. Simon scrambled over the railing, then stopped and took a deep breath. He looked at Kate, gave her a lopsided grin, and said, "I don't think I'll like bridges anymore."

She snorted. "I've never liked bridges myself." She walked over, gave him a hug, and said, "Good job."

He shook his head and said, "If that's what you call it." As he turned to look at Mali, she stood there, staring down at the water, mesmerized. He immediately reached out and put a hand on her shoulder.

She turned, smiled up at him all teary, and said, "I'm

okay. Honest, I am."

"I don't know about that," he said. "You weren't supposed to be here at all. You were supposed to stay home."

She nodded and smiled. "I know, but then he called and said he would give me the proof he's been holding over my head. I came down here to meet him, but it never even occurred to me," she said, "that he would try to do this."

"Well, people being people," Kate said, "you really need to trust your instincts and get away from people like that. Don't listen to what they say. Listen to how they make you feel."

"I know," Mali said. "I get it now. I'll call my mom and talk to them."

"Now that sounds like a grand idea. Maybe you should tell them of the trouble you're having dealing with all this."

She nodded slowly and said, "I really didn't kill my sister."

"I'm glad to hear that," Kate said quietly. "Maybe now you can go get some help and deal with your loss. I'll get somebody to take you home and also see that you get somebody over there to spend some time with you."

Teary-eyed, Mali was led away to a cruiser, where she was put into the back seat and driven off.

SIMON SMILED AT Kate, then downward. "Apparently I'll need some new shoes."

She looked down at his fancy dress shoes with worn-out soles. "Well, you ought to get some running shoes," she said, with a chuckle, "instead of those five-hundred-dollar-dress shoes. Maybe they would hold up better."

"A thousand bucks actually," he said, "and they were on

sale."

"Well, in that case," she said, "maybe you should invest in some cheap runners for when this happens again."

"That's not even funny. Not one bit." But the corner of his mouth kicked up.

She grinned. "It is pretty damn funny," she said. "Hilarious, in fact."

He opened his arms; she walked into them, and they just stood like that for a long moment. "Do you think he could have survived?"

"I don't think so," she said. "The boats and divers are on the way, and they'll go hunting, but, with the temperatures and the height of the bridge, I don't think so. This bridge is pretty unforgiving."

"Yeah, I know," he said, "but tonight the good guys won."

And, with that, she smiled, nodded, and said, "Agreed. Can I give you a lift home?"

"You sure as hell can," he said, and together they walked back to where Rodney stood, staring at them in disbelief.

He reached out a hand and said, "Hey. Simon, right?"

Grinning, Simon shook his hand. "Yeah."

"Rodney. Interesting job you got there."

"It's not my job at all," he said, with a quick shake of his head.

"I don't know," Rodney said. "Seems to me like it's a passion."

"God no. Not a passion I want to pursue at all, but it seems we don't always have a choice. Sometimes we're directed to do things, whether we like them or not."

"I'll feel better when the body shows up," Kate said, with a last glance behind them. "We could really use the closure."

Rodney looked at her and asked, "You going home now?"

"Hell yes, I'm going home."

"Reports?"

She stopped, looked at him, and said, "Everything can wait till morning, don't you think?"

"Hell yes," he said. "Go home and get a good night's sleep for once." With that, Rodney turned with a smirk and walked back to his car.

She looked to Simon. "We can catch a ride with him, if you want."

"I don't know," he said. "It might be easier to grab a taxi."

"Not with the traffic jam we've got going on here." But, as she turned to look around, traffic was moving again, and a cab pulled up beside them.

"Like I said," Simon said, pointing at the cab, "let's take this." He opened up the passenger side, and the two of them hopped in. He looked at the same cabbie from before and nodded.

The cabbie just shook his head and said, "I don't know what's going on, man."

"Don't worry about it. Just take me home," he said. "There's a big tip in it for you. I promise."

At that, the cabbie's face split into a big grin. "In that case, home it is."

Honestly, Simon didn't think he'd heard better words in a hell of a long time.

CHAPTER 21

Kate's Friday Morning

WHEN KATE WALKED into work the next morning, she'd already got a statement from Simon. They did that last night over coffee to get all of their impressions down on paper first.

"That was a hell of a deal last night," Rodney said.

"Yeah, it was," she said, yawning.

"Did you get any sleep?"

She gave him a sideways look. "Some."

"Good job!" he said, with a ridiculous grin.

"What are you? Fifteen?" she said, rolling her eyes. They both filled their cups with coffee and walked back into the squad room, where they were met with cheers.

She laughed. "That was a hell of a night."

"More great news," Lilliana said. "Our drive-by shooter confessed. That is worth a lot too."

Kate sat back, relaxed and happy, and said, "As for the bad news, we've got a ton of paperwork to do to clean all this up. But I'd much rather do the paperwork to put them away, than the guesswork to figure them out," she said, then yawned.

Just then, Colby walked in, nodded at her, and said, "Good job."

"Thanks," she said, and once again yawned.

He looked at her and said, "You could go home and get some rest, you know."

"I could," she said, "but I figured the details on these reports needed to get recorded, while they were still fresh, and we could get as much down as possible."

"Good thought," he said, "but, when you're done, go ahead and take a few days."

"I won't say no to that," she said. "I'm too damn tired."

He grinned and said, "Well, no reason to say no. Just get the reports done up and then get the hell out of here."

She smiled, nodded, and said, "Those are orders I can accept." And, with that, she finished up her paperwork, and by noon she had handed off as much as she could to the others and said, "I'm out of here for a couple days."

Outside she stood in front of the station, stared up at the blue sky and the sunshine, and rotated her neck and shoulders, trying to let out some of the stress of the last few days. As she stood here, she heard a whistle. She turned to see Simon, walking toward her, two cups of coffee in his hands.

"How did you know I was here?" she asked.

"I texted Rodney a few minutes ago, asking where you were, and he said you were out here. Or should be soon. So I grabbed two coffees from a vendor over a block away."

"Got any plans for the day?" he asked, with a bright grin.

"Yeah," she said, "something that has nothing to do with work."

"Sounds perfect," he said. "My place or yours?"

She laughed. "I don't know," she said. "Whichever will be the most comfortable."

"My place definitely," he said instantly.

She rolled her eyes. "My place isn't bad."

"Maybe not," he said, "but it's nothing like mine."

She had to agree with that. "But first," she said, "I want to walk around some and remember all the good things about Vancouver."

"There are a lot of good things here," he said, his voice warm, and she nodded.

"I know," she said. "I just need to be reminded of some of them."

And, with arms linked, they headed off to tour the city.

This concludes Book 2 of Kate Morgan:
Simon Says... Jump.

Read about Kate Morgan: Simon Says... Ride, Book 3

Simon Says... Ride: Kate Morgan (Book #3)

Introducing a new thriller series that keeps you guessing and on your toes through every twist and unexpected turn....

USA Today Best-Selling Author Dale Mayer does it again in this mind-blowing thriller series.

The unlikely team of Detective Kate Morgan and Simon St. Laurant, an unwilling psychic, marries all the unpredictable and passionate elements of Mayer's work that readers have come to love and crave.

Detective Kate Morgan is hot on a new confusing case. A cyclist is killed at the main intersection to the University of British Columbia. At first glance it looks like a hit-and-run, but, as details emerge, it gets much more complicated.

From one day to the next, Simon is blinded by an overload of senses and noises. It's impacting his regular business day, and he seems unable to control when and how these moments occur. Angry and frustrated, he tells Kate but knows she's unable to help. How can she, when he can't help himself?

As Kate struggles to work her way through a gang of arrogant university students, reluctant parents, a defensive dean, and way too many unobservant witnesses, she finds a disturbing pattern of more "accidents" *and* more victims ... Then finally Simon understands why his senses are on overload ... and flips the investigation around.

Third Monday in August

I T HAD BEEN a good two weeks since she'd had a couple days off, and those two days she'd spent with Simon now seemed like a hell of a long time ago. She groaned.

Rodney looked up at her. "What's the matter now?"

"This stupid case," she said. "I'm still tracking down more of the suicides."

"I know," he said, "but all we really can do is give the families closure at this point in time."

"Well, at least that asshole is dead and gone. I'm glad his body was recovered."

"Exactly. And nobody will mourn murderer Ken's death either."

"Good," she said. "Somebody like that, it's hard to not to just toss his file and carry on."

Just then, Dispatch called. "We've got a female DB on the entrance to UBC."

"On the walkway?" Kate asked.

"It's just outside of the university grounds on one of the bike paths," the dispatcher said. "I'm sending you the exact location."

"Crap," she said, as she hopped to her feet. "Hey, Rodney, we've got a woman down on the bike path."

"Out by UBC? Shouldn't the university police have that?"

"This one is a homicide from the looks of it, and it's not on the university campus, It's in the intersection leading up to it."

He looked at her in surprise.

"Vehicular homicide. She's been hit by a car," Kate said.

"Time to rock and roll."

"Another woman was struck by a vehicle up in that area about a year ago," he said, as he stood and grabbed his jacket.

She stopped, looked at him, and said, "What do you mean?"

"Well," he shrugged, "it's not like it's unusual, since that's a high traffic spot."

"Isn't that also where they do bike racing training?"

"Well, they do some of it there. I mean, the UBC campus is full of trails and tracks, so it's perfect for a lot of this stuff. Plus, with all the jogging routes up there, it's great for fitness training."

"*Hmm*," she said, "so you're thinking it was a full year since the last one?"

"Yeah," he said. "Why?"

"I just want to make sure we don't have three in a row," she said on a smile. "Nothing like a serial killer coming back to mark time."

He looked at her in surprise. "I'll look it up."

"Do that," she said. "The last thing we need is another ugly story to mar the beauty of this place."

"You know that there will always be another ugly story," he said. They walked to her car, heading to the location in minutes, as he dug into his coffee while she drove.

"I know that crime lives on," she said, "but, one of these

days, I keep thinking we'll have paradise here."

"Paradise is what you make it," he said, with a laugh.

By the time they drove up to the outskirts of the university campus, she parked near all the cruisers. It looked like the coroner was already on site. "It looks like we're last to arrive," she said in surprise.

Rodney looked up from his phone, frowned, and said, "We did hit a spot of traffic on the way over."

"I guess," she said, with a nod at his phone and the records he was pulling. "Did you find anything?"

"*Hmm.*" He bent his head again, while she hopped out.

She came around, leaned in through his window, and said, "What did you find, Rodney?"

"Nothing good," he said, his tone grim.

She looked at him in surprise. "What do you mean?"

"You were asking about a third?"

"Yeah," she said, her heart sinking.

"How about a fourth and a fifth?"

"What the hell? Where?" she asked.

He replied, "All within a couple blocks of here. And," he added, "all of them on this same weekend. One a year for the last five years."

She stared at him and went, "Shit." Just then her phone rang. She looked down at a text from Simon for her to call him, her stomach dive-bombing at the timing. "Hey, what's up?" she asked. "I've just arrived at a crime scene."

"I know," he said, "and all I'm seeing are bikes, bikes, bikes, and more bikes."

"Yeah, how many of them?"

"Right now, I'd say five."

She swore. "*Great*," she said. "Apparently I'm at a crime scene in a small localized area, where there's been a crime of the same kind every year for the last five years, all on this very weekend."

There was dead silence on the other end, and then his weary voice said, "You'll track this one down, I presume?"

"I won't have a choice," she said.

He whispered, "Neither will I."

"Any more help you can give me?" she asked.

"No," he murmured, "not yet. But it'll come. Don't worry. It'll come."

At that, she hung up, nodding, a grim expression on her face.

Find Book 3 here!

To find out more visit Dale Mayer's website.

smarturl.it/DMSSSRide

Author's Note

Thank you for reading Simon Says... Jump: Kate Morgan, Book 2! If you enjoyed the book, please take a moment and leave a short review.

Dear reader,

I love to hear from readers, and you can contact me at my website: www.dalemayer.com or at my Facebook author page. To be informed of new releases and special offers, sign up for my newsletter or follow me on BookBub. And if you are interested in joining Dale Mayer's Reader Group, here is the Facebook sign up page.
https://smarturl.it/DaleMayerFBGroup

Cheers,
Dale Mayer

Get THREE Free Books Now!

Have you tried the Psychic Vision series?

Read Tuesday's Child, Hide'n Go Seek, Maddy's Floor right now for FREE.

Go here to get them!
https://dalemayer.com/tuesdayschildfree

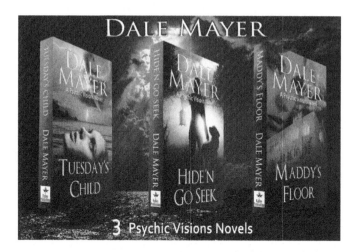

About the Author

Dale Mayer is a *USA Today* best-selling author, best known for her SEALs military romances, her Psychic Visions series, and her Lovely Lethal Garden cozy series. Her contemporary romances are raw and full of passion and emotion (Broken But ... Mending series). Her thrillers will keep you guessing (By Death series), and her romantic comedies will keep you giggling (*It's a Dog's Life*, a stand-alone novella; and the Broken Protocols series, starring Charming Marvin, the cat).

Dale honors the stories that come to her—and some of them are crazy and break all the rules and cross multiple genres!

To go with her fiction, she also writes nonfiction in many different fields, with books available on résumé writing, companion gardening, and the US mortgage system. She has recently published her Career Essentials series. All her books are available in print and ebook format.

Connect with Dale Mayer Online

Dale's Website – www.dalemayer.com

Twitter – @DaleMayer

Facebook – facebook.com/DaleMayer.author

BookBub – bookbub.com/authors/dale-mayer

Also by Dale Mayer

Published Adult Books:

Bullard's Battle
Ryland's Reach, Book 1
Cain's Cross, Book 2
Eton's Escape, Book 3
Garret's Gambit, Book 4
Kano's Keep, Book 5
Fallon's Flaw, Book 6
Quinn's Quest, Book 7
Bullard's Beauty, Book 8
Bullard's Best, Book 9

Terkel's Team
Damon's Deal, Book 1

Kate Morgan
Simon Says... Hide, Book 1
Simon Says... Jump, Book 2
Simon Says... Ride, Book 3
Simon Says... Scream, Book 4

Hathaway House
Aaron, Book 1

The K9 Files

Lovely Lethal Gardens

Psychic Visions Books 4–6

Psychic Visions Books 7–9

By Death Series

Touched by Death

Haunted by Death

Chilled by Death

By Death Books 1–3

Broken Protocols – Romantic Comedy Series

Cat's Meow

Cat's Pajamas

Cat's Cradle

Cat's Claus

Broken Protocols 1-4

Broken and... Mending

Skin

Scars

Scales (of Justice)

Broken but... Mending 1-3

Glory

Genesis

Tori

Celeste

Glory Trilogy

Biker Blues

Morgan: Biker Blues, Volume 1

Cash: Biker Blues, Volume 2

SEALs of Honor

Mason: SEALs of Honor, Book 1

Hawk: SEALs of Honor, Book 2

Dane: SEALs of Honor, Book 3

Swede: SEALs of Honor, Book 4

Shadow: SEALs of Honor, Book 5

Cooper: SEALs of Honor, Book 6

Markus: SEALs of Honor, Book 7

Evan: SEALs of Honor, Book 8

Mason's Wish: SEALs of Honor, Book 9

Chase: SEALs of Honor, Book 10

Brett: SEALs of Honor, Book 11

Devlin: SEALs of Honor, Book 12

Easton: SEALs of Honor, Book 13

Ryder: SEALs of Honor, Book 14

Macklin: SEALs of Honor, Book 15

Corey: SEALs of Honor, Book 16

Warrick: SEALs of Honor, Book 17

Tanner: SEALs of Honor, Book 18

Jackson: SEALs of Honor, Book 19

Kanen: SEALs of Honor, Book 20

Nelson: SEALs of Honor, Book 21

Taylor: SEALs of Honor, Book 22

Colton: SEALs of Honor, Book 23

Troy: SEALs of Honor, Book 24

Axel: SEALs of Honor, Book 25

Baylor: SEALs of Honor, Book 26

Heroes for Hire

SEALs of Steel

SEALs of Steel, Books 1–8

The Mavericks
Kerrick, Book 1
Griffin, Book 2
Jax, Book 3
Beau, Book 4
Asher, Book 5
Ryker, Book 6
Miles, Book 7
Nico, Book 8
Keane, Book 9
Lennox, Book 10
Gavin, Book 11
Shane, Book 12
Diesel, Book 13
Jerricho, Book 14
Killian, Book 15
Hatch, Book 16
The Mavericks, Books 1–2
The Mavericks, Books 3–4
The Mavericks, Books 5–6
The Mavericks, Books 7–8
The Mavericks, Books 9–10
The Mavericks, Books 11–12

Collections
Dare to Be You...
Dare to Love...

Dare to be Strong…

RomanceX3

Standalone Novellas

It's a Dog's Life

Riana's Revenge

Second Chances

Published Young Adult Books:

Family Blood Ties Series

Vampire in Denial

Vampire in Distress

Vampire in Design

Vampire in Deceit

Vampire in Defiance

Vampire in Conflict

Vampire in Chaos

Vampire in Crisis

Vampire in Control

Vampire in Charge

Family Blood Ties Set 1–3

Family Blood Ties Set 1–5

Family Blood Ties Set 4–6

Family Blood Ties Set 7–9

Sian's Solution, A Family Blood Ties Series Prequel
  Novelette

Design series

Dangerous Designs

Deadly Designs

Darkest Designs

Design Series Trilogy

Standalone

In Cassie's Corner

Gem Stone (a Gemma Stone Mystery)

Time Thieves

Published Non-Fiction Books:

Career Essentials

Career Essentials: The Résumé

Career Essentials: The Cover Letter

Career Essentials: The Interview

Career Essentials: 3 in 1

Made in the USA
Coppell, TX
04 December 2021

67108612R00203